CONFESSIONS TO MR. ROOSEVELT

CONFESSIONS TO MR. ROOSEVELT

M. J. HOLT

FIVE STAR
A part of Gale, a Cengage Company

GALE
A Cengage Company

Farmington Hills, Mich • San Francisco • New York • Waterville, Maine
Meriden, Conn • Mason, Ohio • Chicago

LIBRARY OF CONGRESS CATALOGING-IN-PUBLICATION DATA

Names: Holt, Marilyn J., author.
Title: Confessions to Mr. Roosevelt / M. J. Holt.
Description: First edition. | Farmington Hills, Michigan : Five Star, 2019. | Identifiers:
    LCCN 2018040005 (print) | LCCN 2018046727 (ebook) | ISBN 9781432852115
    (ebook) | ISBN 9781432852108 (ebook) | ISBN 9781432852092 (hardcover)
Subjects: LCSH: Federal Writers' Project—Fiction. | GSAFD: Historical fiction
Classification: LCC PS3558.O415 (ebook) | LCC PS3558.O415 C66 2019 (print) | DDC
    813/.54—dc23
LC record available at https://lccn.loc.gov/2018040005

First Edition. First Printing: May 2019
Find us on Facebook—https://www.facebook.com/FiveStarCengage
Visit our website—http://www.gale.cengage.com/fivestar/
Contact Five Star Publishing at FiveStar@cengage.com

Printed in Mexico
2 3 4 5 6 7 23 22 21 20 19

To my mother, Vera, a modern-day pioneer woman

INTRODUCTION

During the Great Depression, the Federal Writers' Project employed out-of-work writers, poets, teachers, and librarians in every state, most U.S. territories, and in Washington, D.C. Their job was to write travel guides and local histories, to collect folklore and songs, and to interview elderly men and women for their life stories. In the states of the Great Plains, ravaged in the 1930s by drought and dust storms, project workers collected the reminiscences of homesteaders and town builders who settled the Plains, had known joy and hardship, and experienced years when the rains did not come. The workers and pioneers portrayed in this book are imagined, but the events they refer to—whether the blizzard of '86, grasshopper swarms, or life in a prairie town—are based on historical fact.

CHAPTER 1
NEAR OPAL'S GROVE, KANSAS, 1870

The back side of the shovel slammed down on soil already tightly packed. John Featherstone ignored the spasm of pain rippling through his old muscles and brought the shovel down one last time. He'd promised the girl he would take care of things. He gave his word, and, once a man did that, he was dutybound. Maybe he'd said what he did because the girl had always been friendly, never making a judgment on him. Or, maybe it was the way she reminded him of someone he'd known long ago.

Didn't matter, he told himself, as he knocked loose dirt from the shovel. The thing was done. He tramped back through the trees to his horse. He stowed the shovel in a leather sheath tied to the saddle. Absently running a hand across the horse's neck, he glanced at the sky. Rain was coming. All day, moisture had been building in the air. Now, it was just a matter of time before heavy, gathering clouds opened a floodgate of spring showers.

Giving the horse one more pat, he mumbled, "Let's get this finished and go home. Fine by you?" The old man eyed the horse, took the shake of its mane as a sign of agreement, and walked back the way he'd come, gathering clumps of winter-killed underbrush to cover the bare earth. He picked his way down to the riverbank, stiff knees creaking, and began gathering rocks the size of melons. It took time to carry these up the embankment and scatter them to look natural. Finally, for good measure, he pulled over a downed limb from a cottonwood tree and angled it crossways on the stones.

Fat drops of rain began to plop against his hat and jacket. Slowly, the rain increased until it fell in a steady shower. John Featherstone stood studying his handiwork. He thought of the girl again and hoped she'd remember to do exactly as he told her when she got to town.

Taking one last look toward the grave now hidden by nature and his helping hands, John Featherstone worked up a good mouthful of spit and sent it flying.

"Rest in peace, you sorry son of a bitch," he growled.

CHAPTER 2
TOPEKA, KANSAS, 1936
ELLEN

An open window allowed a breeze to move the air in the stuffy room. Noises from the street drifted up. Barely visible through a canopy of trees was the dome of the state capitol. Ignoring the view, the sound of automobiles rumbling over brick-laid streets, and the occasional shout of a pedestrian, Inez Fletcher sat behind her desk. She was a stoutly built woman, wearing a dress that strained to contain perspiring flesh. She glanced at the young woman across from her.

"Opal's Grove in Dobbs County will be our base of operations," she began. "It's the county seat, centrally located in the state. Mrs. Iris Hewitt, the president of the local historical society, will be in charge there. She's a real go-getter. Even as I speak, she's signing up the old folks and scheduling interviews."

Ellen nodded. She knew the Works Progress Administration job involved writing down the life stories of people who had settled in the state before 1880 or who had been born there before that date. The project piqued her curiosity. But the prospect of being employed interested her much more. Prosperity was supposed to be just around the corner, but, for Ellen, it seemed a long way off. There was a growing sense of desperation in her search for work.

By nature, Ellen was optimistic, but the last few months of knocking on doors and writing letters that went unanswered or brought rejection chipped away at her confidence. It felt like little pieces of herself were breaking away. She'd gone about her

job search methodically. Months before graduating from college, she began to look for work. Applications were mailed to
every newspaper in the state, and she visited those she could
reach in a day's drive in the aging Packard roadster that had
once belonged to her cousin Louise. When she learned that no
one was hiring a good copy editor or eager young reporter, she
turned to the state's few radio stations, hoping to write jingles
or radio plays. Usually, the people she met were sympathetic,
but the answer was the same. No openings, especially for a
young woman fresh out of school and with no family to support.

Inez Fletcher took a breath. Ellen waited, trying not to glance
at a seam that was beginning to tear along one sleeve of the
woman's dress. "There are seven positions, two of which will be
filled by local writers chosen by Mrs. Hewitt."

The knot in her stomach tightened. While waiting in the
hallway to be called into Mrs. Fletcher's office, Ellen heard
someone say that at least fifty jobhunters had shown up the day
before. With that many applicants, Ellen reasoned, the odds
were not in her favor.

As if reading her mind, the WPA woman veered off the subject
of what was happening in Opal's Grove. "You realize, of course,
that the main goal of the Federal Writers' Project initiated by
President Roosevelt's New Deal is compiling a state guide.
These interviews are only a small piece of the overall project."

Ellen shook her head. She didn't know.

"I've already hired dozens of workers for the guide, because
it must be comprehensive, touching on all sorts of topics.
Highway routes crisscrossing the state." The WPA woman began
to count the subjects off on her fingers. "Town histories and
what one will find in those places today. Points of historical
interest. Manufacturing. Well, I could go on and on. It's not
entirely organized as yet, but the pioneer stories will be included

in some way. Ultimately, we hope for these documents to be housed at the state historical society for future generations to study. Additional workers may be needed for the guide, but at the moment we must have people to conduct these interviews."

Ellen hoped her face did not show her consternation. When she heard from a college professor about the Federal Writers' Project, just the interviews were mentioned. Only now did she realize she had missed the opportunity to apply for work on this guide Mrs. Fletcher seemed so keen on. She pushed back a wave of despair.

"Now," said the woman, staring hard at Ellen. "Let's talk about you. I've read the writing samples you submitted—your articles from the college newspaper and the stories that were published in those pulp magazines. The articles are well done, and I must say I enjoyed the stories in *Ranch Romance* and *Western Romance*. But the ones in *True Confessions!* Oh, my! Surely, those were fiction." The woman fanned her face as if just the thought of what she'd read was too much.

Ellen bit the inside of her lip to keep from laughing. "No, ma'am, the *True Confessions* stories are based on real circumstances. The magazine doesn't mind if you change the names of people and places, but it likes some basis in truth."

"Even the one about the young woman who threw away a fortune to run off with a trombone player? In this day and age, it's hard to believe anyone would turn their back on all that money."

"Believe me; it's true." Ellen had no intention of adding that the woman in question was her cousin, and that Louise had always done things on her own terms. When she fell for the musician, she renamed herself LuLu, waved goodbye to her high-living friends at the Tulsa Country Club, and thumbed her nose at the fortune her father made in Oklahoma's oil fields. When Ellen thought about LuLu, she imagined her sitting in a smoky jazz club in Kansas City or sauntering into a swanky nightclub in Chicago. Wherever she was, Ellen hoped she was happy.

"And the romance stories? Seems to me that if you write about romance, and certainly the way you have, you have some personal experience in the area."

Ellen wished the woman would move on to another subject. Her love life was none of the woman's business. In any case, if she wrote it up for *True Confessions*, the article would be called "I Gave up a Man for a Career." Never mind that she had yet to find a career. And the man in question didn't seem to be pining away for her.

The woman's look told Ellen that she wouldn't be satisfied until she offered something.

"Well, my mother was the inspiration for that story in *Ranch Romance* about the girl whose mother wants to marry her off to the cattle baron she doesn't love. You see, my mother keeps trying to pick a husband for me—the butcher's nephew, the new school principal, the minister's son—and that gave me the idea of a mother trying to force her own ideas of happiness onto the daughter.

"But the girl in the story isn't me," Ellen added hastily. "I'm not interested in marriage right now."

"That's good to know. I don't want any woman hired for this project to be engaged or married. It's a distraction. And I don't want anyone who drinks or smokes. Reflects badly on this project."

Ellen assured her she did neither, omitting the facts that she'd sipped gin from a date's flask at a football game and she'd once tried a cigarette because it seemed to be what modern girls did.

The WPA woman seemed satisfied with Ellen's answers. Tapping the papers in front of her, Mrs. Fletcher turned to the

14

question of Ellen's need for a job. It was a question Ellen expected, and she'd rehearsed the answer over and over again. It was quite simple, she explained. Her family lived in a small town where her father was a mechanic. He had his own garage with a single gas pump out front. Ellen's brother, who was now married and had brought his wife to live with his family, worked with their father and found the occasional handyman job to help out. But times were tough. People couldn't afford to have their automobiles or tractors repaired, so Ellen's father, being the good man he was, did it on promise of payment or for a sack of potatoes or a basket of eggs. As for college, Ellen would never have been able to go if not for her Aunt Viv and Uncle Frank in Tulsa. They had oil money and offered to spend some of it on Ellen.

"No children of their own." Ellen let Mrs. Fletcher's conclusion hang in the air. The less said about Louise, the better.

"So, you see," she finished, "I would just be another mouth to feed at home, and there's the fact that my brother and his wife are now expecting a baby. The best way I can think of to help myself and my family is to find employment."

The WPA woman shifted her weight in the creaky office chair. She stared up to the ceiling as if looking for divine guidance, or maybe, Ellen thought, she was considering the best way to tell her "no." Ellen sat straight in her chair. She clasped her hands in her lap, hoping she looked calm while her worst fears pounded in her head. She was fast running out of options. She couldn't live off the little she made from selling stories to pulp magazines, and the graduation money from Uncle Frank and Aunt Viv would soon be gone. She sent up a silent prayer that the woman's decision would not send her home to face not only her family—but also the town—with her failure.

Mrs. Fletcher roused herself. "You have the job, and I want you to know why. You listened when I talked, which is important when you want people to tell you things in an interview. You appear to be a fine young woman. You don't have painted nails—always a sign of a loose woman in my book—and you're not chewing gum. The last applicant popped her gum so loud, I could barely hear myself think. See Miss Bailey in the next office for the particulars of salary and lodging arrangements in Opal's Grove. Good luck."

Ellen was dumbfounded. Fingernail polish and gum? Then the rest hit her. When she thought about it later, she marveled she had resisted the urge to run around the desk and throw her arms around Mrs. Fletcher. Instead, in a voice she hardly recognized, she calmly thanked the woman, adding that she looked forward to meeting the old settlers and saving their stories for future generations.

CHAPTER 3
TOPEKA, 1936
NANCY

In the time it took to walk three blocks to her automobile, the dazed feeling had been replaced by giddy relief. Ellen could hardly wait to tell Nancy the news. Her friend had cheered her on at every turn and insisted she stay with her at her parents' home until Ellen got on her feet.

She drove expertly through the downtown area. Slowly, stores, restaurants, and small shops gave way to tree-lined streets. Nancy's family lived in a neighborhood of comfortable homes with large backyards. Ellen pulled into the driveway of a brick Tudor-style house. She barely had time to step out of the car when Nancy came rushing from the side door.

"I've been watching for you! Mother and I have been on pins and needles. What happened?"

Laughing, Ellen threw out her arms. "I am officially employed!"

"I knew it!" Nancy clapped her hands like a child given a wonderful gift. "Come inside. I want to hear everything. Mother had to leave for some committee luncheon, but she'll be so happy for you." Nancy steered her friend into the kitchen.

"It's Rose's day off, so you'll have to settle for my sandwiches."

"Bologna and cheese on white bread?"

"Certainly not," Nancy huffed. "That's the soup kitchen specialty, as you well know. I've made enough of those sandwiches to never want to see another."

17

Ellen knew Nancy didn't mean a word of it. She worked at the soup kitchen three times a week, making sandwiches, filling bowls of soup, and handing out cups of coffee. To look at Nancy, you wouldn't expect to find her anywhere near the railyard and its kitchen. But then, people tended to misjudge Nancy. All they saw was a pretty blonde with high spirits, the sort of girl with little on her mind other than deciding which pair of shoes to buy or contemplating which party to attend. That was Ellen's first impression when Nancy arrived at college with two trunks of clothes, a tennis racket, and lots of spending money. Ellen was sure this girl assigned to be her roommate on the whim of whoever directed women's housing must be a snob. Ellen expected Nancy to pledge a sorority and move into one of the Greek houses the moment she had the chance. She was wrong. And with fascination she watched as Nancy managed to sidestep the rituals of sorority rushes and invitations without hurting feelings or losing a place in college social life.

As roommates, they quickly moved from being politely formal to an easy camaraderie. The smooth transition to friendship surprised Ellen, almost as much as her discovery that Nancy intended to have a career after college. Nancy didn't look like the type to think of college as anything more than an entertaining adventure leading to finding a husband. Ellen had soon revised that assessment, promising herself to stop judging people on first impressions.

Nancy, it turned out, had definite ideas concerning her future. Facing the world with a confidence that never considered failure, she had her life mapped out with a step-by-step plan. After college, she would go to law school. When that was completed, she would join the family firm, working alongside her father, uncle, and older brother. And then, she would marry Franklin, who was studying to be a surgeon.

Nancy was well aware that her crowd of friends thought

Franklin a bit of a bore. He preferred playing bridge to an evening of dancing. He'd rather listen to opera than swing music, and his interest in Egyptian archaeology left people baffled. So did his willingness to let Nancy manage their lives. What her friends said didn't matter to Nancy. To her, Franklin was the smartest, most interesting man she had ever met. For his part, Franklin was besotted and quite willing to let Nancy make plans for them both. She had it all laid out. They would marry after she finished law school and Franklin had his medical degree. She'd already decided on what sort of house they would buy. As for children, she thought three would nicely round out their family.

"Don't tell me a thing until I get these to the table." Nancy placed chicken salad sandwiches on two plates, plopping two small bunches of grapes on each as an afterthought. Ellen filled glasses with iced tea, and the two settled into chairs opposite each other.

"Now! I want to know everything. Don't leave out a word."

Between bites, Ellen eagerly recounted the meeting with Mrs. Fletcher.

"It's a good thing I didn't use any of your nail polish." Ellen pointed to Nancy's red-lacquered nails. "According to the WPA, that's a sure sign of a loose woman, and I wouldn't have gotten the job."

"Good Lord!" Nancy threw back her head and laughed. "Hasn't this Mrs. Fletcher heard about the modern woman?"

"Evidently not. Liquor and cigarettes are out, too."

"Well, we both know cigarettes are no great loss. You almost puked trying one."

Ellen groaned. "Don't remind me." She leaned back, her face serious. "I have to say, I feel as if a huge burden just slipped off my shoulders. If this didn't pan out, I was thinking of taking the money Uncle Frank and Aunt Viv gave me for graduation and

19

hopping a train. Maybe go to Hollywood and see if I might get into the business of writing movie scripts."

Nancy believed her. Ellen could be quite stubborn once she'd made up her mind. "I can see you going to New York. But Hollywood"—Nancy shook her head—"it just chews people up and spits them out. Look what happened to the Kansas Wheat Queen."

Veronica Batts, the girl who traveled from town to town promoting Kansas wheat, looked like the girl next door in her newspaper pictures. But Ellen and Nancy remembered a different Veronica, the one who sauntered into that college dance wearing a clingy, white-satin evening gown that showed off every curve. She was on the arm of Jason Davis.

Nancy watched Ellen's reaction at the mention of the Wheat Queen. She hadn't meant to bring up Jason, even indirectly, but she still thought Ellen had made a monumental mistake when she abruptly broke up with him. Nancy was sure that if Ellen had given Jason time, he would have come to accept Ellen's drive to write and earn a living from it. That's how Nancy saw it, but Ellen said she wasn't up to trying to work it out with Jason and get on with a career at the same time.

"Sorry. I didn't mean to mention Veronica. I was just thinking of the scuttlebutt my brother picked up from one of his lawyer friends."

Ellen shook her head. "Look, Jason is over and done with. He was gone from my life even before he showed up with Veronica. Now spill the beans: what happened to the Wheat Queen?"

"Well," Nancy leaned across the table, lowering her voice, "the farm group that sponsors the contest wants to sue the queen. Under her contract, she's supposed to represent the state's wheat industry for a year—you know, visiting fairs and going to community events. But she took off for Hollywood. Going to be a big star."

Nancy made a harrumph noise. "She must not be too bright, or maybe she's just too full of herself. It probably never occurred to her that hundreds of pretty girls who've been queens of something or other show up thinking the movie studios will grab them up. Word is that she barely found work as an extra. Now she's back home. Her folks are furious, and the neighbors are whispering. She's lost her crown and the prizes she won. On top of that, she's got a bunch of farmers ready to take her to court."

Ellen wondered if Jason knew. And would he care? She'd been angrier with herself than Jason when he showed up with Veronica. It had been her idea to end things, but it hurt to see him with someone else. She'd liked him from the day she walked into the college's newspaper office and saw him sitting at the managing editor's desk. A casual cup of coffee at the Student Union led to a movie date, which turned into meeting after classes and away from the school paper. Ellen would never admit it, even to Nancy, but she was crazy about Jason. All the more reason, she decided, to call a halt. If they kept seeing each other, the career could go out the window. She didn't want to look back when she was fifty or sixty years old and wonder what she could have done, who she might have been, if she had stuck to her dreams when she was twenty-two.

Ellen thought she explained this to Jason in a mature, reasonable manner. Looking back, she could see how wrong she was to think he would simply see things her way. She was not prepared for his reaction, which began with disbelief and ended in an explosion of anger before he walked away. They'd left things at that. Only a glance across the aisle at graduation marked their goodbye. Nancy told her more than once that it was a shame, but Ellen wouldn't budge.

Nancy began to clear the table. "Now, I'm going to bring something up you probably don't want to think about, but how are you going to tell your family? Telephone?" An impish grin crossed her face. "How about a postcard? That way, the mail carrier will see the card, and if he's anything like our Mr. Jenkins, who can't help but look over what he drops in the box, half of your hometown will know about your job before your family. Of course, your mother will have a fit—not just because everybody will know her business, but because she had another plan for you."

They burst out laughing. Over the past four years, Ellen had regaled Nancy with tales of the men, most of them unsuspecting, thrown in her path by her mother.

"The job starts a week from Monday, and I should get settled beforehand in the boardinghouse the WPA picked out. Still, there's time to go down and see the family. I should give the news in person. Dad will be happy for me. He may not understand what I'm aiming for—sometimes I don't, either— but he'll back me up. So will Eddie and Maryanne, although it will have as much to do with getting my bedroom for the baby they're expecting. I think we can predict what Mother will say."

"She might surprise you. People can be unpredictable."

Ellen hoped her mother might come around, but she was doubtful.

CHAPTER 4
OPAL'S GROVE, 1936
AGATHA AND IVY

The two women sat rocking on the front porch. Half-finished glasses of lemonade sat on a table between them. The two had been friends for over seventy years. It seemed a mismatched friendship to those who knew them in the old days. Agatha, wife of a banker, moved in the social circle of women who had maids and cooks. Ivy, married to a farmer, often worked alongside her husband, raised chickens, and did her own housework. Their differences in social standing hardly mattered these days. To anyone catching a glimpse of the women sitting on Agatha's porch, they were simply elderly widows enjoying the late afternoon breeze.

If truth be told, Agatha's house was the plainest one in what was considered the fashionable part of town. The house was attractive and well cared for, but it lacked the stained-glass windows, turrets, and gingerbread decoration seen on other homes. The simplicity was intentional. When Thomas Bright built the house for his bride in 1869, he wanted the townspeople to know that, as a banker, he stood for financial stability, not overindulgence. Agatha was new to the town, but she understood the value of appearances.

Agatha glanced at her friend and smiled. She didn't have to say this was her favorite time of day; Ivy knew. All the sharp angles of the noonday sun were gone. The light was softer now, dappling grass and leaves in shades of light and shadow.

They were silent. There was no need to make constant

conversation, although Ivy had something on her mind. For a good part of the last hour, she had put it off, but it was getting late. Her daughter-in-law would arrive soon to drive her home. She took a deep breath, but before she could utter the first word, the quiet was interrupted. The jarring sound of something being dragged along the sidewalk was accompanied by boyish voices, one complaining that it was his turn to pull the wagon.

The women exchanged surprised looks. "What on earth?" They both leaned forward, trying to look beyond the big locust tree in Agatha's front yard. In just moments, ten-year-old Jimmy Picketts and his younger brother, Timmy, came into view. Jimmy pulled a faded red wagon, the front wheels wobbling badly from one side to the other. A pouting Timmy followed behind.

"Hey, Miss Agatha. Miss Ivy." The boys trailed along the white picket fence until they reached the open gate. "We brought you a pie, Miss Agatha." Jimmy grinned and beamed with pride. Timmy pointed at the wagon and gave the women a big smile. A front tooth was missing.

"My goodness! What a wonderful surprise!" Agatha brought both hands up to the sides of her face to emphasize her amazement.

"Mama said to thank you for the roast you sent over, and she baked you this pie."

"Well, you tell your mama that I was just glad she took that roast off my hands. I don't know what got into Martha, making such a big Sunday dinner when she knew there was just going to be three of us." Agatha began to push herself out of the rocker, her cane in one hand. Ivy motioned for her to stay put and made her way down the front steps to the sidewalk where the boys waited.

"I'll take it up to her," she half whispered to the boys like a conspirator. "She just got that cane, and she's still learning how to use it."

The boys peered around Ivy to stare. "Did she break her leg?" the older one asked.

"No, no. She's got arthritis, and the doctor said she has to use the cane." Lifting the pie out of the wagon, she gave the boys a look. "Can I peek under the cloth?"

"Oh, yes. It's a strawberry pie. The berries came out of our own patch in the backyard," Jimmy answered.

Ivy held the pie with one hand on the bottom of the tin and pulled the cloth up at one corner. "Well, it's just about the most perfect pie I ever saw." She turned back to Agatha, carrying the pie with both hands as she climbed the steps. "I may have to stay for supper just to get a slice of this."

Agatha folded the covering back for a look and made appreciative noises, but the boys were already moving down the street. Ivy opened the screen door and headed into the house, where she was met by Agatha's cook halfway down the hall. Martha showed no surprise. Inevitably, families that received Sunday dinner from Agatha, accompanied by the lame excuse of Martha overdoing, sent something in return. Once it was a sack of turnips. Another time, a bunch of onions.

When Ivy rejoined Agatha, she gave her friend's hand a little pat as she settled back into her rocker. "That was a real nice thing to do."

Agatha shrugged. "The father fell off a stack of pallets at work and broke his arm. They're keeping him on halftime doing little jobs, but that's not enough to feed a family of six. It's a ticklish business sending over food, but I don't think I hurt anyone's pride when I accept what they bring in return."

She straightened stiffly in her chair and wagged her finger at Ivy. "And you're one to talk, sending Thelma out into the night to leave a sack of clothes at one place, a bag of underwear or a pair of shoes at another."

"*I'm* sending Thelma?" Ivy shot back with a smile. "While

she's delivering my goods, she's also leaving the bags of groceries you give her." Ivy shook her head. "We're quite a pair, trying to ease away the problems this Depression brings people."

"More like that story of the Dutch boy trying to hold back the floodwater with a finger in the dike." Agatha rocked for a moment, letting Ivy get settled.

"Now, before Constance shows up to cart you home, you better tell me what's on your mind. You're fretting over something, and that's not like you."

Ivy sighed. "It's those interviews Iris Hewitt talked to us about. I've been thinking about Wheat and feel bad no one will hear the things he could have told them. Your Thomas, too."

Agatha nodded. "Thomas and his family lived in a tent until they got a house built. His father opened his first bank out of a wagon."

"I just wish the WPA had picked some other place. I'm not sure I'm up to talking about the past."

"Oh, for heaven's sakes," Agatha interrupted. "Somebody asks you a question, and you answer. If you don't want to answer, don't. You tell what *you* want, and leave out the rest. I certainly will, and I've never known you to be shy about saying just what's on your mind."

Ivy had no argument for that. She'd always been plainspoken, an attribute not everyone admired.

"I'm worried about Nettie. There's no telling what will come out of her mouth."

Agatha gave her friend a long stare and bristled. "I don't give a fig about Nettie Vine, or anything she might say. I learned how to deal with her long ago. But it just galls me that my husband, and now my son, ended up being guardians for that old woman. I don't know what possessed Sylvester Vine to put that in his will. And another thing . . ."

Ivy laid a hand on Agatha's arm. "Settle down. It was a credit to Thomas and to the bank that Mr. Vine trusted them with Nettie's affairs. Goodness knows neither she nor her mother could have managed things."

Agatha was only slightly mollified. Ivy was sorry she'd given voice to her misgivings. It was just all this sudden talk about the old days. Ivy remembered much of those times with fondness, but some things were better left unsaid and forgotten.

"Ivy, I don't think anyone will give much credit to anything Nettie says. People here abouts know her and her ways. Every town has to have an eccentric, and she's ours. I doubt most folks ever give her a moment's thought unless Stella Castle—who in my book is a saint and should have a stained-glass window named for her at the Baptist Church—has to go hunting for her. Last week Stella called the police when Nettie was nowhere to be found. Martha told me one of the deputies found Nettie sitting in that ramshackle building that used to be John Featherstone's store."

Ivy felt a chill. John Featherstone. Nettie remembered him well enough to end up at his old place.

Agatha eyed her friend. "Don't fret. That sort of behavior only proves—as my grandson would say—that she's not all there." Agatha tapped a finger to her forehead.

Despite herself, Ivy laughed. "How in the world did she get to Mr. Featherstone's? It's almost out of town."

"She walked. She was always quick on her feet."

"Wandering around town like that." Ivy frowned. "That's what I mean; she's unpredictable. She still does whatever she likes, and she could say anything."

"And no one would believe it, even if it was true." Agatha banged the cane. "Forget Nettie. We promised to talk to these WPA people, and we will."

Ivy gave in. "By the time we're finished, people will think we were the bravest and smartest pioneer women this country ever saw."

Agatha's laugh was low and throaty. "Well, don't overdo it. Think of it this way: it's sort of like us handing out food and clothes. We're fighting Old Man Depression. Those people being hired to do the interviews will have their jobs just a little longer if we talk to them."

"True enough. I guess we have to think of our children and grandchildren, too. They're expecting us to take part. They're proud of us being 'old settlers,' and Constance is already counting on using my interview as her stepping-stone to being president of Kansas Daughters. She's been wrangling for years to get that position. This just might do it, or so she thinks."

The two women burst into laughter. Ivy's daughter-in-law was a source of amusement, and sometimes exasperation. When their children were young, Agatha and Ivy talked about how wonderful it would be if Agatha's daughter married one of Ivy's two boys. But the children only seemed to notice each other when they kicked at one another under the kids table during family get-togethers. Agatha's daughter married a lawyer in Topeka. Ivy's oldest boy got a job with the railroad, moved to Santa Fe, and married a woman there. Ivy's other boy, Dell, married Constance soon after he came home from business school.

As if the mere mention of her name caused her to materialize, Constance pulled to the curb. The car screeched and lurched before coming to a complete stop.

"And they say I'm a hazard behind the wheel," mumbled Agatha. It still rankled that her son sold her Oldsmobile after that one tiny accident. Anyone could have wound up crossways on the sidewalk blocking the steps to the Methodist church.

Constance got out of the car, gave a big wave, and joined the women on the porch. A tall woman in her fifties, Constance carried herself with an air of importance and purpose.

"Sorry I'm late, but the meeting just went on and on." Constance was on practically every committee and board the town could devise. Her parents had once thought that her purpose in life would be as a missionary to China, but when Constance met Dell, she decided all those people in foreign lands would have to hear about the Baby Jesus from someone else. Being the best wife to Dell and improving the town of Opal's Grove became her mission field. Since the death of Ivy's husband, Constance had made Ivy one of her special projects.

Ivy eased her long, thin frame out of the rocker, took the covered plate of sliced pie from Martha, who had suddenly appeared at her elbow, and followed Constance down the steps. She turned back to Agatha and shimmied her skinny behind. "Do you think anyone will believe I used to dance at the Hurley-Burley?"

Constance gaped in shock, sending the two old friends into a paroxysm of laughter.

The Hurley-Burley had been notorious. Located outside the city limits and just barely inside the law, the place was a saloon with gaming tables and a stage where three or four dancers of various sizes and talent entertained the fellows. Although respectable people weren't supposed to know about what went on there, they did. Just as they knew the crowd favorite was Arlette, who could walk across the stage on her hands, do a flip, and end up in the splits.

"You never did!" The color drained from Constance's face.

"Of course not," Ivy managed to say through her laughter. "Don't you know when you're being teased?"

Constance scowled. "Well, I hope you can be serious when you're interviewed and just stick to the facts."

"I'll do my best," Ivy mumbled, waving over her shoulder to Agatha.

CHAPTER 5
OPAL'S GROVE, 1936
ELLEN

A large storage room in the basement of the Dobbs County courthouse had been converted into office space. Someone had managed to find mismatched chairs and battered desks. They contrasted sharply with the almost-new typewriters rented from the local high school. The odor of cleaning solutions mixed with the musty smells of damp and age. Iris Hewitt—president of the local historical society, director of the public library, and head of the WPA project in the county—stood just inside the door, introducing herself to each person.

Ellen shook the woman's hand, found a seat, and watched as the others filed into the room. She had arrived in town on the previous Saturday, after spending a few days at home. The visit hadn't been the disaster she'd envisioned. She'd surprised them at supper when she pulled into the driveway. Her brother, Ed, met her at the door and pulled her into the house. Ellen's family wasn't the kind that hugged. Her brother thumped Ellen on the shoulder with a loose fist, the way he did when they were kids. Her sister-in-law giggled and squeezed an arm. Her mother patted her on the back as she eased Ellen into a chair at the dining table. Her father smiled and nodded. She hadn't wanted them to think she was home to stay, so she broke the news right away. There was just a moment when Mother seemed ready to launch into the usual lecture about matrimony and its benefits, but she stopped herself. Whether it was her father's slight shake of the head or her mother finally surrendering to her daughter's plans, the subject was dropped. Ellen was grateful that over the next few days, family conversations revolved around her mother's garden, the coming baby, and the work her brother and father did on her automobile to keep it in top-notch running condition.

It was only when Ellen was packing to leave that her mother made a last half-hearted attempt to change Ellen's mind. "I hate seeing you churning up all this misery for yourself," she began. "You're chasing a pie-in-the-sky dream, and when it doesn't happen, you'll be hurt. I just don't want you to be bitter, and a bitter old spinster at that."

Those words hung in Ellen's head and made her smile as she glanced around the courthouse basement and the group there. She turned to Audrey Varns, her new roommate at Miss Jewell's boardinghouse, and smiled. "Here we go," she whispered.

Iris Hewitt stepped to the front of the room. A woman of middle years, she wore her muddy-brown hair fixed to the top of her head in a complicated arrangement of bobby pins and tight curls. A pair of reading glasses dangled from a chain around her neck. She clapped her hands sharply as if bringing a group of misbehaving schoolchildren to order. She welcomed the group, encouraged them to read up on local history, and pointed to manila folders arranged on a small table to her left. Inside each were the names and addresses of old settlers assigned to each interviewer.

With the skill of someone accustomed to being in charge, the woman went over the guidelines for transcribing and typing up the interviews. She had taken the liberty of arranging the times for each interview, making it clear she was to be consulted on any changes. "Now, as I call your name, please come forward, pick up the folder with your name on the front, and introduce yourself to your colleagues."

Ellen was glad to be one of the first. She took her folder,

faced the group, and introduced herself. "In college I worked on the school paper, and some of my short stories have been published. I don't know where writing will take me. I just know it's what I want to do." With that, she slipped back to her spot and studied the others. It seemed an unlikely group, thrown together by chance and unemployment.

There was Mae Swenson, whose poetry was published once a week in the local paper. The woman had a sweet smile but a rather vague expression, as if her muse were calling to her even at that moment. Ellen wondered how the woman would ever be able to focus on asking questions and listening to the answers. Then there was the man who looked to be in his thirties and introduced himself as Cowboy Joe. He penned cowboy poetry, but his one great hope, he confided, was to go on the radio to sing his songs. Joe had the assignment of traveling throughout Dobbs and surrounding counties to record songs on a special machine.

The science-fiction writer spoke next, saying little about himself and a great deal about the imaginary planet Xandabar. Iris Hewitt skillfully cut him off and called Audrey to the front. Audrey gave her dark, short-cropped hair a pat and offered the group a wide smile before introducing herself as an out-of-work librarian who'd turned to writing children's books that no one wanted. "Oh, there was one publisher," she added rather wistfully. "But the company went bankrupt a week after I signed a contract." When one or two in the group groaned in sympathy, Audrey shrugged. "But something will turn up. This job did. So, I'm not discouraged."

Heads nodded, encouraging Audrey's optimism. The mood was just as quickly dampened by the man Ellen guessed to be in his mid-thirties. Wearing a tweed jacket too heavy for the warm weather, he scanned the room with a dour expression, as if evaluating a freshman class. He cleared his throat before introducing himself as a temporarily unemployed college teacher who wished to be addressed as Professor Reynolds.

"Oh, boy," Ellen muttered.

The young man next to her leaned across and whispered, "You got that right. He'll get booted out of the county if he uses that snotty tone with an old farmer and tells him to call him 'professor.' Serve him right, too."

He grinned and extended a hand to Ellen. "Jess Smith, high school graduate."

Ellen gave his hand a business-like shake just as Jess was called to the front. He was a local hired by the WPA. "I just graduated from high school," he began, "and maybe I'll have a chance to go to college, but what I really want to do, after three years of covering sports news for both the school and town papers, is to be a sports reporter in a big city."

He glanced at Iris. "But, for now, I'm being sent to the far end of the county, where I'll stay with a great-aunt I haven't seen since I was twelve, but whose house, as I remember it, smells of camphor, cats, and old socks. I'm happy to have this job, but I sure don't look forward to Aunt Sissy." Laughter, including Mrs. Hewitt's, followed Jess as he took his seat.

Iris Hewitt announced the meeting was ended, but she expected that beginning the next day, everyone would begin their interviews as scheduled.

As people began to mill around and leave, Ellen tucked her folder into her worn leather satchel and walked to where Audrey was engaged in a one-sided conversation with the professor.

"Do you want a ride back to Miss Jewell's?" Ellen asked. Audrey had arrived in Opal's Grove driving a rusted, dented Ford that didn't look as if it could go another mile. "After lunch, I plan to track down the addresses for my assignments. We could look for yours, too."

"No, thanks," Audrey turned and flashed a grin. "I appreciate the ride getting here this morning, but I think I'll look around downtown. My first interviews are all at one place—the old folks' home on the west end of town." She gave the professor a sweet smile. "Me and Professor Reynolds are both assigned there for a couple of days."

Audrey put enough emphasis on the name to make it sound ridiculous. Ellen thought she saw the man flinch.

"You can call it an old folks' home, but we both know it's the poor farm," he huffed.

"Then we should take a good look at the place. See what it's like, because we might end up there if this Depression keeps on." Audrey's look dared the man to say more.

Ellen mumbled that she'd see Audrey later and followed the others into the hall. On the stairs she found herself next to Jess.

"I was wondering," she said as they reached the first floor, "how are you getting to wherever it is you're going?"

"The place is Boxley. It's not much more than about ten houses with a general store, post office, and gas station. And I get there on a motorcycle."

He laughed at Ellen's look of surprise.

"Yep. It belongs to my brother, but I'm riding it while he's out in Idaho at a CCC camp."

"Idaho? I've heard people talking about a bridge project just outside town. Why isn't he here working on that?"

"The bridge is WPA, although they brought in some CCC boys to clear brush and haul rock. Some are local boys, but most are from somewhere else. They live in a camp down near the river." He shifted his folder from one hand to the other, anxious to be on his way. "Well, bye. I'm going over to the library. Mrs. Hewitt's big on local history. She and the historical society set up what they call 'the Kansas Room' and filled it with history books and old things people have donated. I don't want to look stupid when I talk to these old-timers, so I've been reading up since last week."

As he started for the door, Ellen hurried to catch up and asked if she could tag along. She knew some state history, but nothing about the county. A browse through some local history wasn't a bad idea.

Jess gave a shrug, trying to appear nonchalant, but he looked pleased to have Ellen along. On the short walk to the library, she learned that Jess had played basketball and baseball on the school teams. He wanted to learn the game of golf, if he ever had the money to buy clubs, and he was dead serious about being a sportswriter.

The library sat on a corner lot just off the courthouse square. Built of limestone, its double front doors of dark wood were flanked by stone columns. Ellen's eyes widened in surprise. "I was expecting something less grand. The library in my hometown is located in the old two-room grade school."

"Wait till you see the inside." Jess reached for the door. "One thing you can say about this town, when people decide to do something, they do it in a big way."

Ellen stepped through the door, scanning the central room. To the right, an ornately carved staircase led to the second floor. To the left was a large, highly polished desk. Behind it sat a woman with the ramrod posture of a commanding general and the sharp eyes of a store detective.

"Hello, Miss Riley." Jess stepped up to the desk.

"Hello, Jess." The pleasant tone of the woman's voice contradicted her physical presence. "I thought you started that job today," she said, putting aside a file of library cards.

"Yes, ma'am, I did. I've just come over from the courthouse. This is Ellen Hartley, one of the other WPA people." He turned and motioned Ellen forward.

Ellen murmured a "pleased to meet you," and let Jess do the talking.

"She wanted to see the Kansas Room, and I'd like to read some more before I head out to Boxley this afternoon."

"That's fine." The woman's nod was curt. "Mrs. Hewitt must still be over at the courthouse, but you know where things are. If you need anything, please don't hesitate to ask for assistance. We don't approve of people riffling through the books in that room." She glanced at Ellen, including her in the warning.

"You don't have to worry, ma'am. I'll be careful." Jess led Ellen past shelves of books to a room at the back. When they were safely out of the woman's line of sight, he grinned.

"She's a real character, isn't she?"

"I'll say. She's like a guard dog. Does anybody have the nerve to come in and check out books?"

"Oh, she's okay. You just have to get used to her." He pointed toward an arched doorway. "The Kansas Room."

Ellen followed him. A table with four chairs sat at the room's center. Bookshelves lined two walls. Another wall was covered with framed portraits of important local men, as well as historical photographs of Opal's Grove. Under two sets of windows, glass-topped display cases filled the remaining space.

While Jess selected his books, Ellen examined the cases. The miscellaneous collection of branding irons, hand tools, hats and gloves from bygone days, and pieces of china and silver held no interest for her. The items and the names attached to them with small labels meant even less. About to turn away and join Jess, her eyes caught the contents of the last case.

At least one hundred arrowheads, of various sizes and colors, were arranged in perfect rows. Next to them were larger pieces, ax heads and grinding stones. At the far end, and easy to overlook because of their size, were two carvings, no bigger than a person's thumb. A small yellowing label identified one of the carvings as a bird, the other as a turtle.

"Oh, my." Ellen barely breathed the words. When she was eight years old, she had found an arrowhead in a recently plowed field. After her father explained what it was and who made it, Ellen felt a tremendous sense of wonder that she had found such a treasure. She never discovered another. Now, here in this case, was a collection that must have taken years to unearth.

Straightening, she took in the whole effect. A large hand-printed label across the top of the case identified the collector as J.S. Featherstone. Beneath his name was smaller printing: "All items were found along the Big Muddy River. Mr. Featherstone believed these items proved an Indian village once existed along the river, but the exact location eluded him."

Ellen called to Jess and motioned at the case. "Is there anything about this Featherstone in any of those histories?"

"Not much, but I read about him just the other day." He thumbed through a book, finding the page he wanted. "Says he was born in Kentucky but left home early and headed west. Became a mountain man and once lived among the Sioux Indians. He also drove supply wagons for the army and acted as a scout for survey teams. Died in 1875. It doesn't say when he settled in the county."

He closed the book, disappointed there wasn't more.

Ellen shrugged at the short biography. "Too bad he's not around to interview. I'd love to hear his stories."

Jess agreed and went back to his book. Ellen took a chair across from Jess and opened one of the histories he'd pulled from the shelves. She skimmed through the accounts of the county's early settlers, the coming of the railroad, and the homesteads that began to dot the landscape. Shutting the book, she pulled Mrs. Hewitt's list from her satchel and began to leaf through the pages of the county biography Jess had used to find

Featherstone. She began to search for family names that matched those on her list of people to interview. She found one name and then another.

A light tap on the doorframe interrupted the quiet.

"Sorry to bother you." Iris Hewitt walked into the room. "Miss Riley told me you were back here."

"Hello, Jess." She nodded in his direction. "Still reading up on your history. Good for you."

"Yes, ma'am, but I better get going." He looked at the watch that had been his graduation present.

"And, Miss Hartley," the librarian turned her full attention to Ellen, "I'm so pleased that at least one person from the group this morning took my advice about visiting our little history collection."

Ellen started to explain she'd just tagged along with Jess, but Iris wasn't finished. "Inez Fletcher was very impressed with you, which is why I assigned you to interview people I consider most important to this project. Now, I'm sure it was the right thing to do."

"And I get Aunt Sissy," Jess broke in good-naturedly.

Ellen gave him a smile of gratitude. Mrs. Hewitt had taken her by surprise, and she still wasn't sure how to respond. Although she'd gotten the job, she still found it difficult to believe that the WPA woman in Topeka had been impressed.

"I'll certainly do my best," she finally managed, thinking that, while Iris Hewitt seemed nice enough, the woman would be watching her, maybe more than the others.

CHAPTER 6
IVY

Ivy Hamilton lived on a quiet street west of the courthouse square. Her trim brick bungalow was fronted by forsythia bushes. A detached garage sat back from the house. It wasn't a big place like Agatha's, but Ivy was more than satisfied with the house she and Wheat built when they decided to sell the farm and move to town. It was time, Wheat had announced one day. The work was getting to be too much, and, since the boys didn't want to raise cattle or plant crops, better take the good money being offered for the property and go to town, where the only farming he wanted to do was keep a vegetable garden. That was in 1920.

Ivy watched as an automobile pulled into the driveway and a young woman emerged with a battered satchel. She opened the screen door before Ellen took two steps across the porch. Ellen felt the woman taking her measure, just as she tried to hide her own appraisal of Ivy Hamilton. Ellen knew the woman was in her mid-eighties, but she seemed younger. It was the gleam in her eyes and her open smile, Ellen decided. The effect made her feel welcome, as if she were just the person Ivy was hoping to see that day.

She felt herself relax as she followed the woman into the house. The Hamilton name hadn't come up in the county histories she'd read, and within minutes Ellen guessed the reason. The histories mentioned the area's great agricultural potential, but said very little about people like the Hamiltons, who ran the farms and ranches. Ivy explained her move to town as she led Ellen through the living room and past a dining room.

Ivy came to a stop in the kitchen and pointed through a side door to the left. "I told Wheat I only wanted two things in the new house. There had to be a room for my sewing and a screened-in porch where we could sit and catch the breeze without being bothered with flies and mosquitoes."

The woman suddenly stopped her commentary. "Oh, dear, I didn't ask if the porch would suit you. Maybe you'd rather go into the living room."

Ellen assured her that the porch was just fine and followed the woman to the wicker chairs arranged on either side of a small table. As both women settled themselves, Ivy waved toward the backyard. "We had seven good years in this place, and then Wheat up and died. Out there in the garden. He just keeled over in the lettuce. I've never been so mad at anybody in my life. Leaving me alone like that."

Ellen stopped rummaging in her satchel for paper and pencil. "I had an aunt who said the same thing when her husband passed on. For weeks, she'd stand in the kitchen, throw back her head, and shout as if he were hovering over the house and could hear every word."

Ivy laughed. "That's the way I felt. And it's too bad he's not here to tell his story."

Ellen got her pad and pencil ready. "Well, tell me. I'll include it with yours, if you like."

Ivy liked the idea. "Wheaton Jefferson Hamilton was his full name, but nobody called him anything but Wheat. He had so many experiences. He was born on a ranch in Texas but left home when he was just fourteen. You see, his mother died and the father married a widow lady with two boys who made Wheat's life a misery. The father never stood up for Wheat. Afraid of losing the wife, I suppose. One day, Wheat just up and left. He got a job at one place, and then another. Three years or so later, he was working for an outfit driving cattle from Texas to Kansas. It was hard work, but he liked it. Some of the tales he told were beyond belief. Sometimes, I teased him that half of them were too wild to be true."

Ellen nodded and jotted down the woman's words in the shorthand she learned in high school and perfected while working on the college newspaper.

"Let's talk about you, Mrs. Hamilton."

"I think you're going to get to know me well enough to call me Ivy, or Miss Ivy."

"All right, Miss Ivy, and you call me Ellen."

The two women nodded to each other as if making a pact.

Ivy sat back, looking like a student who had been asked to recite a lesson. "I came to Kansas from Illinois in 1868. I arrived with my Uncle Nate—he was my mother's younger brother—and Nate's wife, Clara. I was seventeen years of age, full of excitement at the adventure I was on. I wasn't in the least bit frightened." She laughed. "If I had any sense, I would have been scared out of my shoes."

Glancing at Ellen, she asked, "Is this what you want to hear?"

Ellen looked up. A tentative smile played around her mouth. "You're doing fine. I'm the one who's nervous. You're my first interview."

"Well, don't worry; we'll get along fine. I could talk about all the changes I've seen in my lifetime. Young people today can't imagine not having talking pictures or telephones or automobiles, but I can recall when people rode in horse-drawn carriages and lit their houses with candles and oil lamps."

Ellen scribbled in her notebook. "I like that. Now, maybe you could tell me more about how you and your relatives decided to settle in Kansas."

Ivy nodded, reaching for a pair of glasses on the table. Then she rummaged through a cloth bag on the floor beside her, finally pulling out a child's dress. "I have to do something with my hands. I never could just sit. So, while I talk, I'll work on this dress hem. Some of us ladies at the Methodist Church started a clothing bank in the basement. Anybody who needs things for themselves or their children can pick up donated clothes we've repaired or the things some of us made from scratch."

"That's wonderful! I'm sure people really appreciate it."

Ivy nodded as she threaded a needle. "It does my heart good, too. There was this one family I'll never forget. The boy of about eight or nine didn't have one thing to wear but a sister's hand-me-down dress. Oh, my, the look on his face when he got a pair of overalls just made you want to cry."

The story pulled at Ellen's heart, but there was a job to do. She steered Mrs. Hamilton toward it. "You were going to begin with how your settlement came about."

"Well, I guess you could say I ended up in Kansas because of the Battle of Shiloh during the Civil War. My father, Herbert Williams, was in the 18th Illinois and wounded on the battle's first day. One minié ball ripped across his left shoulder. Another grazed his scalp and tore off part of an ear. He was knocked unconscious. When he awoke during the night, he could hear the horrible sounds of the wounded and dying all around him. As he later told it, he thought he would die there, too, but a Mr. Graham from his company came out early the next morning, found Father, and carried him back to a field hospital. That may be too grand of a way to describe it. I heard Father once tell our hired hand it was the closest thing to hell he ever hoped to see.

"Now you're wondering how this led to Kansas." Ivy looked up, her face crinkled in a smile. "Getting to that. Father recovered from his wounds, but after he returned home, he kept thinking about Mr. Graham, who came back from the war, packed up his family, and headed to Kansas to homestead. He wrote letters encouraging Father to do the same. And he might have done just that, but Mother wouldn't hear of it.

"You see, ours was a prosperous farm. Father didn't have to go into the army. He could have paid someone to take his place. That was allowed, but he felt compelled to go. I don't think Mother ever forgave him for that, and she certainly had no intention of uprooting the family and leaving a comfortable home to start all over again."

When Ivy stopped to find another spool of thread, Ellen asked, "What about Uncle Nate?"

Ivy smiled. "Ah, Nate. You couldn't find a kinder man. He went off to fight near the end of the war, but mostly it was over before he saw or did anything. He felt like he'd been cheated, but he wasn't going to miss out on the adventure of going west. By that time, Father had read every book and pamphlet he could find on Kansas, passing them on to Nate, who was wild to homestead. So was his wife, Clara. She was a tiny thing, but absolutely fearless. Homesteading was like a fever. Father had it. Then, Nate and Clara. Their friends, Caleb and Hannah Henson, caught it, and finally me.

"Nate and Clara were agreeable to me coming along. They knew it would take a lot of work to build up a homestead, so another pair of hands was welcome. I had the idea, too, that I could help out by making money as a seamstress. I was just a girl when my grandmother and mother began teaching me embroidery and handstitching. I learned to operate a sewing machine when Mother bought one after the war.

"Whether I sewed by hand or with that machine, I had a talent I've never been able to explain. Just like some people can hear a piece of music and then play it note for note, I can look at a picture of a skirt or cape or shirtwaist, and I know how it is

43

constructed and what fabrics work best."

Ellen kept writing, her squiggles and swirls of shorthand filling up page after page. Without looking up she said, "It sounds as if your father, aunt, and uncle agreed to you going along. Your mother, too?"

Ivy put down the dress. "If I tell you this, you can't write it down. When Mrs. Hewitt set up these interviews, she told us some of the stories might be printed in the county newspaper, and I surely don't want people knowing my mother only agreed to my leaving because she thought I'd find a husband."

"No!"

Ivy nodded as she pushed herself out the chair. "Let's get some iced tea." She led Ellen into the kitchen, where Ivy got glasses from a shelf, directing Ellen to a pitcher of tea sitting in the icebox.

After they returned to the porch with their drinks, Ivy began. "My mother's goal in life was to marry her two daughters off to well-bred professional men. Toward that end, after the war, she enrolled me and my sister, Violet, in a nearby female academy. Mother did not care if we learned Latin, the sonnets of Shakespeare, or how to properly serve tea. She believed young men of a certain caliber looked for such cultivated backgrounds when they chose their wives.

"Violet was very accomplished in all the social niceties, and, without any instruction, she just naturally seemed to have perfected the art of attracting suitors. She had a way of smiling at a young man and making him think everything he said, no matter how idiotic, was the most interesting thing she'd ever heard. It was no surprise when Violet married a young lawyer who had just been elected to the state legislature."

Ivy sipped her tea before continuing. "As you might imagine, Mother was thrilled with Violet's marriage. Then, she would look at me and sigh. I could never master the manners of flirtation. And truth to tell, I didn't make a great effort. To make matters worse, at least in my mother's eyes, I had this appalling habit of saying what I thought. Young ladies, even those better educated than most, were not encouraged to openly express their opinions regarding issues of the day or important events. I was considered attractive, but . . ." Ivy stopped mid-sentence, considering Ellen. "You know, I'd say your pretty brown hair is very much like the color of my own, before this gray settled in."

Ellen was pleased with the compliment. She'd always thought her hair was a nice shade of brown, although few ever commented on it.

"Anyway," Ivy returned to her story, "that's why she allowed me to leave. She'd heard the men outnumbered women in the West. Surely, she thought, I could find a bachelor homesteader to marry."

Ellen choked on her tea as she tried to stifle a laugh. "Miss Ivy," she sputtered, "I apologize. I'm certainly not laughing at you, but your mother and mine must have been taken from the same mold. My mother is constantly trying to play matchmaker. The last one was a mortician."

Ivy's laugh rolled across the porch and through the screens. "Oh, you should have seen what came courting me. Mother was right about all the spare men. We hadn't been on the homestead but about two weeks when this boy about my age showed up. He stood out in the yard, kicking at clumps of dirt with his bare feet and digging into an ear with his pinky finger. Later, I heard that the boy's dad sent him over to propose before somebody else grabbed me up. Then, there was a man who'd just lost his wife and needed a new mother extra quick to look after his three little children."

Ivy shook her head at the memory. "Oh, there were one or two others." For a fraction of a second, her eyes narrowed before the sparkle returned. "But I just couldn't be interested."

"Until Wheat?"

Ivy nodded. "The first time I saw him, he was being chased by a cyclone. It was a Sunday afternoon in the spring of '69. We were visiting Caleb and Hannah Henson, who took a homestead adjacent to Nate's. The day was hot and sultry. You just knew from the feel of the air a storm was brewing. We kept glancing toward the southwest where clouds were building and starting to roll in our direction. The sky took on a dark-greenish hue. The wind rose to a howl. We took shelter in the soddie, the children wailing. Hannah's little boy was not quite two, and by that time, Clara had her own little boy. Hannah and I delivered that child, and let me tell you, it made me wonder about going through that myself. Then, I went and had two of my own.

"But I'm getting away from the story. There we were, with the wind blowing and the children crying. Just as Caleb started to push the door closed, Hannah shouted there was a rider coming our way. As it turned out, that was Wheat, riding like the devil was on his heels. He barely got his horse under the lean-to and himself into the house before the storm hit with such force I thought it would carry us all away."

Ivy smiled, remembering. "That was the first time I saw Wheat. He looked like he'd been whipped around every which way. His hair stood in clumps. His clothes were bedraggled. The man was long and lanky, and he had the silliest lopsided grin you ever saw."

She sat back. "While we waited out the storm, Clara got the children quieted, and Hannah plied Wheat with food and coffee. I just happened to look up as I was cutting off a wedge of pie, and he was staring at me. I almost had a heart attack. That man had the bluest eyes I've ever seen, and they were looking straight at me.

"My goodness, I was flustered. When I put the slice of pie down in front of him, he nodded his thanks, but his attention was on what Nate and Caleb were saying about finding a good place to start a farm. Wheat told them he was finished with riding the range, herding cattle. He wanted to settle and put down roots. When he left that day, he didn't put any more meaning into saying goodbye to me than he did the others, and I wondered if I would ever see him again."

"But you did."

"At the town's Fourth of July picnic." Ivy pointed at Ellen's notebook. "You might want to record how we celebrated back then. It was really something. Patriotic speeches were given from the courthouse steps in the morning. Then people would load themselves, with huge baskets of food, into carriages and wagons, and we'd all ride south out of town, like a big parade, to the river. Lots of the vehicles were decorated with flags and bunting. The town band rode in a farm wagon, playing the whole way. There were lots of trees and shade along the river, but it became customary to hold the annual picnic in one particular spot among the cottonwoods.

"That Fourth of July with Wheat stands out in my memory. I wore a sky-blue dress with puffy half-sleeves. I'd seen the design in a *Godey's Lady's Book* illustration, and I was a little proud of myself for looking so fashionable. Wheat wasn't any fashion plate, but anyone could see that his clothes were brushed and his boots cleaned."

Ivy motioned for Ellen to stop writing. "I don't know if I'd want people to know about the details of our courtship. When Wheat spied us in the picnic crowd, he came right over, shook Nate's hand and then Caleb's. His grin was as lopsided as I remembered. He'd found a place to settle in the northern part of the county and thanked the men for their advice.

"Then, looking straight at me, but speaking to Nate, he asked for permission to escort me to the table where lemonade and cool water were being served. I couldn't have been more surprised, but Nate didn't blink an eye. Permission was granted, and I was walking beside Wheat, not caring one whit if we ever reached the lemonade.

"Our conversation was not what you would call romantic. He asked what I thought of cattle ranches, and I replied that since I had never seen one, I could not express an opinion other than to say it seemed risky to put all your eggs in one basket. It seemed to me a man would do well to also plant grain. Maybe not corn, because it didn't seem to do so as well in Kansas as it did in Illinois. Maybe wheat was a good crop to have.

"That stopped Wheat Hamilton in his tracks. He gave me a long look, that grin playing around his mouth, and asked what I knew about such things. I talked right back, letting him know I had grown up on a farm, and even if I didn't pay attention to lots of things, I had learned quite a bit listening to Nate and Caleb. He looked surprised, and I wanted to kick myself for spouting off. Just once, I thought, couldn't I have heeded my mother's advice to 'govern my tongue'?

"Then, the most extraordinary thing happened. Wheat laughed in that quiet, almost embarrassed, way I came to know so well. As it turned out, he didn't mind a woman that spoke her mind, and heaven knows he heard lots from me over the years. But there was more to it than that. From the very first, we felt comfortable with one another. That was the beginning of our courtship, although it wasn't the romantic sort you read about in books."

Ellen leaned forward. "Why do you say that?"

"Well, for one thing, Wheat never said flowery words to me." Ivy paused. "Thank goodness!"

Ellen laughed along with Ivy.

"And we didn't go out on long buggy rides or to many town entertainments. In fact, we didn't see each other for stretches of time. He was busy getting his farm organized. There were fences to build, land to plow, and cattle to buy. And he was building a long, low ranch house of limestone that resembled a place he'd seen and admired in Texas.

"When he could, Wheat visited me out at the soddie, chaperoned by Nate and Clara. We might go to the country church that stood near Hannah and Caleb's place, and a few times we rode to his farm. Wheat was anxious that I approve his ideas for the house. Ours was a very quiet courtship. We married in May of '70."

Ivy took off her glasses, rubbing the bridge of her nose before putting them back in place.

Ellen picked up her notebook. "Maybe, you could tell me about what it was like at the very first when you and Nate and Clara were just starting out."

"Nate and Caleb came out ahead of us to locate claims and break the ground for early planting. They drove out wagons filled with our worldly goods. Two milk cows were tethered behind. We ladies made the trip two months later. Father took us in a wagon to the ferry that crossed the Mississippi River to St. Louis. From that city, which was so alive with people and sounds I didn't know which way to look, we took a boat up the Missouri River to Kansas. The river trip was so wonderful I could understand how some people want to live their whole lives on the water. But we were going to be prairie folks. Once back on firm ground in Kansas, we boarded a train to Opal's Grove.

"At times our travel was tedious. Sometimes it was difficult. Hannah's little boy was only a babe, and Clara was in the early stages of pregnancy. Still, we never despaired. Never once did I regret leaving Illinois. When we arrived here and saw the men waiting for us at the train depot, we cheered."

"On that first day in Opal's Grove—before you went to the

claim—was there anything that stood out in your mind about the town?"

Ivy shook her head. "Not the town, no. I didn't really see it because the depot is south of the square. From the depot, we took the road south toward the river and then west to the claim. But at the depot there was one thing that struck us all." Ivy paused, as if considering her words.

"Yes?" Ellen prompted.

"I don't know if I should say, but you might as well write this down, because I've no doubt it will be mentioned in someone else's interview. It was a common occurrence for Nettie Vine to meet trains arriving from the East. Of course, we didn't know that at the time. On the day of our arrival, I saw this girl, no older than me, standing on the platform. She waved wildly, like she was trying to get our attention, and she shouted greetings to everyone coming off the train. It was an odd spectacle, and I remember Clara giggling at the sight of a near-grown girl carrying on in such a way."

Ellen looked up. "Nettie Vine?"

"Marie Antoinette Vine," Ivy corrected. "Only her mother called her Marie Antoinette. To everyone else, she was just Nettie."

Ellen started to say that the name was on her interview list, but something in Ivy's voice made her hold back.

Ivy didn't seem to notice Ellen's hesitation. "I guess you or somebody else will be interviewing her because she's still around. Back then, I had no idea who she was until I met her by accident about a month after we arrived. You see, I was anxious to work as a seamstress, but being in the country was a handicap. I needed a place in town where I was visible. And, to be honest, even though I was a great help to Clara, especially with her expecting, she and Nate sometimes needed a little more privacy than they were getting with me around.

50

"I came up with this idea. I went to the Archers, who had an empty space in back of their dry goods store. I offered to work in the store for free if I could use the extra room as a workshop. I could pull a curtain across the back half of the room and have a place to sleep when I didn't want to ride the five miles out to the claim."

"That showed a lot of initiative," offered Ellen.

"I thought it was a good idea, but Mr. Archer didn't like it one bit. He didn't mind getting free labor or letting me set up shop, but he was dead set against a young, unchaperoned girl staying alone. Lucky for me, his wife had a real nose for profit. In less than ten minutes she'd talked him into having me stay at their house in a little room off the kitchen that was barely bigger than a closet. And she made him see how it was to their benefit having a seamstress right in their store.

"Of course, there was ready-made clothing available, but a lady doesn't like to walk into church or a big social event and see two other women wearing the same thing. Mrs. Archer understood that. I was counting on it. Ladies coming in to see me would walk by shelves of bolts of fabric and sewing notions like buttons and lace trim. They'd buy their goods from the store, and when I wasn't sewing, the Archers got free labor."

Ivy shook her head. "Looking back on it, I'm surprised the plan worked. Of course, I still helped Clara when I could, and there were more times than I can count when I rode alone between town and the claim. For protection, I carried Father's war pistol holstered at my side. Nate taught Clara and me to shoot, just in case some desperate type came to the soddie when he wasn't around, or we encountered snakes or other varmints. You can't imagine the freedom I felt! My mother would have been mortified, but I worked under that old assumption that what she didn't know wouldn't trouble her—or me, for that matter.

"Well, as I was saying, the day I approached the Archers is the day I met Nettie. She came waltzing into the store to pick up some parcel for her mother. When she saw me, she came right over to introduce herself. She was very social. Not long afterward, she came out to the claim, driving that pony cart of hers along the track just as fast as she could make that poor animal go. She wanted to invite me to a lawn party the coming Saturday afternoon. Other young people living on claims close to town were invited. I would have a chance to meet my neighbors, as well as people my own age living in town.

"I went, with the Archers' permission to take off work, and thoroughly enjoyed myself. There were about twenty of us, but there was no doubt Nettie expected to be the center of attention. No one seemed to mind because she was so vivacious. Most anything she suggested, whether it was croquet or musical chairs, we happily agreed to."

Ivy looked out toward the backyard. "You can keep that part," she told Ellen, "but leave off this last. There were other parties and get-togethers. Nettie arranged many of them, but not all. There were times when a bunch of us would just decide on the spur of the moment to go down to the river on a Sunday afternoon or to meet at someone's home. This bothered Nettie, because she considered herself the leader. She felt snubbed, even when she came along. It's not a kind thing to say, but the more I got to know Nettie, the less I wanted to be around her. If things didn't go her way, she could be quite unpleasant. She would pout or say hurtful things to whoever was closest at hand.

"As it worked out, I became too busy to do much socializing or to think about Nettie. When I wasn't helping Clara on the homestead, I was working at the Archers' and sewing. People began to come to me with all sorts of requests, and I obliged, whether it was reworking out-of-style clothes to make them look new or stitching up dresses and shirts from scratch. Then, of course, Wheat and I began to court."

"When you married, what happened to your business?"

"I closed it, but when someone asked me to sew up something for a special occasion, I tried to oblige."

"Did you regret giving up something you'd worked so hard for?" Ellen couldn't stop herself from asking.

"Of course not." Ivy shook her head as if the very idea was absurd. "I was proud of myself because I'd made a success of it, but the business wasn't the most important thing to me. Wheat was."

That settled, Ivy asked the time as she bent over the hem's last few stitches.

When Ellen checked her watch and told her, Ivy let out a little gasp.

"I had no idea it was getting so late! I've got to iron this dress, and my daughter-in-law will be here in a few minutes. She's going to take me to the church so we can organize the clothing bank for this weekend. I was never very confident about operating an automobile. After Wheat died, I gave our Ford to my grandson. Now, I have to rely on others to get around."

Ivy reached across the table to pat Ellen's arm. "Time just flew, didn't it?"

"Yes, it did. You've given a wonderful interview." Ellen tucked the notebook and pencil away, trying not to show her disappointment that their time together was over.

"I could ask Constance to wait if you want to hear more, but that would just raise a stink. She has every minute of her day organized and hates to be put off stride." Ivy leaned over, giving Ellen the impression they had become close confidantes. "She was a little miffed when Iris Hewitt was asked to head this interview project, but Constance doesn't know a thing about history—or writing, for that matter. To tell you the truth," Ivy continued, "Constance and I have our tussles. Since Wheat

53

died, she gives me more attention than I want. She means well, but sometimes I just want to throw something at her."

Ellen couldn't help but laugh. She could see Ivy Hamilton doing just that.

"You best be going, but could you come back?" Ivy's expression was hopeful.

Ellen brightened. She would very much like to see the woman again. She pulled out her assignment list. "Yes, I would like that, but I can't do it this week. Mrs. Hewitt has given us pretty full schedules. Would next Tuesday afternoon be okay?"

"I was just thinking if you came Saturday afternoon, after we close the clothing bank, I could show you the old soddie." She rose to walk Ellen to the front door. "I saw you have an automobile. You could drive us out there and get an idea of the place I'm talking about."

Ellen agreed enthusiastically but hesitated when Ivy suggested she come for lunch first.

"You'll eat better than at Miss Jewell's," Ivy cajoled. "You are staying there, aren't you?'

Ellen nodded, suddenly reminded that Opal's Grove was no different from other small towns. People noticed newcomers, like the WPA workers. Ellen suspected they had been discussed from the courthouse to the barbershop to the post office.

"The room and board includes breakfast and dinner. If we want lunch, it's extra."

"All the more reason to eat with me. Miss Jewell is a good cook, but on Saturdays she brings out leftovers from the week before and calls it potluck."

They agreed Ellen would come to the clothing bank, take Miss Ivy home for the promised lunch, and then set out for the soddie.

At the door Ellen again thanked Ivy for the interview. She

was already looking forward to Saturday. She liked the woman and felt sure Miss Ivy had much more to tell.

CHAPTER 7
ELLEN

Ellen arrived at the courthouse buoyed by the morning's interview and feeling comfortable with finding her way around town. Except for the railroad, its depot, and a hotel for travelers on the southern edge of town, everything centered on the courthouse square. Two state highways, one running north-south, the other going east-west, intersected on the square's northeast corner. Unlike so many towns the Depression had turned into sad, abandoned shadows of what they once were, Opal's Grove remained fairly prosperous.

She checked her watch. Before her afternoon interview there was enough time to go to the WPA office, type up her notes, and then get lunch at Miss Jewell's. She got out of the car, swiping at the back of her dress where it stuck to her legs. The temperatures for June were already above normal, and if the trend continued, said forecasters, the summer would be even hotter than the one before. After another tug at the dress, Ellen hurried across the street to the courthouse. She nodded hello to the men sitting on benches under large shade trees. Some sat here most of the day, spitting tobacco, gossiping, and talking politics.

The front and back doors of the courthouse stood open, allowing air to circulate. Despite the basement's musty smell, Ellen welcomed its dank coolness. Halfway down the stairs, Ellen heard a snatch of voices and then laughter. Hope disappeared of having the place to herself. Stepping through the door, she put on a smile, ready to greet her fellow workers. She stopped short. The professor stood with his arms braced on a desk, leaning toward Audrey. Both were laughing.

Audrey looked up, still smiling. "Well, hello. Sit down. You have to hear this. Ralph just told me the funniest thing."

Ralph? Ellen's mouth dropped open. The man who insisted on being called Professor Reynolds was now Ralph?

"So, what is it?" She tried to regain her composure and busied herself with pulling out a chair.

Audrey prompted the professor. "You tell her. It's your story." But the man looked away, clearly flustered.

"Oh, for heaven's sake," Audrey protested, shaking her head. "This morning the elderly gentleman Ralph was interviewing asked if it was true that Mr. Roosevelt was going to read each and every story we collected. Somehow he got the idea that FDR is just sitting in the White House waiting for these interviews to land on his desk." Audrey's laugh rolled against the basement walls.

"What did you tell him, Professor Reynolds?" Ellen wasn't going to call him by his first name unless invited to do so.

"I said it was doubtful, and the old guy perked up. Seems he's been a Republican all his life and didn't want any Democrat, even if he is president, knowing his business."

Ellen detected a slight smile slip across the man's face.

She chuckled along with Audrey as she arranged her notebook and put paper into the typewriter. She still had some time before lunch. Soon she was completely focused on interpreting her notes as she typed. She tuned out Audrey and the professor until she became aware of Audrey at her elbow.

"We're going across the street to the lunch counter at Kresge's." Audrey raised her voice to be heard over the typewriter's clacking keys. "Want to come?"

Ellen shook her head and continued typing. "Thanks. Some

other time. I'm going back to Miss Jewell's."

"See ya later then." Audrey gave a backward wave, following Ralph out the door.

Ellen did not want to tell Audrey she was watching every penny, even if it was the fifty-cent difference between lunch at the boardinghouse and Kresge's. She had to save her money. Her father had said as much when he refused her offer to send him a portion of her weekly earnings.

Her father wanted Ellen to try her wings. "Don't come home unless you really want to," he'd told her as she getting ready to leave. "I don't want you to be miserable trying to fit in with your old friends and maybe marrying one of those men your mother keeps bringing up. No, you save that money."

Ellen looked at her watch, gasped at the time, and began to place the pages she'd typed and her notebook back into the satchel. Typed interviews were supposed to be left in the office. Mrs. Hewitt had gone to a lot of trouble, labeling files and setting up an organizational system. But, Ellen rationalized, the interview wasn't finished. She had more information to collect. Besides, she didn't want to leave her work out for just anyone to see.

She covered the typewriter, grabbed her things, and hustled out to the car. The heat wrapped around her. By the time she reached Miss Jewell's, she felt wilted.

The boardinghouse was on a nondescript street of unremarkable houses. Miss Jewell, who refused to be called by her first name—Jerusalem—kept her yard neat and the house painted a crisp white. She had three regular boarders, all teachers. But, as she explained to Ellen and Audrey, the teachers were gone for a few weeks of their summer vacations. Two were visiting relatives. The third had set off with friends for the Grand Canyon.

Ellen found Miss Jewell in the kitchen, cutting potatoes. She hummed a little tune as she peeled and sliced. The woman was middle-aged, softly round like bread dough, and unfailingly cheerful. Her mother started taking in boarders after Jerusalem's father died, and, now that her mother was gone, Miss Jewell carried on. She was proud of the way she ran the house and secretly delighted in the stories her boarders brought in from the outside world.

When the woman saw Ellen, she shouted out a "hello" and waved for her to sit. It was one of the house rules. Boarders should be treated as guests and served in the dining room, even when there was only one for lunch.

Ellen felt ridiculous, but she knew not to argue as Miss Jewell set a glass of tea and a food-laden plate in front of her. "I made a chicken salad, with some cottage cheese and pickled beets on the side."

Ellen nodded. Leftover fried chicken from last night had become a salad. Miss Jewell, like Ellen's mother, knew how to stretch a meal.

"Why don't you join me?" Ellen asked the woman. "Even if you've already eaten, I'd love the company. I guess Audrey's not coming back for lunch."

"No. She told me this morning she would probably just grab something downtown. I don't mind getting off my feet for a few minutes." Miss Jewell sat down heavily opposite her boarder. "This heat is a killer."

Ellen took a bite of salad. It was very good. "Stifling. I'm glad I drove to my appointment this morning. Otherwise, I might have passed out on the street trying to walk in this heat. That's why I'm going to drive to the one I have this afternoon, although it's not far."

"Who are you going to see, if I can ask?"

Ellen assured Miss Jewell it was no secret and told her the woman's name.

"You got a plum there. I don't know her personally, you

understand, but people think a lot of the family. Been around since the town began and always been big supporters of anything that makes it a better place to live." Miss Jewell nodded approvingly. "Yes, ma'am, you got a plum."

CHAPTER 8
AGATHA

Ellen admired the Bright home as she made her way up the walkway and across the porch. Moments after she rang the bell, a figure appeared on the other side of the screen door. "You must be Miss Hartley here to see Miss Agatha." As Ellen moved closer, she saw a woman about her age. "Come on in." She pushed the door open to allow Ellen inside.

The young woman was thin and angular. A wide smile revealed a dimple in her right cheek and a small gap between her front teeth. "Just this way." She pointed toward a door immediately to the right. The room was done in pastel shades of pink and green. Curtains, pulled away from the front and side windows, allowed the breeze to circulate through the room. Agatha Bright, dressed in a short-sleeved dress of pale yellow, sat in a wingback chair to one side of a green-tiled fireplace. Her snow-white hair was pinned into an elegant twist at the back of her head. Her figure, although thickened with age, still suggested the curves that had once given Mrs. Bright an hourglass figure without the benefit of corsets and stays.

The first word that came to mind was "regal." Ellen walked around a sofa facing the fireplace. She took Mrs. Bright's extended hand and introduced herself. For a fleeting moment, Ellen felt the urge to curtsy.

Mrs. Bright dropped the offered hand and smiled. "Excuse me for not getting up to greet you, but the arthritis is giving me a terrible time today." She fingered an ebony-colored cane

hooked over the chair arm. With the other hand, she waved Ellen to a chair opposite hers. "Thelma can bring us something to
drink if you like."

When Ellen declined, Thelma nodded and turned back into
the hall. Over her shoulder she called, "Just ring the bell if you
want anything, Miss Agatha. I've got to get to Kresge's, but Sis
will hear ya."

Agatha smiled after the girl. "That's Thelma Weaver. Her
father does my yardwork. Her mother cooked for me until her
arthritis got worse than mine. Now Thelma's older sister does
the cooking, and Thelma helps out here when she can. In the
afternoons she works behind the dry-goods counter at Kresge's."

Ellen took the offered chair and pulled out pad and pencil.

"Thelma's getting married in the fall, and saving every cent
she can," Agatha continued. "Going to marry that deputy
sheriff, Bill Snyder."

The room turned silent. Mrs. Bright fingered the top of her
cane. "I've been wondering what I'd say in this interview about
the old days," she confessed. "You know, there are some around
town that think you WPA people are wasting your time talking
to old folks like me who lived in town and not out on a
homestead. Well, I say pooh to that. The blizzards didn't stop at
the edge of town. The grasshopper plagues didn't pass us by,
and death sure didn't stay away. I lost two children to diphtheria
and counted myself blessed I didn't lose the two others."

Ellen took this down, surprised at the note of strong convic-
tion in the woman's tone.

"I see you writing this down in those squiggles," Agatha
continued, her voice lighter now. "I saw my dear friend Ivy
Hamilton this morning after you left her house. She and her
daughter-in-law picked me up to go to the church. I've never
been much at sewing, but I help separate the items into sizes
and so forth at the clothing bank."

She gave a little sigh. "I used to drive everywhere, but then I had that unfortunate accident. I tried to tell my son it really wasn't my fault the automobile ended up on the front steps of the Methodist Church. Nobody was hurt, but he got rid of my beautiful Oldsmobile anyway."

The image of an elegant Mrs. Bright bouncing her car onto the church steps made Ellen smile as she struggled to bring both herself and Mrs. Bright back to the reason for her visit. "And you talked to Mrs. Hamilton about her interview?"

The woman nodded. "She said you won't put anything down if I ask you to leave it out." She cocked her head to one side as a question.

"That's right." Ellen nodded. "I don't think Mrs. Hewitt or Mrs. Fletcher in Topeka will mind as long as what we do write down is interesting and useful."

"What about Mr. Roosevelt?" Ellen detected a mischievous gleam in the woman's eyes. "You know, some of these old pioneers think the president himself is going to read what they have to say."

Ellen smiled and nodded. "So I've heard, but I would be very surprised if that happened. I think the president has other things on his mind." She paused. "Now, Mrs. Bright, are you ready for me to write or just listen?"

"Call me Miss Agatha, if you don't mind. Most everybody in town does."

The woman seemed to relax but remained silent for a moment, fingering the cane. Ellen's instinct was to remain quiet. Some people, she knew, needed time to gather their thoughts. Peppering them with questions only pushed them away.

Agatha took a deep breath and looked straight into Ellen's eyes. "One of these days, I'm going to be gone. Ivy, too. When that happens, no living person will know the story of who I was before I became Mrs. Thomas Bright. My children don't know, and certainly not my grandchildren. I hadn't made up my mind if I was going to tell you, a stranger, but since my talk with Ivy at the church, I've been thinking I would like someone to know about me after I pass on. But there is a great deal I don't want written down or ever repeated."

Ellen felt the seriousness of the moment. She had the odd feeling of suddenly stepping into a confessional, but it wasn't an entirely unknown situation. She'd once been assigned the job of writing about a much-beloved spinster teacher, never imagining that during what began as a rather boring interview, the woman would suddenly reveal that she had been married for twenty years to the man who posed as her mother's hired hand.

Ellen never told anyone the teacher's secret. Nor would she breathe a word of Miss Agatha's. She said just that, adding that she felt it was an honor for the woman to confide in her.

Agatha nodded and leaned back, satisfied. "Well, this is the listening part, and maybe you'll understand more as I explain. People have a particular picture of who I am. I'm a member of the upstanding, comfortably-fixed Bright family, and I've worked most of my life to be that person. But when I first came to Opal's Grove as a bride, there were some nasty rumors about my background. These were spread about by a certain someone who is still alive and still as meanspirited. One breath in this interview of my humble beginnings—and believe me, they were—might start this person off again."

Ellen stopped herself from jumping in and asking who this was and why he or she would do such a thing. Better to let Miss Agatha tell things her own way. Questions could come later.

"I couldn't abide that, and I don't wish to have my family embarrassed by whispers and innuendo. My daughter is married to a prominent man who advises the governor, and Tom Junior runs the bank that was started by his grandfather and carried on by my husband. People think highly of my son, because when other banks failed, he kept this one going. I won't have his reputation tarnished."

Ellen put aside the notebook and sat back. "Whatever you tell me goes no further than this room. I promise."

Agatha nodded and took a deep breath and began to talk about her parents. "They lived in a mining village in Wales. Dad worked the coal mines. Ma was a scullery maid in the mine owner's fine house. But Dad got into trouble. Had a fight with the owner's son and left him so bloody that Dad's family and friends pooled their money to get Dad safely away from the man's wrath and, quite possibly, jail. But he wouldn't leave without Ma. He got a minister to say words of marriage over them and then beat a hasty path to the closest port for passage to America.

"That was two or three years after gold was discovered in California, and Dad became obsessed with joining in the rush to find his pot of gold." Agatha shrugged. "My parents were closemouthed about so many things. I never knew how they made their way to California, where I was born. My three brothers, too." Agatha shifted her gaze toward the front window.

"From the time I was five or six, I had this idea I was born into the wrong family. We moved from one mining town to another, one claim to the next. Then Dad traded California for Colorado. An image that will never leave me is a little cottage I spied as we traveled through a mountain town. It wasn't a big house, but there were lace curtains in the windows and hollyhocks by the front door. I wanted to be the little girl living in that house."

Agatha sighed. "It's a mystery to me how my brothers and I survived our childhoods. When we were sick, we were dosed with whatever homemade remedy came to mind. If things seemed really dire, Dad found someone who claimed to have doctoring skills. Otherwise, my parents were fairly indifferent toward us. They seemed to live for each other in their own world. I could swear Ma sometimes looked at her children with surprise, like she was wondering what these little urchins were doing in her kitchen. So, when we weren't doing chores, my brothers and I explored caves, climbed trees and rocks, and played in abandoned shacks. If there was a school going, we might attend, but it was hit and miss.

"I liked the freedom of doing whatever came to mind, but even a little kid knows when things are out of kilter. I had this yearning to learn from books and to find out how people lived in those nice houses I sometimes saw. Help wouldn't come from Dad or Ma. I was eight years old when I decided I had to do it myself. We were in California when this revelation came to me, and I asked the wife of a Methodist minister in the camp if she could teach me to read. This went on from place to place. Someone else began my lessons in writing. Another showed me how to do simple sums. A gambler taught me a smattering of French while teaching me the finer points of blackjack and poker." The amusement returned to her voice. "I never had the opportunity to display my card-playing skills, but the French was useful, if for nothing else than impressing Thomas's parents.

"In another camp, two bachelor miners loaned me books, explaining the words I didn't understand. Sometimes, they read to me. Shakespeare. Dickens. I loved Dickens. In a mining town—by this time we were in Colorado—I had my first real lessons in manners and the social graces." Agatha paused for a long moment. "My teachers were two whores."

Agatha stopped and eyed Ellen. "Does that shock you?"

Ellen fought to show no reaction. She wanted Mrs. Bright to continue, no matter what. "I would say surprised." It was the mildest word Ellen could think of when, in fact, she was reeling between stunned and astonished.

Agatha continued, leaving Ellen to feel she'd passed some sort of test.

"I was rather vague on the particulars of what these women did with their male visitors. In fact, I hadn't given them much thought. They were as common in mining districts as prospectors going bust. Then, a woman bent on reform came to our shack, wanting Ma to sign a petition to rid the town of these 'soiled doves.' Ma pulled her hands out of the washtub where she'd been scrubbing Dad's overalls and gave the woman a long look before she refused. She wasn't going to bring more trouble to those women, she said. At least a few had once been genteel ladies. Under other circumstances some of them would be having tea with this busybody woman. That's what Ma called her, a 'busybody.' "

Agatha chuckled. "Ma had her faults, but I admired her for standing up to that do-gooder. Now, this gave me an idea. If some of those women had once been genteel, they would surely know good manners, and I desperately wanted to learn. In that town, there were six houses with ladies. I went to the backdoor of four of them before I found two women willing to teach me some social graces. One, who called herself Lizzie, claimed to have been a maid in a fine house before her employer ruined her. The other, known as Billy Belle, was the widow of a Union soldier. At first they laughed at me. And who could blame them? I was a scrawny ragamuffin.

"The woman that ran the bawdy house came charging into the kitchen swinging a broom and cursing like the devil to chase me away. Well, that didn't work. The woman was too fat to swing very far. And the cursing didn't shock me. You couldn't be in a mining camp and not hear the worst kind of language. Lizzie and Billy Belle had practically collapsed from laughter by then, but they finally managed to get themselves under control. And to my surprise, they talked the fat lady into letting me visit.

Until we moved on to another camp, I went two or three times a week.

"They fussed over me, treating me like a pet. Billy Belle often brushed out my hair. It was as black as the coal Pa mined in Wales, and it was beautiful when it was done up right. Lizzie brought out a fringed shawl for me to wear so I felt dressed up for a tea party. I practiced walking like a lady from the kitchen door to the table. I learned to sit with my back straight and knees together. They taught me to daintily drink from a china teacup and to take small bites from butter-smeared slices of bread we pretended were little cakes and sandwiches. Over the years, I've thought fondly about those women."

Agatha sat back, fanning her face with a lace-edged handkerchief. "I think I would like some lemonade." She reached for the bell on a small side table.

When Thelma's sister arrived, Agatha briefly introduced Martha. Ellen guessed she was a good ten years older than Thelma, but Ellen saw a sisterly resemblance in their smiles.

After Martha returned and left two sweating glasses of lemonade, Ellen again reassured Miss Agatha that none of what she had said would be put on paper. "I understand your reasons for not making this public, but I think it's inspirational. Look at all the people today who are trying to improve themselves and get ahead. You're proof it can be done."

"Pooh." Agatha drank deeply from her glass. "Lots of people helped along the way, but things changed for me because the family's fortunes improved. By the time I met Thomas Bright, we were a respectable family, living in a modest but nice house with lace curtains. I was a long ways from being little Aggie from the mining camps." She placed her half-empty glass on a side table.

Ellen took another sip of lemonade before setting her glass aside. Sensing the time had come for Miss Agatha's official story, she sat ready to take it down. When Miss Agatha didn't object, she began to write.

"Dad made his strike in 1866. None of us could believe it. Oh, he'd had some success over the years, but this one was different. And Dad was no fool. The prospector's life was wearing him down. Ma, too. He took the money and moved us to Denver, where he set up a business. My brothers worked with Dad, freighting supplies to the mines that no train could reach and working in the store he opened to sell mining equipment.

"It was in Denver I met Thomas. He was there on business for his father's bank, looking for investments or some such thing." Agatha's mouth formed a beautiful smile as she remembered, and, once again, Ellen caught a glimpse of the beauty the woman had been in her younger days.

"My, he was handsome! He stood over six feet; the top of my head barely reached his shoulder. He had a wonderful sense of humor, but only the people who knew him well ever saw that side of him. To the outside world, he was a serious banker, because that's what people expect. That's what they trust. Thomas Bright only did one impulsive thing in his entire life, and that was marry me."

Ellen's hand wavered over the notebook. She expected Agatha to ask to strike that last part because it was too personal. In the few seconds it took to realize that wasn't going to happen, Ellen asked how Agatha met her future husband.

The woman's laugh was low. "I bumped into him. Or maybe it was him running into me. My father had bought a piano for our front parlor, thinking this was the kind of thing a successful businessman would have in his home. No one was actually expected to play the thing, but I wanted to improve myself and took up music lessons. I had a terrible singing voice, but it turned out I had some aptitude for the piano. On the afternoon I met Thomas, I was walking home from a lesson with Mrs. Arbantrout, whose countenance and exacting ways terrified students. I was no different, but I was determined to please her. So, there I was, walking along and replaying in my head the day's lesson when Thomas and I collided. Sheet music went flying, and I was saved from a hard fall by Thomas grabbing my waist. He insisted on seeing me home, and at the doorstep asked if he might call that evening to assure himself I was unhurt.

"He came every night for the next two weeks. At the end of that time, he asked Pa for permission to marry me. There was no objection, and for the first time I could remember, my folks made an effort to notice me. Pa gave me a small, but quite adequate, dowry. Ma threw herself into planning the wedding dinner and ordering flowers for my bouquet. Less than two weeks after Thomas proposed, we married on a bright April afternoon in 1869. I was eighteen. He was twenty-two. The ceremony took place at home in the parlor. A Methodist minister conducted the ceremony. My dress was pearl gray with a gray-and-white-striped underskirt. There was lace at the collar and at the wrists."

Agatha smiled at the memory. "We were a handsome couple, even if I do say so myself. And the best part was we truly loved each other, even though we had known each other for such a short time. Now, you're wondering if he knew about the way I'd grown up."

Ellen nodded, putting down her pencil. Without being told, she knew this was not for public consumption.

"I became so fond of him so quickly that at first I was afraid I'd never see him again if he knew. He obviously came from such a different background. But I couldn't deceive him, so I mustered up my courage and told him about tramping from camp to camp, how wild we children were, and finding teachers in the most improbable places. I even told him about Lizzy and

Billy Belle."

Agatha tilted back her head and chuckled. "My, you should have seen the look on his face when I mentioned that. Then he did the most remarkable thing. His face broke into a smile that got wider until he actually shook with laughter. Then, he took my face in his hands and kissed me. After he pulled away and I was trying to breathe again, he said he was even more in love with me than he had imagined. He was like you, saying he admired my spirit.

"We never spoke again of my childhood. Thomas gave his parents a brief sketch of my father as a prospector who struck it rich and then settled in Denver as an honest and prosperous businessman. In the long run, I guess it didn't matter all that much what Dad did for a living. He died of pneumonia two years after my marriage. Ma followed him four months later. The doctor couldn't identify the cause, but I knew. She couldn't imagine living without Dad and just up and died."

Agatha pointed to Ellen's notebook and nodded. "When Thomas brought me to Kansas, I was anxious about his parents. After all, the first they knew of their son's marriage was the telegram he sent from Denver. But they were wonderful to me. Even Thomas's sister Julia, who, he warned, was too wrapped up in her books to be social, was very kind. When she decided to attend a women's college in the East, I truly missed her company. All in all, I considered myself a very lucky bride. I adored my husband, and I had a new family that welcomed me as a daughter. We lived with Thomas's family while this house was being built for us and got along beautifully."

With no more to say on the subject, Agatha looked expectantly at Ellen, ready for a question.

"You mentioned Mrs. Hamilton is a close friend. Could you tell me how you met?" Ellen prompted.

The woman nodded. "Actually, that fits in rather nicely with

71

the story of my first days in this town. My in-laws decided to have a reception to honor us newlyweds. As you might imagine, I was nervous, wondering about the impression I would make. For several days, I went back and forth over what to wear. Julia and Mrs. Bright were right there with me, trying to decide. Finally, we agreed upon a dress that had a summer-green bodice and matching skirt. It also had just a hint of a striped silk underskirt. I had purchased the dress, along with three others, just a few days before my wedding. But the dress needed some alterations, especially around the neckline, which Mrs. Bright assured me was too daring for the good people of Opal's Grove.

"That's where Ivy came in. She may have told you that even before she left Illinois, she had the idea of being a seamstress."

Ellen nodded. "She explained about her arrangement with the Archers, and I got the impression she was successful."

"Well, you'll have to ask her the details. But when I arrived, she had a business going. Although there were ladies that thought her too young to be very skilled, she had many clients. Mrs. Bright swore by her. So a message was sent to Ivy, and in an hour or so, she appeared at the door. Seeing someone about my age was a bit of a surprise, but she proved in a short amount of time she knew what she was about. She listened to Mrs. Bright's concern and then walked around me as I stood in the center of Mrs. Bright's dressing room, modeling the dress. Finally, she turned to my mother-in-law and said quite seriously that she didn't see anything wrong. The dress was in the latest style, and if the townspeople pretended to be shocked over a hint of décolletage, they had better quit stampeding to the opera house every time Polly Armstrong and her Theatricals came to town."

Agatha laughed, remembering that day. "You wouldn't know about Polly Armstrong, but the woman had this traveling show. She wore short tunics over tights when she and her troupe acted out Shakespeare, and when she took to the stage to sing popular tunes, her evening gown allowed for a considerable display of bare flesh. But I knew my mother-in-law wasn't happy. Ivy knew it, too, so she took the dress away and returned with it the next day. She'd cut fabric from the underskirt where it wouldn't show and applied it around the neckline as a little stand-up ruffle. I wasn't completely covered up, you understand; there was simply less to see.

"Ivy was quite clever. I liked her from the first. I admired her straightforward way of speaking. You've met her so you know what I mean when I say you just have this great feeling in her company. Over the years we've shared so much, and, even though I lived in town and she married a farmer, we always found ways to visit back and forth. And you might think this strange, since we lived only about twelve miles apart, but we kept in touch with letters. We exchanged news about our children, and we told each other the most ordinary things. I knew what vegetables she was getting from her garden in any given week, and she knew what I wore to church when the new minister came to town."

Agatha sighed. "We've seen each other through good times and bad. I don't know what I would have done without her when Thomas died during that influenza epidemic in 1918. He was such a robust man, but in a matter of days, he was gone." Her hand fluttered for a moment over her cane before she smiled at Ellen. "And to think, she became my closest friend because of a dress."

Ellen finished jotting the last and glanced at her watch. She was shocked to see how much time had passed and more than a little troubled at the small amount of written material that represented her interview. Iris Hewitt would be disappointed, what with Mrs. Bright being a prominent member of the community. She glanced at the woman and wondered if she was tiring. Squaring her shoulders, she told Agatha the problem.

"Is there one event you might talk about? Maybe you could mention something that every settler endured."

Agatha, head tilted to one side, considered the possibilities. "Well, I absolutely refuse to talk about the grasshopper plagues. Just the thought of how those pests got into everything, including your hair and clothes, makes my skin crawl."

Ellen blew out a breath and tried another topic. "The droughts?"

"No." Agatha shook her head emphatically. "The droughts were bad, but blizzards always terrified me more than anything else. The one that stands out in my mind happened in '86."

Ellen felt a flood of relief. Here was something that represented the settlers' endurance. She nodded, encouraging Miss Agatha to continue.

"It came in early January, not too long after New Year's. The temperatures had been bitterly cold, but then the weather turned mild, almost warm. People went out without coats or shawls. Tom Junior, who would have been fourteen at the time, went off with his friends. They were chomping at the bit to try out the baseball mitts and bats they received as Christmas gifts. Caroline had just turned eight. She and two of her little friends were having a doll party on our front porch. Clouds began to build to the west and north. At first I thought nothing of it, but as the afternoon wore on, I felt this growing sense of dread.

"There are people who claim to have premonitions of bad things coming. Well, I never had one before, but I just had this feeling. I couldn't concentrate on anything for two minutes, and I kept walking to the front door to check on Caroline and to watch for Tom Junior's return. When the wind began to rise, I broke up the doll party as calmly as I could. I left Caroline with our cook, Bess, and walked her little friends to their homes. Then I went looking for Tom Junior. An overwhelming panic seized me. I almost collapsed from relief when I met my son coming down the street.

"My husband and his father arrived shortly afterward. Snow had begun to fall by then, and the wind was stronger. They'd closed the bank early and sent the three employees home. My serious, level-headed father-in-law had the same sinking feeling I was experiencing. Maybe it wouldn't amount to a thing, he said, but he would feel better if we all went home with him.

"It wasn't far to go. Just across the street. By that time, the snow was coming down heavier and blowing sideways. We bundled up and packed a few things, intending to stay the night. Then, in a tight little group that included Bess, we pushed our way across the road. As it turned out, we were there two days. We kept the fireplaces roaring in the two downstairs parlors, keeping the heat in by closing the pocket doors that led to the entry hall. Bess and Mrs. Bright's domestic help, a Swedish girl named Inga, kept the kitchen stove going and somehow managed to feed us all. We were uncomfortable, but we didn't suffer half as much as the people who were caught out in their sod houses and dugouts.

"For days—even weeks—after the storm, reports came in of people found dead, frozen to death. Some died huddled in their homes. Others were caught out on the open prairie. Animals died, too. Some cattlemen, especially those farther west, lost most of their livestock. Thomas worried about the effect on the bank, but our biggest concern was the fate of friends. Until I learned Ivy and her family were safe, I couldn't sleep. Although they had a substantial house on their farm, I still imagined them huddled against the freezing cold or caught unawares out in the storm. That happened to Sylvester Vine. He started out that January morning to visit a man about the sale of his farm and was found four days later, his buggy pulled up against a rock outcropping. Everyone assumed he tried to save himself and his horse by getting out of the wind, but the cold was too much for both man and beast."

Ellen recognized the name. The county history she'd read had sung the man's praises. There had been a photograph, too, although the only feature Ellen could recall was the man's overly generous beard.

"Sylvester Vine . . . one of the town's founders?" She was rather proud of herself for knowing the name.

Agatha nodded. "He was the primary investor in the town company. He named the town for his wife. And don't write this down, but she was a lot like that busybody I told you about in Colorado. Opal Vine made just about everything her business, whether it was organizing a literary society, building a decent school, or starting up a public library. There were many people who wanted those things and worked for them. Mrs. Bright and her daughter, Julia, for instance, devoted countless hours to raising funds for a library.

"I joined their cause after moving here. In fact, I gave two or three piano recitals to raise money. We had a lovely new piano in that parlor across the hall." Agatha pointed with her cane. "Thomas and I grandly called it our 'music room.' It was my mother-in-law's idea to hold afternoon teas at which I performed. For the privilege of being culturally elevated by the few pieces of classical music I could play without mangling them, the ladies gave a donation." Agatha chuckled and shook her head.

"Mrs. Vine attended, but you knew from her pinched expression she wasn't happy. She had this idea that she alone could bring 'civilization' to this town. My sweet-natured mother-in-law once confided she thought Mrs. Vine was a 'pill.' That was the worst thing I ever heard her say about a person, and I could have said much worse, knowing all those naughty words I'd heard in the mining camps."

"Sylvester and Opal Vine," said Ellen. "They would be the parents of Marie Antoinette Vine. Correct? She's on my interview list," Ellen added.

Agatha's face tightened.

Ellen realized she had unknowingly blundered. Whatever the mother was to Agatha's mother-in-law, she thought Marie Antoinette was to Miss Agatha.

"Yes, she's Sylvester and Opal's daughter," said Agatha, her mouth a tight line. Ellen noticed Agatha's white-knuckle grip on her cane.

Agatha cocked her head. "I have a word of advice. She can be difficult. You tread lightly with her."

"Yes, I will," Ellen murmured, sorry the interview seemed to be ending on a sour note. As she put her things away, she thanked the woman for talking with her.

Agatha nodded with the grace that once again reminded Ellen of a queen acknowledging her subjects. "I'd love to have you drop by again to visit."

The tension Ellen felt just a moment earlier was gone. "I'd like that very much."

When Agatha started to rise, Ellen waved her to stay. "I can find my way out."

"Come back and see me," Agatha called after her. "And keep in mind what I said about Nettie."

As she stepped onto the porch, Ellen heard Agatha's bell ring for more lemonade.

Ellen considered the interview as she walked to her car. Perhaps it was just coincidence that Nettie Vine had come up in Ivy's interview and then in Agatha's. After all, they had all been in Opal's Grove since the town was young. Yet the two women didn't talk about Nettie Vine as a friend, but as someone they kept at a distance.

CHAPTER 9
ELLEN AND AUDREY

Ellen intended to type up Miss Agatha's interview, but the day's heat was wearing her down. A hot wind blew in waves through the car's open windows. Few people were out on the street. Even the gossipers and tobacco spitters had been driven off their benches by the temperature. Ellen started to park near the courthouse but suddenly changed her mind. She had never cut a class in college. It wasn't like her to shirk anything, but she suddenly felt drained by the unrelenting sun and exhausted from a day of listening and writing. She reversed the car and drove to the boardinghouse.

It was quiet when she arrived. She didn't hear Miss Jewell in the kitchen, and Audrey was not in their shared room. Ellen stripped off her clothes, draped the dress across the back of a chair, wrapped herself in a cotton robe, and padded down the hall to the bathroom. She stood in the tub under the shower, letting cold water run over her. After several minutes, she felt refreshed and toweled dry. Combing tangles out of her hair, she examined her face in the mirror. People said she took after her father's mother—those high cheekbones and squared chin. Ellen supposed she was pretty in a way most girls were, but she didn't fool herself into thinking she had the beauty that turned heads.

Returning to the bedroom, she pulled a white short-sleeved blouse and a faded blue skirt out of the closet. Through the open bedroom windows, Ellen heard the sound of voices in the backyard. She hurriedly dressed, pulled on a pair of sandals, and took the stairs down to the kitchen. Miss Jewell was just coming through the backdoor.

"Let me fix you a nice glass of iced tea," offered the woman. "I just came in to get another."

Ellen thankfully took the offered glass and held the screen door open for Miss Jewell to pass.

"I convinced Miss Jewell to take a break from that hot kitchen," Audrey called. She was stretched out on a canvas-backed deck chair under an arbor of honeysuckle and trumpet vines. She wore a sleeveless blouse and cotton trousers rolled up to her knees. She held a glass of tea in one hand. A cigarette in the other.

Ellen gave her a long look as she pulled a lawn chair into the shade and took a seat.

"You don't approve?" asked Audrey as she brought the cigarette to her lips. Her look said: *I dare you.*

"It's not that. I tried it myself." Ellen shrugged. "I was just thinking you could lose this job if Mrs. Hewitt found out and told Mrs. Fletcher. And maybe I would, too. You know, guilt by association. And what about Miss Jewell?" Ellen cut her eyes in the woman's direction.

"Don't worry." Audrey blew out a perfect ring of smoke. "Miss Jewell doesn't mind. I asked before lighting up. And nobody can see me under this arbor."

"That's right," chimed in the landlady as she took a seat. "One of my teacher boarders makes use of the arbor on a regular basis. If she was ever seen, she'd be fired."

"Miss Jewell is the soul of discretion." Audrey took another puff.

"Just be careful," Ellen warned. "As tired as I am after two interviews, I still don't want to lose this job."

"Hard day?"

Ellen shook her head. "No, it was good."

Before she could say more, Audrey broke in. "Well, mine was a pip! My first interview was with a man who came here when he was ten years old. His stories about fighting a prairie fire and going out with his brothers to gather buffalo bones gave me some wonderful ideas for a children's book. The afternoon interview wasn't so great. Mrs. Clancy couldn't talk about anything but recipes and how to prepare things like squirrel and prairie dog." Audrey wrinkled her nose. "I told Ralph being assigned to the old folks' home wasn't going to be as easy as he thought."

Ellen raised an eyebrow. "Ralph? He made such a point at the meeting about being called Professor Reynolds. And you get to call him Ralph?"

"I didn't ask permission. I just told him he was being a stuffed shirt, and, whether he liked it or not, I was calling him by his first name." She ground the cigarette into an upturned canning lid. "He's really pretty nice, but he's having a tough time right now. He was teaching at a little college when it closed for lack of funds, and he hasn't found another school to take him."

"Too bad he got off on the wrong foot with the group. He should realize all of us are worried about what happens next. Maybe a little scared, too."

"I'm not scared," countered Audrey. "I was, though. When they let me go at the library because there wasn't any money for my salary, I was plenty scared. But not anymore. Something always comes along."

She pointed a finger at Ellen. "Ralph's problem—and, I bet it's yours, too—is that you can't see yourself any other way than what you want to be. I got over thinking of myself as a librarian. I had to, if I wanted to eat. I worked behind the concession stand at a movie theater, and for a time I cooked greasy burgers at one of those highway joints truck drivers like."

Audrey tilted back her head and drained the last of her tea.

Ellen sipped her own tea while she thought this over. Audrey was five, maybe six years older. She'd obviously had more experience in the real world, but Ellen wasn't ready to concede Audrey's point.

"But that's giving up on your training and what you really want."

"Not at all. I'm still writing my stories, and one of these days I'll find somebody to publish them. Maybe another library will hire me. But it doesn't matter if I'm a dishwasher or working for the WPA, I'm still who I am."

They'd forgotten Miss Jewell until she broke in. "You'll be fine. You've got spirit."

The landlady turned to Ellen. "How was Mrs. Bright?"

"Wonderful. Just as you said she'd be. So, was my first interview, Ivy Hamilton."

Miss Jewell beamed. "My goodness, you got two of the nicest ladies around these parts. Who do you see tomorrow?"

The woman's smile faded when Ellen gave the name, Marie Antoinette Vine.

Miss Jewell leaned forward, lowering her voice. "You know, I don't gossip. If I did, I wouldn't have any boarders. I go by the rule that if you can't say something nice about somebody, don't say anything." Miss Jewell sighed. "But I'll break that rule for Miss Vine."

"I was told she can be difficult."

The landlady snorted. "Difficult! Ha! She's mean as a snake. Let me tell you about Miss Vine."

Ellen and Audrey exchanged glances. This was a different side of Miss Jewell.

Looking around as if the neighbors were hanging over the fence to catch every word, Miss Jewell kept her voice low. "My mother's family was poor as dirt when they came to this town.

My grandfather mucked out the stalls at the livery stable and did any other nasty job no one wanted. My grandmother took in laundry. My mother was just a little slip of a girl, but she sometimes went with her mother when she went around to the big houses."

Miss Jewell took a breath. "One day, Grandmother's at the Vine house, delivering clean linens or whatever, when Nettie Vine comes driving into the yard with that pony cart she had. My mother was six or seven at the time, and you know how some kids just love animals. She ran over to the pony, with the idea of patting it. She barely put her little hand on its nose when Nettie jumped down from the cart and slapped Mother away. Hit her right across the face, hard enough to send Mother sprawling on the ground."

"Holy cow." Audrey swung her feet to the ground and sat upright.

"That's terrible!" Ellen was outraged.

Miss Jewell nodded. "Grandmother was so mad! She swore she'd never wash another thing for that family. Of course, there were one or two other laundresses, but my grandmother was the best. Mrs. Vine apologized several times and made her daughter do the same. But Grandmother wouldn't change her mind, not even when she was offered more money. And my mother made sure I heard that story as a lesson to stay away from the Vines. When I was a girl, I'd cross the street if I saw Miss Vine coming down the sidewalk toward me. I was that scared of her."

"And that was the end of it? No one punished Miss Vine for hurting a child?" Ellen couldn't believe Nettie had gotten away it.

"Of course, nothing happened," Miss Jewell sniffed. "Remember, this is the high and mighty Vine family. They could do anything they wanted." She put a hand over her mouth and dropped her eyes. "Sorry. The story still rankles when I think of it."

"Are you going to ask her about it tomorrow?" Audrey flashed a wicked grin in Ellen's direction. "That should spice up these old settler interviews."

Miss Jewell, regaining her composure, laughed at the idea as she pushed herself out of her chair. When the landlady was back in the kitchen with her radio on and a pot of boiling potatoes on the stove, Audrey tilted her head toward the kitchen. "Do you think Miss Jewell's right?"

"About the story?" Ellen couldn't imagine the woman would make it up.

"No, no. What she said earlier about things turning out all right." She stopped as if deep in thought. "You know what we should be doing? We should be thinking about what happens after this job ends. There's no guarantee it will go on to another county, and there's no promise we can move on to that state guide some writers are working on. In a month, we could be right back where we started."

Ellen agreed, although she admitted that, since coming to Opal's Grove, she felt too busy to think ahead. She saw herself back home and felt a shiver of dread.

Audrey leaned toward Ellen, elbows on knees. "I bet the first thing that just popped into your head was packing it in and going home to the folks."

Ellen gave a slight nod.

"I thought about it when the library let me go, but by then, I'd been on my own for some time. Going back to the bedroom I shared with my sister when we were growing up and rocking on the porch with the folks after supper seemed worse than living in a cheap rooming house and frying up greasy hamburgers. Besides," she continued, "it would be admitting defeat. I couldn't do that after my folks made sacrifices, especially Mom, who was determined her daughters have an education. Dad went along with my sister studying to be a nurse and me going to library school, but Mom had a tough time with Dad's family. They thought it was foolish to educate girls when we'd just end up getting married."

Audrey smiled wryly. "I used to tell myself that my sister and I stayed single just to prove them wrong. But the truth is, I like being on my own. Why else would I turn down two marriage proposals?"

"Two?" Ellen blinked in surprise.

"Well, you don't have to look so shocked. I know I'm no beauty queen, but I do have personality." Audrey tossed her head.

Ellen started to apologize, but Audrey cut her off with the wave of a hand. "Never mind. We have to concentrate on the problem of what comes after this job." She lit another cigarette and reclined on the deck chair. "The main thing is to make a plan. We can't just hope something will happen. We have to help things along."

Ellen watched Audrey concentrate on blowing a series of smoke rings. Audrey, she decided, was a nudger. She'd poked at the professor until his façade began to crack. Now, she was pushing at Ellen.

CHAPTER 10
NETTIE

Nettie Vine lived in the house built by her father. It stood on a large corner lot just two blocks from Agatha Bright's, but the Vine home was unlike any other in Opal's Grove. It had the look of a mansion, a monument to Sylvester Vine's success. Constructed from limestone, with red granite lintels set over each window, the massive house was topped by a cupola. The yard was enclosed by an ornate wrought-iron fence.

Ellen parked on the street. Somehow, pulling into the driveway seemed like an intrusion. She took a deep breath before leaving the car and unlatching the gate that brought her to a stone-paved walkway. She approached the house with trepidation. Miss Jewell's story and Agatha Bright's words kept running through her head. She tried to forget them. A good journalist, she reminded herself, had to leave preconceived notions behind.

She took the three wide stone steps to the front door. Unable to locate a door bell, she rapped the oversized door knocker. She waited and was beginning to wonder if she should leave when the door was answered by a middle-aged woman in a black uniform with a white apron. Introducing herself as the housekeeper Mrs. Castle, the woman invited Ellen inside. With a muttered request to follow, the woman led Ellen into a marble-paved foyer, through a second set of massive wooden doors, and into a large hall dominated by a central staircase.

"Miss Vine is receiving this morning in the front parlor,"

intoned the woman, indicating Ellen should go to the left through a set of pocket doors.

Ellen blinked. Every surface of the room was covered with some sort of decorative piece. An ornate clock bracketed by silver candlesticks sat on an oversized mantelpiece. Tables were cluttered with porcelain figurines and faded arrangements of dried flowers under domed glass. Wilted peacock feathers sprouted from a large Chinese vase in one corner, and gilt-framed paintings obscured much of the dark paisley-patterned wallpaper. Lace curtains, overhung with heavy velvet drapes, barely moved as the morning breeze tried to push through half-opened windows. It wasn't enough to alleviate the room's sultry climate. Ellen felt beads of sweat begin to form along her brow.

Standing in the center of the clutter was a diminutive woman. Like the room, she seemed out of another era. Her ankle-length, white organdy dress was trimmed along the collar with embroidered pink rosebuds. She wore white high-top shoes, pointed at the toe and buttoned along the side. The woman's faded yellow hair wrapped around her head in a braided crown.

She stepped forward to greet her guest, gracefully lifting a bird-thin arm. Her fingers lightly touched Ellen's outstretched hand.

Ellen found it difficult to imagine this frail woman ever had the strength to knock down a child. Still, she didn't doubt Miss Jewell.

"Would you be wanting any refreshments?" asked the housekeeper, who hovered at the door.

Nettie Vine barely moved her head to indicate she'd heard. "This is not a social meeting, Mrs. Castle. It's business."

Ellen gave the woman a small smile. "Nothing for me, but thank you for asking."

Nettie gave a small wave that took in the room. "Welcome to my home. Please be seated." Nettie indicated a small sofa, its velvet upholstery faded and creased from wear. The woman settled onto a matching couch across from Ellen.

Ellen glanced around the room. Its décor left her dizzy, but she managed to say, "Your home is impressive, Miss Vine."

"My parents always wanted the best." She sat back, her bow-shaped lips forming a little pout. "You know, I should be cross. My father founded this town. It's named after my mother. I should have been the very first person interviewed in Mrs. Hewitt's little project."

"It's very gracious of you to see me now. I've read about your father. He was a very important man." Ellen felt like a character in a comedy of manners. Miss Vine ducked her head, accepting the words as nothing less than her due.

Watching Ellen pull out her notebook and pencil, the woman straightened. "I hope you have my correct name in that little book. Although my close acquaintances call me Nettie, my formal, given name is Marie Antoinette Vine. My mother adored the French and their culture. She said it was only natural that I be named after the country's most famous queen. My brother was christened Rex Louis."

Ellen tried to nod seriously, as if the choice of names was understandable. But they struck her as absurd. The urge to laugh almost got the better of her. She dared not look at the woman and feigned great concentration in writing until she felt she had regained control.

"What an interesting choice of names." She almost choked out the words. Taking a deep breath, Ellen pushed on. "Mrs. Hewitt failed to mention that you had a brother."

Nettie's face took on a studied expression of sadness. "Oh, poor Rex Louis. He died, sweet child. It was not long after we arrived here. Father had given me a pony cart. I warned Rex Louis he was too young to ride with me out on the prairie. But I couldn't resist his pleadings. It was so sad. The cart overturned, and my little brother hit his head on a large rock." Nettie cut her eyes toward Ellen. "Of course, I was devastated, but Mother and Papa urged me not to blame myself. I was their only child now, and it was important to put the whole thing behind me."

Ellen wrote, wondering if Nettie would ask that it be omitted. But the woman seemed more interested in smoothing her skirt across her lap.

Aware of the warning that Nettie could be difficult, Ellen turned to something she hoped was more pleasant. "It would be interesting to learn about your early experiences in this new town. You were in a special position to see the changes and progress." Ellen wasn't exactly proud of appealing to the woman's vanity, but it was clear Nettie Vine expected deference.

As if on cue, Nettie's face brightened. "The town was formed in 1866. Papa was a major investor in the town company, although he had many other interests. There was the shipping and trading business, begun by his grandfather in Philadelphia. Papa's family—Mother's, too—were among the first in that city. Mother also had very important and successful cousins in Boston." Nettie's words and demeanor left no doubt that she took pride in a family history of wealth and commerce. "Mother never imagined that Papa's interest in a Kansas town would actually bring us here. On numerous occasions, I overheard her ask why Papa couldn't manage his investment from a distance, but he wanted to be on hand. He wanted to take an active part to protect his interests. Originally, the town was called Grove— for the stand of oak trees along the town's northern boundary— but Papa said if Mother would come to Kansas, he'd change the name to include hers. And he promised to build an elegant home, one even grander than the one we had in Philadelphia's most exclusive section of town."

Nettie looked past Ellen as she recalled those days. "Papa also appealed to her sense of duty. This was a rough prairie town crying out for women of culture. Mother could be a guiding light. Despite her reluctance to leave family and friends behind, Mother agreed. Early in 1867, Mother, my brother, and I arrived in Kansas. Traveling with us was Mother's maid and Mr. and Mrs. Ross. She was our cook. He was the butler and Papa's manservant." Nettie plucked at a sleeve. "After about a year, the maid left us to get married, and Mother was at her wit's end trying to find a replacement. Satisfactory help was so difficult to find, especially when all that seemed available were the immigrant girls."

Ellen winced. While her own father's family traced its roots back to the Revolutionary War, her mother's people were the sort of immigrants Nettie obviously dismissed as inferior. She took a deep breath. "Once you were settled, what were some of your mother's projects?" Ellen had already heard this from Agatha Bright, but it had to be asked.

"Oh, any number of things. The first, as I recall, was raising funds to furnish the town's school. The building itself was funded with donations from the townspeople, and there were two rooms, one for the younger children and one for the older students. Teachers were hired, but, before classes could begin, the classrooms had to be filled with desks and the many other things a proper school required. Mother rallied other ladies to hold fundraisers and raffles to raise money."

"After the school opened, did you attend?"

Nettie's eyes widened, horrified at the thought. "I had just turned fifteen and had already completed my education in Philadelphia. In addition to attending a private school for young ladies, my parents hired tutors who came to our home. One instructed me in French. Mother insisted on that. Another was a dancing master. A young woman of my position had to be adequately prepared to go out into society."

Ellen nodded as if she completely understood the ways of the privileged class. "Your mother felt she had a role to fulfill for this town. Did your father envision any duties for you?"

"I asked Papa that very question." A smile spread across the woman's face at the memory. "We were right across the hall in his library, which also served as his office. I remember him sitting at his desk, considering. Finally, he said that, while I might help Mother in her endeavors, I would have a special responsibility. I was to cheerfully greet every newcomer. If people felt welcome, they would want to settle in town or take claims in the county. I decided I could best accomplish this responsibility by meeting trains coming from the East. I often stood on the platform, calling out words of welcome. Papa thought this a lovely idea."

Nettie paused before continuing. "Of course, I did other things. I was the leader of my social set, just as Mother provided an example of refinement among the ladies of her acquaintance. With Mother's assistance and Papa's approval, I organized parties and picnics and afternoons of croquet or ice cream socials or taffy pulls for the boys and girls around my age. We had some wonderful times.

"I was quite popular. One boy, his name was Simmons, wrote a poem comparing my eyes to cornflowers and my hair to the bright sun at noon." Nettie smiled dreamily. "Wasn't that sweet of him? There were several suitors, and I must mention the English duke who stopped to visit Papa while touring the American West. We held an elegant dinner party here for him and his two companions, who were also from titled families.

"The dinner was lovely. The crystal and silver sparkled in the candlelight. I wore my first grown-up dress. It was pink with pale-green florets that began along one shoulder and trailed down one side of the skirt. The duke was quite charmed with me. I believe he wanted to ask for my hand in marriage, but Papa must have had told him in private that I was too young.

When the duke left, I was disappointed, but then Mother reminded me of the young men right here in Opal's Grove. Several were entranced with me. They jockeyed with one another to sit by my side. They lined up to dance with me."

Ellen stopped herself from asking about these suitors, but she did wonder what had become of them. From the information supplied by Mrs. Hewitt, Ellen knew Nettie Vine had never married. She thought this rather odd, but perhaps it was as simple as Nettie being more inclined to collect admirers than to take any of them seriously.

Ellen saw the woman flinch, as if struck by the same thought. Feeling as though she were walking on eggshells, Ellen searched for another line of questioning.

The safest path was to ask something innocuous. "Is there something in particular you would like the people who read this to know about the early years?"

"Mr. Roosevelt's not reading this, is he?"

Ellen let out a breath as she promised Nettie this was not the case, but the look on the woman's face remained skeptical. Ellen repeated the question.

Nettie put a bony finger to one side of her face, as if considering. "When we first arrived, the town was very raw. The courthouse was not quite completed. The trees planted on the courthouse grounds were spindly little things, tied to thick sticks for support. The only sidewalks were around the square, and they were wooden planks. When it rained, the streets turned into a mire of mud. Only Papa's drive and determination changed that. The downtown streets were paved with bricks. Later, many of the residential streets were paved. Papa convinced farmers to settle in the county, and businessmen to open stores and offices in town. People should remember Papa as a great man.

"As to later years, I don't know what to say." Nettie let a

hand drift in the air. "Mother continued with her committees and afternoon get-togethers with friends. I often went along. But we also traveled. For almost two years, Mother and I did the grand tour of the Continent—London, Paris, Rome, Vienna, and other cities of cultural importance. Mother and I adored Paris. Many of the beautiful things in this room were purchased on that trip. On other occasions, I spent extended periods back East with Mother's family. One such time was after Papa died in that horrible blizzard." Her voice broke.

"I'm sorry," Ellen said. "I had no intention of bringing up unhappy memories."

Nettie lifted her head. "Mother considered moving back to Philadelphia after that, but in the end, she felt we should stay here to remind the townspeople of Papa's influence and contributions." She sighed. "It was such a sad time. Even now, I must remember Mother's admonition to be brave. Papa would have wanted that."

"I'm sure that's true." Ellen didn't want to dwell on the demise of Sylvester Vine. She moved to a topic that should bring back happier times.

"It seems there were several girls near your age in the early town. Perhaps you might want to mention your closest friends."

Ellen expected the woman to readily recall at least a few of those young women who were part of Nettie's crowd. Surely, she hadn't forgotten Ivy. But Nettie let several moments pass before she answered.

"Certainly, there were girls who came here for parties and afternoon visits and who, in turn, invited me to their homes. As for close friends, I don't know how to answer that. Delia Sanders and I spent a good amount of time together. She was entertaining, in a mischievous sort of way, but I knew that anything said in her presence would be repeated. She simply couldn't help herself. She was a terrible gossip."

Ellen's hand faltered over the page.

"Oh, don't worry about insulting dear, homely Delia. She and her family left Opal's Grove long ago. Besides, everyone knew she couldn't keep a secret, just like everyone knew Julia Bright was too bookish to be any fun at a party." Nettie plucked at a sleeve.

"Of course, I tried to befriend Julia, but she was hopeless with all that talk of poets and great literary authors. I confess she bored me to tears. I can't say she was terribly missed when she went back East."

Ellen kept her head down, pretending to write. She didn't want Miss Vine to see that she was appalled by the casual way the woman discarded the girls with whom she professed to be friends.

"And there was Millie Lakin. The only reason for her popularity with young men was her willingness to kiss most anybody, and allow other signs of affection." Nettie raised an eyebrow, suggesting Ellen knew what she meant.

Ellen pulled herself upright, determined to move on. "Perhaps there's one social event or party that stands out in your mind, other than the dinner for the British duke."

Nettie nodded, willing to be led down another path. "That would easily be the party Papa gave in the autumn of 1869. It was October. Mother and I had returned from spending several months with our Philadelphia relatives, and Papa threw a huge affair to welcome us home.

"I remember that night as if it was yesterday. I wore my hair up, dressed with a blue silk flower that matched my gown. The beading on my evening dress glittered in the candlelight reflecting off the crystal chandelier. A string quartet, brought out from Kansas City, was positioned on the landing at the top of the stairs, and waiters moved through the crowd serving glasses of champagne. Papa knew that some people would object to the alcohol, but teetotalers, he said, could drink our cook's 'god-awful' sarsaparilla punch laced with cherry syrup."

Nettie giggled, giving Ellen a glimpse of the long-ago Nettie. Ellen could imagine Nettie descending the mansion's staircase to make a grand entrance at her own party, then plucking a champagne glass from the tray of a passing waiter.

"My crowd was impressed with the champagne. Most everyone from our gang was there. I don't think I ever laughed so much as when Will Pascall pulled me into the middle of the hall and tried to imitate a courtly minuet as the quartet played, and then there was Millie, who almost tumbled into the potted palms after just one glass of champagne. I was never sure if she was inebriated or just lost her balance while flirting outrageously with this new man who had recently arrived in town . . ." Nettie's voice trailed off.

Ellen waited for her to continue, but Nettie seemed to have retreated to a place only she saw.

Minutes passed before Ellen asked if there was anything else Miss Vine wanted to add. The woman shook herself out of her reverie. "I don't want people to forget what my father—Mother, too—did to make this a good town. Lots of town companies failed, but not Papa's." With the last words, Nettie's voice rose.

Ellen said she would be sure to include that in the interview and quietly closed the notebook. Mrs. Hewitt might be disappointed with the result, but Ellen decided her job was finished. She'd interviewed one of Mrs. Hewitt's prominent people. She had something to type up and put into the waiting file. The interview had been a strain, and she couldn't think of any reason to continue. Just as she began to thank the woman for her time and say goodbye, the mantle clock began to chime.

Nettie Vine looked startled and then stricken. "Mrs. Castle! The time! Mrs. Castle! I'll be late! The train!"

Ellen bolted from her seat, taking a step toward the woman,

who was struggling to stand.

The housekeeper intervened, stepping between her charge and Ellen. She put an arm around Nettie's waist, helping her to her feet. Ellen suspected Mrs. Castle had been hovering near the door during the entire interview.

"No, no. There's plenty of time to get to the depot." The woman kept an arm around Nettie while glancing sideways at Ellen. "If you wouldn't mind letting yourself out, Miss Hartley." The woman nodded toward the door.

Ellen grabbed up her bag, stuffing in paper and pencil as she hurried through the double doors into the sunshine. Walking back to her car, she turned once to stare back at the house, wondering exactly what had happened. She heard the sound of doors slamming and the start of a car's motor. Ellen got to her own car just as an old Ford backed out of the Vine driveway. At the wheel was Mrs. Castle. In the passenger seat was Nettie Vine. Ellen shook her head. Surely a woman in her eighties didn't still greet passengers.

Ellen felt sneaky, and a little idiotic, following Mrs. Castle. She could turn off onto another street and go back to the courthouse, but she didn't. She had to see for herself. The Ford pulled into a space near the train station. Ellen slowed and parked in front of a ramshackle diner offering "cheap eats" to travelers. She walked to the depot's street-side entrance. The sound of a train's whistle sounded in the distance. Cautiously, she peeked around the door. Nettie and her housekeeper sat side by side on a bench. Mrs. Castle leaned close to Nettie, saying something into the woman's ear. Then, she drew back. They sat silently as the westbound train drew into the station.

Ellen almost expected Nettie to hurry out onto the platform and wave to arriving passengers. Instead she sat, shifting her gaze from the passengers boarding the train to the arrivals entering the station. When the last one passed, Mrs. Castle put an arm around the woman's small shoulders, helped her to her feet, and turned toward the exit. Ellen jumped back unseen and went to her car. She had no explanation for what she had just witnessed.

CHAPTER 11
OPAL'S GROVE, 1870
NETTIE

Nettie stood at the top of the staircase, peering around the banister for a glimpse of Malcolm. He saw her and gave her one of his devilish smiles just as the maid ushered him into Sylvester Vine's study. Nettie clapped her hands in excitement and hurried back to her bedroom.

She tried to imagine the scene downstairs. Papa would be seated behind his heavy mahogany desk, his fingers steepled in the manner he always assumed when discussing weighty issues. Malcolm would be offered the good leather chair. They would ask after each other's health and then touch on the weather. Finally, they would turn to the matter at hand.

Nettie moved to the mirrored vanity and studied her reflection. She pinched her cheeks, although they were already rosy with anticipation. Malcolm was at this very minute asking her father to consent to their marriage. Impatiently, she paced to the window. Did this sort of thing usually take so long? Surely, Papa would have sent word by now that she and Mother were to join them in the study to celebrate the news and perhaps discuss wedding details.

Unable to stay in her room, Nettie silently crept to the top of the staircase. Her mother was just crossing the foyer, dressed to go out.

"Mother! Where are you going? Father will be calling for us at any moment." Nettie flew down the stairs.

Opal Vine slowly turned to face her daughter. "Marie Antoinette, please lower your voice. Mr. Mahan has left by the study door. Your father has refused."

"That's impossible!" Nettie stood to block her mother's way.

"My dear, you and that common laborer could have saved your father from this ordeal. After all, we made it clear some time ago that we do not approve of him as a suitor." Opal spoke slowly, as if explaining something complicated to a small child.

Opal Vine stepped around Nettie, fussing with her gloves. "Please, don't make a scene. It will do you no good. I was thinking we should go back East. It is time you were married to someone befitting your station. I'm going to write your Aunt Ruth."

The idea of returning to family in Philadelphia and Boston left Nettie cold. Her last visit had been miserable. Instead of being the center of attention, she felt overlooked. She wasn't the prettiest, the most popular, or richest girl in her relatives' wide circle of friends and acquaintances. It had been a shock, as had the realization that many regarded her as an unpolished country cousin. She had no desire to repeat the experience.

"I don't want another trip. I want Malcolm."

Opal Vine shook her head. "Don't be ridiculous." With that, she sailed through the door, bound for an afternoon visit with a neighbor.

As if nailed to the floor, Nettie stood in disbelief. Mother had to be wrong. Papa never refused her. She crossed the hall to her father's study. She knocked on the door and entered the room.

"Papa . . ."

Sylvester Vine, his face drawn into a long frown, stopped her with a look. "The matter is settled, dear girl. That man's name will not be uttered in this house again. Now, go to your room and rest, or whatever it is young ladies do when they behave foolishly." He dismissed her with a wave of a hand and returned to the open ledger before him.

Nettie backed out of the room in shock. As she quietly pushed the door closed, she felt as if she were being swept down into a bottomless pit. Her parents had turned against her. Malcolm was gone.

No! Malcolm isn't lost. Without stopping to throw a cape around her shoulders or tie on a bonnet, she raced from the house. She had to find him. Pulling up her skirts, she ran down the street toward the town square. She would try the lumberyard first. If he wasn't there, she would go to Malcolm's boarding-house. Let people talk if she was seen there. She didn't care. She was Marie Antoinette Vine. She deserved to have what she wanted, and Malcolm had been hers since she first spied him across the room at her homecoming party.

Stopping to catch her breath when she reached the square, she stood on tiptoes, craning her neck for a glimpse of Malcolm. Surely, he came this way. She was about to turn in the direction of the lumberyard when she spied him. He was talking to Ivy Williams, a smile flashing at something she said. Nettie's hands clenched in anger. More than once, she'd seen him make a point of speaking to Ivy or finding an excuse to stand near her.

A hot flush of rage coursed through her. Nettie barely registered the woman with a shopping basket or the old farmer she pushed past to reach Malcolm. By the time she came to a stop, Ivy was across the street.

"You can't keep away from her, can you?" Nettie gasped, catching her breath.

Malcolm's head swung around, and, before she could say more, he grasped her hand, tucking it under his arm and pulling her next to him in a vise-like grip. "Let's walk," he commanded in a low voice. "You don't want to draw attention."

"I'd be pleased to walk you home," he said louder for anyone passing them to hear.

Nettie seethed but let him draw her to the side street, away from the square.

He winced as Nettie dug her fingers into his arm, but he refused to release her.

"What were you doing with that seamstress?" Nettie hissed. "I've seen you talking to her before, all charm and smiles."

"Jealousy does not become you, Miss Vine." Malcolm kept his voice even. "If you must know, I was offering her my felicitations on her upcoming marriage. She's marrying that cow herder. Surely you and your friend Delia know all the news about town."

"Of course, I know it. It's all some of Mother's friends talk about. I could scream listening to them praise her skills and worry over who'll do their sewing after she's on that farm." Nettie tried to pull away but failed.

"You once tried to court her. I know that." Nettie persisted.

"No." He would never admit that Ivy had caught his eye early on, but that was as far as it went. His confidence in wooing her was derailed in short order when she rebuffed him at every turn.

His long stride pulled Nettie along. "I have spoken to her on many occasions, but I have courted you. And for that I have been shown the door by your father." He suddenly released Nettie and turned to walk away.

She reached for his arm, pulling him to a stop. She was not going to give up Malcolm. Mother didn't understand that. Neither did Papa.

"I don't care what Papa says. If he won't give his blessing, we'll run away. When we're married, they'll have to accept you."

"They will never accept me." Malcolm's voice was edged with anger. "Your father didn't even have the decency to offer me a chair. I had to stand, hat in hand like a beggar. It was humiliating."

He stuffed his hands in his jacket pockets. "I'm leaving town."

"You can't!" Nettie stamped an elegantly clad foot.

"I won't stay in a place where people will soon know that Sylvester Vine doesn't think enough of my character to allow me to marry his daughter." He started to walk away. "There are lots of other places to find work. I think I'll head west. Maybe I'll go all the way to California."

Nettie caught up with him. "I'll go with you. I've some money. At least, Papa has money that he keeps in his study safe. I know the combination. That will get us started."

He shook his head. "Normally, your spur-of-the-moment impulses are amusing. But this? I know you well enough to see this would just be an adventure to you. You'd soon tire of it, and of me. It makes no difference how much money you manage to filch from your father. The money will run out, and I can never give you the things you take for granted."

Nettie protested that nothing mattered but being with Malcolm.

Malcolm turned to look at Nettie squarely. Her face was flushed with excitement. He lowered his voice to a whisper. "We have to discuss this somewhere else. The neighbors are probably peeking out their windows as we speak. Meet me in our spot down by the river in an hour. We'll make our plans. Perhaps we could leave on the Wednesday morning train." He turned and walked away before Nettie could say more.

She watched him until he turned down a side street. She fought the urge to laugh and spin like a pinwheel. Self-control was not in her nature, but for Malcolm, she would behave as if she accepted her parents' decision. She took measured steps walking home. She slowly made her way up the driveway to the barn at the back of the property. Her pony cart and her father's buggy sat inside to the left. The remainder of the ground floor contained stalls for two horses and Nettie's pony.

Nettie told the hired man polishing the buggy to hitch up her pony. He doffed his hat, waiting until she was well on her way to the house to spit a wad of chewing tobacco in her direction.

Passing through the kitchen without a word to Cook, Nettie headed to her father's study. Since the accident that killed Rex Louis, Nettie's parents insisted she tell them when she was going out in the cart. This was no time to disobey the rule and draw attention to herself. She knocked at the study door. When no answer came, she opened it a crack. Her father's coat and hat were missing from the peg next to the side door. She slipped inside. With her father out of the house, this seemed an ideal time to check the desk drawer where money was kept. If there was enough, she wouldn't have to worry about opening the safe.

Nettie moved around the desk, sat in her father's chair, and reached for the bottom right drawer. As she pulled at the handle, she noticed the open ledger on the desk. The money drawer forgotten, she studied the last entry made by her father. She knew little about business or reading columns of numbers, but she understood the final notation well enough. Three hundred dollars to Malcolm Mahan. It took a moment for the meaning to take hold, but there could be no other explanation. Sylvester Vine had given Malcolm a good amount of money.

She stared at the ledger. Malcolm hadn't said a word. She raced out of the room to find her cape and hat. He would explain everything, she was sure. Hadn't he agreed to run away? The train on Wednesday. That's what he said. Now, all that had to be done was talk out their plan for leaving.

CHAPTER 12
ELLEN

Friday was payday. Audrey accepted Ellen's offer of a ride to the courthouse but fidgeted with impatience when Ellen insisted on stopping by the post office to mail the short, chatty notes written to her parents and the aunt and uncle in Tulsa. A much longer letter was addressed to Nancy.

"Stop fussing." Ellen slid back under the wheel. "We're early as it is."

Audrey tapped a finger on the edge of the open window as Ellen maneuvered the car into traffic. "I know, but I can't wait to get my hands on that money. I've been thinking about going to a beauty parlor to get my hair cut properly. It's a mess and getting worse every time I take those dull scissors to it. And I wouldn't mind having a new dress to wear when I sit down with Mrs. Hewitt tomorrow."

Audrey wasn't wasting any time in her search for the next job. Her plan was to make Iris Hewitt an ally. "I bet she goes to library meetings and conferences around the state," Audrey said as she explained her plan to Ellen. If anybody knew about job openings, it would be Mrs. Hewitt.

Ellen agreed, offering only one piece of advice: Audrey should visit the woman's pride and joy, the Kansas Room.

After Ellen parked the car, she turned and gave Audrey an appraising look. She was wearing a dreadful dark-purple dress printed with giant cabbage roses. Ellen suppressed a comment about Audrey's taste in clothes. After all, she was still wearing hand-me-downs from Louise, many of them looking somewhat threadbare and faded after almost five years of wear.

"Go to the beauty shop we saw just off Main Street. In fact, I'll go with you. My hair could do with a trim," Ellen said. "But don't buy a dress. Come with me to the Methodist Church tomorrow morning and look for something at the clothing bank."

Before Audrey could object, Ellen went on. "Miss Ivy would be thrilled to meet you, and she'd love to help."

"Really?"

Ellen nodded. "Now, let's get this meeting over with."

Iris Hewitt was once again standing just inside the door to the basement office. As Audrey and Ellen stepped in and began to look for a place to sit, Iris pulled Ellen aside. Ellen waited for the woman to chide her for not turning in Ivy's interview. She had her explanation ready, but Iris had other things on her mind.

"I'm so pleased you were able to interview Miss Vine. I wasn't sure she'd actually do it when the time came," she said. "Grover Calley at the newspaper is going to start featuring the interviews next week, and it will get everything off on the right foot to have Miss Vine's in the first issue. Of course, hers will appear along with our other leading citizen, Mrs. Bright."

Remembering the look on Agatha's face when Nettie's name was mentioned, Ellen knew that teaming the two together was a mistake. She had no idea what history lay between the women. She simply knew Agatha would hate being paired with Nettie Vine.

"Of course, Miss Vine should be first," Ellen conceded. "But perhaps the other person should be a man. That way, readers will have a man's perspective of the pioneer years, along with a woman's. I don't think Mrs. Bright would mind being in a later edition."

Iris beamed. "An excellent idea. I'm sure Grover will agree."

The room was filling up, and Ellen grabbed a chair next to Audrey.

Mae Swenson, the poetry lady, wandered in looking confused. Ralph Reynolds followed, his expression smug.

Ellen leaned close to Audrey's ear. "What's with Ralph?" She'd decided to stop calling him "professor."

"He's got a line on a teaching job," she murmured back.

"Now that we're all here . . ." Iris clapped her hands to begin the meeting. Ellen tuned out the woman's praise for the group's overall efforts and disappointment that one or two were falling behind in their assignments. Mae Swenson sniffled at that. A general restlessness in the room stopped Iris from saying more. Abruptly concluding her remarks, she began to hand out the checks.

Ellen tucked hers into the satchel, planning to open an account at the Bright bank and send a check to her brother with instructions to put it toward buying a baby carriage or bassinet. Her father may have refused her offer to send money to the family, but he couldn't complain if it was meant for the baby.

"Hey, Jess." She stopped him at the door. "How's Aunt Sissy?"

He grimaced. "About what I expected. But I played baseball one night with the fellas in Boxley, and the interviews have been okay."

"That's good. I wanted to ask you about the town newspaper. Does it have all the old papers in storage?"

"Sure. Every year is bound up in oversize volumes. Mr. Calley, the owner and editor, is very particular about that. I'm on my way over to see him. He sent a note to the house saying he wants me to stop by as soon as possible. Come with me."

Ellen matched his stride. The newspaper building sat in the middle of the block on the square's north side. As they crossed the street, Jess cocked his head back toward the courthouse. "I heard Mrs. Hewitt say something to you about the interview with old Miss Vine."

"I was worried because it wasn't very long, but Mrs. Hewitt was happy I got anything at all."

Once they reached the far sidewalk, Jess stopped. "When we were kids, Miss Vine always seemed like a scary old woman. Not exactly a witch—you know how kids make things up—but somebody you stayed clear of. Nobody ever took the dare to go past that wrought-iron fence and right into her yard. There were all sorts of stories about what would happen if you were caught."

He seemed to shiver, just remembering. "Then, I'm down in Boxley interviewing this man named Simmons. Nice old gent. I ask him what he and his friends did for fun when they were my age. He starts telling me about living here in Opal's Grove before he married this girl from Boxley. He talked about parties at the Vine house. He said Nettie Vine was the belle of the ball." Jess shook his head, as if he still found that difficult to believe. "Anyway, after Simmons tells me he had a crush on her, he says something kind of odd."

"About Miss Vine?" Ellen held her breath.

"Yeah. He said that for all her good-natured high spirits, she was 'nutty.' That was the word he used. I didn't know if I should leave that in, seeing as how it's sort of an insult to Miss Vine, so I asked Mrs. Hewitt. She told me to delete it."

"Did he say exactly why she was nutty?"

"That's the other part I took out. Mr. Simmons said he and another fella got into an argument over who would sit beside Nettie at one of her ice cream parties. And she said they'd settle it with a duel. She ran into the house and came out with a couple of her father's pistols. Simmons thought it was a joke, but when he checked the chamber of the one she handed him, he saw it was loaded."

Jess held a hand over his heart. "So help me, that's what he said. He never went to the Vine house again."

Ellen leaned in close as Jess opened the door for her. "I'll tell you a secret, Jess. I believe it, and you're not the only one to delete something. Miss Vine said unkind things about some people she knew long ago. If those were printed, it might cause hurt feelings. I took them out of the interview, but I didn't ask Mrs. Hewitt for permission."

Ellen stepped into the newspaper office. It was much as she expected. The secretary seated behind the counter glanced up, smiled, and continued typing. A middle-aged man sitting at a desk waved in their direction as he continued taking notes over the phone. A few feet away, a woman of indeterminate age and a bad permanent wave pounded away on her typewriter.

Jess walked around one end of the counter, motioning Ellen to follow him up a wrought-iron staircase. At the top of the stairs, Jess yanked a thumb toward a closed door to the left. "Dell Hamilton works in there. He's the accountant."

"I interviewed his mother. I liked her very much."

"Yeah, she's a nice lady." Jess turned to the right and knocked at the door with the name *Grover Calley* stenciled in black.

From behind the door a voice boomed, "Go away."

"He always says that. Likes to make people think he's cantankerous." Jess laughed and opened the door, motioning Ellen in. "Hello. Got your note. Oh, and this is Ellen Hartley. She's doing some of the interviews and wants to see the morgue."

The editor was in his shirtsleeves. An electric fan on a side table ruffled the man's white-blond mane of hair. He took off a pair of wire-rimmed reading glasses and nodded to Ellen before turning his full attention on Jess. "Glad you got here. Got something I want to talk about."

Ellen started backing out of the room, but the man told her

to stay. His business with Jess should only take a couple of minutes.

"Now, here's the deal." Calley leaned back in his desk chair. "I was talking to a friend at the *Kansas City Star.* He's sending his two best sportswriters to Berlin for the Olympics, and he's going to be shorthanded. He's going to take on some stringers, and I suggested you."

Ellen realized that for the first time since she'd met Jess, he was speechless. She stepped up beside him and gave him a poke with an elbow. "Snap out of it! This is a wonderful break for you."

"Yes. Thank you, Mr. Calley, sir." The words came out in a stutter that the editor ignored.

"Now, here's what I want you to do. The eastbound train leaves at 1:30. It'll get you to Kansas City in time to meet this fellow."

Calley stood. He pulled a money clip out of a trouser pocket, counted out some bills, and handed them to Jess. "This should pay for the train ticket and your expenses for staying overnight. I don't want to hear that you spent it on booze or women." The man didn't crack a smile.

Calley leaned over the desk, jotting down some information. "This is who you're going to see and the newspaper's address. This," he said as he finished writing on another piece of paper, "is the telegram you send before you get on the train. It will let my friend know you're on your way."

Jess took the papers, staring from one to the other.

"Well, get going!" Calley yelled.

Jess stumbled from the room in disbelief.

Ellen turned back to the editor as Jess's pounding steps echoed on the stairs. "That was a very nice thing to do."

Calley ignored the remark. "You wanted to look at some of the old editions in the morgue?"

Ellen was about to say she could come back at a more convenient time, but Calley was already taking his gray suit jacket off a coat rack in the corner and jamming his arms through the sleeves. He glanced at himself in the small mirror hanging on the back wall and patted his hair in place.

"It's not vanity. You show your respect for others when you try to look your best for them."

Ellen was too surprised at this bit of homespun philosophy to respond.

"So, you want to see the old papers. Doing research?" Satisfied with his appearance, he walked around the desk and motioned Ellen toward the door.

"I suppose you could say that. The interviews this week have made me curious."

He gave her a glance before leading her out of the office. She followed him down the stairs and around a corner to a door opening to the back of the building, past a linotype machine and the printing press, past the worktable where a man was laying out an ad for used cars, and past a gigantic roll of newsprint. Through another door was the morgue, stacked with every edition of the Dobbs County paper. Each year was bound in dark leather.

"Ever been in a newspaper office?" Calley asked suddenly.

"I worked on the college paper and visited the printing plant a couple of times," Ellen answered, hoping she didn't sound like she was showing off. Calley didn't seem to be the sort of person to put up with braggadocio.

"Guess you want to be a reporter. Seems like I get thirty or so letters every year from people who want a job, and I don't have any work. I can barely afford to keep this place going."

He gave Ellen a long stare to ensure he had her attention. "My granddad started this paper when this town wasn't much more than a few houses and a railroad depot. My dad kept it going. Now it's my turn, but it's tough. Do you know what happens in a Depression? People stop buying subscriptions. I lose money from advertisers because they close their businesses, or if they stay open, they don't buy ads like they used to."

Ellen knew all this, but it had been an abstraction. Calley and his troubles made it real, and the odds of her finding a reporter's job looked dismal. She didn't tell him hers had been one of the thirty or so letters he'd gotten in the past year.

Walking into the morgue, Calley indicated a table and chair in one corner.

"Those oversized volumes aren't easy to handle. If you have trouble, ask Maynard. He's the one out there at the worktable."

As Ellen began to thank him, the man turned on his heel and left. She laid the satchel to one side of the table and began to scan the shelves. She was looking for 1869. Agatha's story had piqued her curiosity. She carefully moved editions off a shelf until she could extract the one she wanted. By the time she finished moving the heavy volumes, her white blouse and navy skirt were smeared with flakes of old leather and decades of dust.

"Wonderful, just wonderful," she muttered, trying to flick some of the dirt off her skirt.

She sat and began to page through the volume until she came to April. She scanned each page, looking for the first mention of the Bright marriage while she got a flavor of the town that greeted Agatha when she arrived.

Her eye caught an advertisement, and Ellen smiled with delight. There, in the upper right-hand corner of page four, among advertisements for ointments and elixirs, bonnets, pianos, and plows, was a small ad announcing Ivy Williams offering her services as a seamstress. Inquiries could be made at the Archer Store. Ellen ran a finger around the advertisement's boxed outline. She imagined a seventeen-year-old Ivy walking into the newspaper office with a determined step and putting coins on the counter to buy the advertising space.

The paper had a predictable format. The society news of ladies' meetings, attendance at the literary society, and who had traveled out of town was always on page three, and that's where she came upon the first mention of Thomas and Agatha Bright. It was a small paragraph tucked between a report on the last meeting of the Methodist Ladies Club and the names of children attending a birthday party. The marriage announcement was short and to the point, with the barest of particulars. Ellen was disappointed. She wasn't sure what she expected, but this was a letdown.

She moved to the next issue and then the next. Finally, she found what she'd hoped for. In a story several paragraphs long, details of the newlyweds' reception were captured for posterity. The reporter painted a picture of blazing candles casting a honey-toned light on the entire party, with an extravagant buffet of hearty fare and any number of hard-to-find delicacies. The groom's parents, noted the article, beamed. The new husband had the look of a happy man. As for the bride, the writer could not say enough about her gracious charm and beauty.

Ellen smiled. If the writer's enthusiasm was any indication, Agatha made a brilliant impression on the people of Opal's Grove.

She reread the article before glancing over the other society news, stopping abruptly. Near the bottom of the page, a single line reported that Mrs. Opal Vine and daughter had departed for an extended visit with Eastern relatives.

Ellen drummed her fingers on the table, rolling this over in her mind. Rather than stay in town for a glittering social affair, Nettie and her mother left. Perhaps a family member was gravely ill back in Philadelphia. Maybe there had been a death. The snippet didn't say, which Ellen thought odd since the paper seemed to report every detail about any little happening. Of one thing, Ellen was sure. Mother and daughter left in the spring of 1869 and returned in the fall, when Nettie enjoyed her own welcome-home party.

Ellen paged through the volume, slowing when she came to October. It took a few minutes before she found the write-up of the evening Nettie had described. Much was said about the food, the drink, and the musicians brought all the way from Kansas City, but Ellen detected a slight contrast in tone from the description of Agatha's welcome to the town. While the writer had fairly gushed in that article, there was a note of restraint in this one.

Still wondering about the differences, Ellen put the volume away and took out the one for the next year. She wanted to see what the paper said about Ivy's wedding. She intended to go straight to May of 1870 but found herself caught up in the earlier issues and their reports of events in Opal's Grove. Another group of Swedish immigrants had arrived in the county. A children's choir was being formed at the Methodist Church, and the Baptist Sunday School was rehearsing an Easter program. A cartload of pigs overturned, sending the animals in a squealing rush across the courthouse grounds and into several businesses, including the millinery shop, where a woman fainted when confronted by a boar blocking the aisle.

Ellen stifled a laugh while chiding herself. She didn't have time to read each issue, but it was addictive. She turned the pages, forcing herself not to stop, but then another article caught her eye. It recounted a "delightful recital given by one of the town's most gracious and accomplished young matrons." Ellen knew it was irrational, but she felt a proprietary pride in Agatha Bright.

Ellen resolutely moved on. Finally, she found the write-up of Ivy's wedding. It was brief, but the reporter must have had some affection for the couple. Ivy was described as the "town's well-liked seamstress" and Wheaton Hamilton as a "progressive rancher." Ellen sat and thought about the couple beginning their lives together, as she absently turned pages back to earlier issues. Just as she started to close the volume, another paragraph in the society column caught her eye. A month earlier, Mrs. Sylvester Vine and daughter had once again boarded a train for the East. The writer alluded to a sickness in the family but gave no details. Again, Ellen wondered about the Vine women and their travels.

Ellen checked her watch. She really had to go. She had one more thing to do before returning to Miss Jewell's. The idea had been percolating since she'd seen what Mr. Calley had done for Jess. After shelving the volume, she walked to the front and stopped to speak to the secretary, who was just preparing to leave for lunch. "Is Mr. Calley still in?" she asked. "I just want a quick minute of his time."

The secretary glanced at an oversized wall clock. "He'll go home for lunch soon, but you have time to go up." The woman gave Ellen a warm smile. "But first, you'll want to duck into the washroom and wipe that smudge of dirt off your face."

"Thank you." Ellen raised a hand to one cheek and followed the woman's directions to a small restroom tucked under the stairs.

She washed her face and ran a comb through her hair before climbing the metal stairs. If she didn't do this now, she wasn't sure she'd have the courage later.

She knocked on the closed door, ignored Mr. Calley's shout to "go away," and walked in.

He glanced up and then back to the papers in front of him. "Find what you wanted?"

Ellen thanked him. "Mr. Calley"—she took a breath—"Jess got me thinking about being a stringer. I wonder if you know of any editors I might apply to."

Calley took off his glasses. His expression was dour. "Depends on what you're capable of writing. If it's the ladies' page or society beat, forget it. There are too many angling for those spots already."

"Those don't really interest me," Ellen answered. "I could show you my clippings." Her portfolio was back at the boardinghouse, under her bed with her typewriter.

The man grumbled, running a hand across his face. Ellen was sure he was about to turn her away.

"No, forget the clippings. Show me what you can do." He sat forward, resting his elbows on the desk.

"We're going to start publishing some of the interviews you folks have been doing, but it's got to have some context. I need a lead article that explains the background of the WPA project. Iris Hewitt gave me a write-up, but I doubt Iris has all of her facts straight. And her writing leaves a lot to be desired. Bring me something I can use. Then we'll talk stringer."

"Thank you, Mr. Calley." Her smile was so big, her cheeks ached. "I'll have it on your desk Monday morning." She took the stairs with a bounce in her step.

Smiling at the woman at the desk, she left the building already writing the article in her head.

"Hey, girl! You there!"

She stopped with a jolt. Nettie Vine was pointing her parasol in Ellen's direction and walking toward her as fast as her pointed-toe shoes would allow.

Nettie drew up in front of Ellen, slightly out of breath. "I've been looking for you. You're that girl that came and talked to me."

Ellen nodded.

"And you talked to Ivy Hamilton and Agatha Bright. I know you did; don't lie."

Nettie's voice rolled over Ellen's protest that there was no reason to lie. "They probably said awful things about me. Never liked me. Well, I could tell a few things about them, too. I'd wager Agatha never mentioned I was the one that should have married her precious Thomas." The woman stopped to take a breath.

Ellen was speechless, aware of the stares from passersby. They were spared another diatribe when a harried Mrs. Castle appeared, slipping one arm around Nettie's waist.

"I'm so sorry. I just turned my back for a minute, and she was out of the house. She's been doing that quite a bit lately. Haven't you, dear?" She patted Nettie's back, gently propelling her toward the Ford automobile Ellen had seen earlier at the Vine mansion. Nettie allowed herself to be maneuvered into the front seat.

When the housekeeper was satisfied Nettie was settled, she walked back to Ellen. "I hope you won't write about Miss Vine's little upset today. Or her behavior the other day. I've been with her for almost fifteen years, since my husband died, and in all that time, she's hardly ever slipped away or wanted to go to the depot."

"Mrs. Castle," Ellen reassured her, "there's no need to worry. I didn't put anything in the interview about her 'upset,' as you call it."

The woman continued as if she hadn't heard. "Since the day Iris Hewitt came and talked to Miss Vine about being interviewed, she's been edgy. It's remembering the old days that's got her worked up. Sometimes, she gets confused and thinks she's back there."

Ellen repeated that the woman wasn't to give it another thought.

"Well, good. Thank you." Mrs. Castle stepped back. "The

minister and his wife are coming to the house for lunch with Miss Vine. We'd best be on our way."

CHAPTER 13
AGATHA

On her way back to the boardinghouse, Ellen's thoughts seesawed between the article for Mr. Calley and Nettie Vine's sudden appearance. The train incident and then today's confrontation nagged at Ellen. There was nothing to do about it, she decided, but to talk to Ivy or Agatha. Maybe she was being a snoop, sticking her nose where it didn't belong, but she wouldn't be able to concentrate on the newspaper article until she could put Nettie Vine out of her mind.

At Miss Jewell's, she found Audrey already beginning her lunch, chattering with the landlady about going to the Beauty Hut. Inwardly, Ellen groaned. She'd forgotten about their appointments with the mother-and-daughter hairdressing team that promised to work them in on their busiest day.

"I was afraid you'd be late," Audrey said when Ellen walked into the dining room.

"Of course not. I just got waylaid." Ellen took the plate Miss Jewell offered and sat across from Audrey. As they munched on cold fried chicken and hot potato pancakes, Ellen reported her conversation with Mr. Calley. Her excitement returned with the telling.

"We'll head to the Beauty Hut just as soon as I make a phone call," she told Audrey.

She peeked around the kitchen door and asked Miss Jewell for permission to use the phone, handing the woman a nickel for its use. The landlady installed the pay rule years before, believing it made her boarders think twice before they tied up the phone.

With her contact list in one hand, Ellen picked up the hall phone and dialed Ivy's number. When there was no answer, she pulled out another coin for Miss Jewell and rang Agatha.

Through Martha, who answered the phone, Ellen arranged to see Agatha after three that afternoon. She realized she would rather talk to Ivy about Nettie Vine; Agatha seemed more agitated by the woman's very name. Still, Ellen decided to plow ahead.

Martha met Ellen at the door, directing her into the same pink and green room where Ellen first met Miss Agatha. The woman, dressed today in a turquoise dress with a white bow tied at the collar, put aside a pair of reading glasses and a worn, leatherbound book when Ellen entered the room.

"I'm so pleased you wanted to visit. Can Martha fetch you something cold to drink?"

Ellen declined, as Agatha waved Ellen to a chair. "After our talk the other day, I began thinking about how much I loved Dickens. Haven't read him in years, but Martha helped me find this in Thomas's library." She tapped the book on the side table. *The Old Curiosity Shop.* You know, they say when the ship arrived in New York with the story's next installment, people thronged the dock shouting 'Is Little Nell Dead?' "

Watching Agatha's face light up as she talked about the book's characters, Ellen lost her nerve. In this sunny room, with Agatha chattering away, Ellen couldn't bring herself to broach the subject of Nettie Vine.

"Now," said Agatha, ending her analysis of Nell's fate, "tell me about your week."

Ellen skirted around her real reason for the visit, telling the woman instead about Mr. Calley's offer.

"Well, he must think something of you. I've known him all his life, and he doesn't go out of his way for just anybody."

Agatha sat back, considering Ellen with a knowing look. "Now that you've told me the good news, tell me what's bothering you. I'm a good people watcher, and I can see you're troubled by something."

Ellen nodded glumly. "I like your company, Miss Agatha, really, I do. But I came to talk to you about something you might find unpleasant."

"Maybe it's unpleasant. Maybe not. We won't know until you tell me." She gave Ellen a small smile.

Ellen took a deep breath and launched into the story of following Nettie to the train. "I'm ashamed I spied on them. I almost expected Miss Vine to wave to the passengers. Then, she stopped me on the street this morning. Her housekeeper showed up and took her home, but not before making sure I hadn't included any of what she called Miss Vine's 'upset' in the interview. She said Miss Vine hasn't done that sort of thing for a long time."

"As far as I know she hasn't, although years ago she was down there most every week. People around here are used to such goings-on, but I can understand how it might startle you." Ellen caught an undercurrent of strain in Agatha's voice.

"There's more." Ellen decided if she didn't tell it now, she never would. "I went to the newspaper office this morning to read some of the early papers. That's how I happened to meet Mr. Calley. Anyway, after I read the wonderful write-up about the reception for you and your husband—it must have been just elegant—I noticed a little blurb about Mrs. Vine and her daughter going back East."

Ellen usually came right out with her questions when putting together a newspaper article, but she felt tongue-tied facing Agatha.

119

"It just seemed odd, their leaving when one of the social highlights of the year was about to take place. And then, this morning, Miss Vine said she should have married Thomas Bright."

Ellen stopped. It had been a mistake to call on Agatha. This was none of her business. Her curiosity had simply gotten the better of her. "Mrs. Bright, I apologize. This is absolutely none of my business. I got carried away." She started to rise, but Agatha waved her down. The room was so quiet that the buzz of insects could be heard outside.

Finally, Agatha broke the silence. "Poor Nettie. I didn't think it would come to this. Perhaps I should have told you when we talked before, but dragging up old hurts and worries is never easy."

Ellen leaned forward.

"The other day, I mentioned there was someone who might say some ugly things about me. As you might have guessed, it's Nettie Vine. I didn't know it at the time I married Thomas, but she planned to have him for herself. Her mother fed the idea. So, when he brought me to Opal's Grove as his bride, she was incensed." Agatha stopped. "No, that's too mild a word. To put it bluntly, she was hell-bent on ruining my name. With the help of a girl named Delia Sanders—who followed Nettie around like a puppy—she put it about that my father wasn't a respectable businessman. He was a drunk who ran a disreputable saloon for miners, with me working behind the bar. And, maybe I was doing something more upstairs. The rumor also suggested I had somehow spotted Thomas on the street, lured him into the bar, gotten him drunk, and then married him before he knew what was happening."

"That sounds so ridiculous it would be funny if it hadn't been so hurtful to you." Ellen knew it was a small thing, but she was glad to have kept the two women's interviews from appearing side by side in the upcoming edition of the newspaper.

"My mother-in-law heard the whispers and knew exactly the source of the rumors. She and Thomas's sister were well aware of Nettie's many attempts to attract Thomas before we married. Julia told me later they had been amused when Nettie made a show of sitting in the front row when Thomas took part in literary society debates, and when she suddenly pretended an interest in Julia. My sister-in-law did not care for Nettie. She told me she went along just for the pleasure of watching Nettie's eyes glaze over as Julia talked about *Plato's Republic* or the symbolism in *Pilgrim's Progress*.

"Both Julia and my mother-in-law knew Nettie had a spiteful side to her. They never doubted Nettie was behind the rumors. Thomas was livid, and intended to march into the Vine house and have it out with the whole family. But my mother-in-law prevailed. She went to her husband, who was quite upset but managed to direct his anger into a methodical plan. He first visited the Sanders home, where Delia, stared down by both her father and Mr. Bright, confessed her part. With this information in hand, my father-in-law then paid a call on Sylvester Vine. We were never told what was said, but very soon after, Mr. Vine whisked his wife and Nettie out of town."

Agatha gazed out the window for a moment. "I was terribly hurt. Remember, I had been in town only about a week. The Brights were preparing the big reception for us newlyweds. The kitchen was bustling with deliveries of food and drink; extra china and glasses were borrowed from three of Mrs. Bright's closest friends; extra help had been hired. And ruining our happy anticipation of the evening was this ugly thing Nettie started.

"The party went on as planned. I told you earlier that Ivy and I became friends because of that dress, but there was more to it. The evening of the reception, she arrived early. Her excuse was the off chance the dress might need last-minute alterations, but her real purpose was to see me alone. She gave me a real talking to. Told me not to worry about what people might have heard. She refused to leave my dressing room until she was sure I was ready to hold my head high. And that's what I did. At the end of the evening, after all the guests were gone, Thomas said how proud he was for the whole town to see I was a charming, refined young lady." Agatha chuckled.

"But, you *were* a refined young lady," Ellen protested.

"Yes, I was." Agatha lifted her head a shade higher. "During the time Nettie and her mother were away, I realized I had gained esteem in the eyes of the town, while Nettie lost a good bit. I did not forgive her for what she tried to do, but, when they returned, I made a point of inviting Nettie to my home when I hosted ladies for an afternoon of visiting. I always acknowledged her when we met in public."

"You took the high road."

"Not necessarily." Agatha chuckled again softly. "My revenge on Marie Antoinette Vine was to treat her with kindness. I took satisfaction in knowing it irritated her to no end. She once tried to get the best of me by using her schoolgirl French. You should have seen her face when I answered in kind."

Ellen couldn't stop herself from smiling. Agatha didn't follow the route many others would have taken, snubbing her antagonist at every opportunity. Ellen was about to say this when she realized Agatha had more to add. "Over the years, things went on much as they had before. My father-in-law had business dealings with Sylvester Vine. My mother-in-law mixed in the same social group as Mrs. Vine. But, more than once, I caught Nettie watching me with outright malice in her eyes.

"When these interviews began, I wondered if her animosity would rear its ugly head. I don't think she's ever forgiven me for taking away Thomas, although he was never hers to begin with. Of that, I have always been sure."

"People would no more believe her now than they did then," Ellen said.

"I suppose that's true, but sometimes old feelings die hard. You've seen how she can be." Agatha reached for the bell to ring Martha. "Stay and have some lemonade. You can explain to me what a newspaper stringer does."

Ellen clearly understood the message. The subject of Nettie Vine was closed.

CHAPTER 14
IVY

Ivy Hamilton sat in the passenger seat, looking like an excited girl. Ellen worried she had done too much. Before having lunch at the woman's house, the morning was spent in the church basement, handing out clothes. Audrey had her dress, beige cotton with a simple white collar, and Ellen, pressed by Ivy to take a navy print recently donated by Agatha's daughter in Topeka, found herself with an almost-new dress.

Ellen met the other women working at the clothing bank. Frances Teller, wife of the minister and mother of five grown sons, was in her element, helping out in the men's clothing section. Agatha's daughter-in-law Carol manned children's clothing. As Ellen watched her put mothers at ease and shower attention on shy girls and reluctant boys, she thought the woman couldn't be more different from Ivy's daughter-in-law, who stood stationed at a long table laden with shoes of every type and size, slips and girdles, hats and handbags. From her little command post, Constance dispensed advice with an authority that brooked no contradictions. As the woman began to grate on Ellen's nerves, she marveled that Miss Ivy had the patience to deal with the woman, day in and day out.

"Are you sure you still want to go for this drive?" Ellen asked, as Ivy made herself comfortable. "It's been a busy day already, and the sun is beating down something fierce."

"I'm fine. In fact, I've been looking forward to this little trip."

Only partly reassured, Ellen drove downtown and took the

highway south toward the river. The road was closed three miles out of town for the bridge construction, but Ivy said not to worry.

"I checked with Dell. The highway is closed just past the county road we want."

They saw the barricades and warning signs before Ivy pointed to a gravel road off to the right. "The turn is just up there."

Ellen slowed to a crawl. To the left in an open field, a dozen or so white canvas tents marked the CCC camp. A few men could be seen lounging in the sun or walking between the tents and the temporary wood-frame buildings that comprised the kitchen and bath facilities. But it was the construction site ahead that drew the women's attention. A massive road grader and several farm wagons stood in line, as if ready to march when given the order. Piles of rock and sand formed hills.

"That is a lot of rock," Ivy said, shaking her head.

Ellen agreed. "I heard someone at the courthouse say the workers have to dig even more from along the river to shore up the bridge embankments. Something about not enough bedrock and too much clay and sand." She made a slow turn down the country road, which had once been nothing more than a wagon track following the natural break between woods on the left along the river and open prairie on the right.

Ivy warned Ellen it had been some time since she'd been this way, and the soddie had been going to pieces even then.

"I'd still like to see it," Ellen said as they bumped along the road.

Ivy pointed. "It's up there on the right." Ellen saw a mound of earth surrounded by a field planted in wheat.

"You can pull over to the side," Ivy directed.

Ellen did as she was told. Ivy hadn't understated the disrepair of the old homestead. One end of the soddie bulged, slowly crumbling back into the earth. The roof was long gone. The windows were nothing more than gaping holes. The door had been torn off or simply rotted away with time.

Ellen went around the car to help Ivy step out and then cross a dry, dusty ditch. Brittle prairie grass broke beneath their feet as they moved to stand beside a barbed-wire fence. Ivy rested a hand on a rough-hewn post. She turned her face toward what remained of her first Kansas home.

"I feel like a girl again. I can remember the wind whipping my long skirt around my legs and the prairie grass bending in waves with just the slightest breeze."

Ivy sighed, adjusting a wide-brimmed straw hat more firmly on her head. She turned to Ellen, who stood ready with pencil and notebook. "Morton ought to pull that soddie down instead of letting it die a slow death, but I suppose he's got other things on his mind."

"Morton's family bought the place?"

Ivy nodded, her big hat bobbing against a stout southern breeze. "Like I told you at lunch, Nate and Clara stayed on the place for the five years required by the homestead law. Once they had clear title, they sold it and moved on. I wasn't all that surprised when they announced they were going to Oregon. They both had an adventurous streak and were itchy to move. They wanted Caleb and Hannah to join them, but they were pretty well situated and didn't want to start over again. I was glad they didn't. They were like family, and it was a comfort to have them near."

Ivy gave Ellen a wistful smile and turned back toward the ruins. "You've got to have a good imagination to see the place the way it was. Over to the right was a lean-to barn and behind that a corral. There was a big potato field behind the house. Of course, there was a garden, and a well. The trees Nate planted are gone. I think Morton's father took them out when he decided to go into planting wheat in a big way. There was a time the crop made good money.

"So many good memories are here. On the day Wheat and I married, we said our vows at the little country church down the road. Then we came here with Nate and Clara and a few friends for our noon meal. There was even a wedding cake, baked by Hannah. Agatha and Thomas were here, and the Archers."

"Tell me about your wedding dress."

"Of course, I made it, using a design I'd seen in a magazine. The dress wasn't white. Most weren't back then. It wasn't practical to spend money on a dress you'd wear only once, and, even if you planned to dye it, you couldn't be sure the fabric wouldn't be ruined.

"My dress was a light shade of rose, with lace at the neck. The back of the skirt had insets of a light-blue print with tiny rosebuds. Matching ribbons were braided into my hair, which I wore pinned up."

Ivy smiled. "I was beautiful, and that dress got worn and made over to copy newer fashions until the material just wore out. I've got a scrap of it in a box of mementos."

She glanced again at the soddie. "Clara was fond of flowers. She had wisteria and red roses she'd started from a cutting brought from Illinois. We had a pretty bowl of the early roses on our wedding table."

"Mr. Calley let me look through old newspapers, and I saw the mention of your marriage. The write-up called you the 'town's well-liked seamstress.' There wasn't very much detail about the wedding, the way some write-ups are today with their descriptions of what the bride wore and the names of brides-maids."

Ivy smiled. "That's the way most of the marriage notices were back then, although some were more elaborate if you were somebody real important in the community. I have that little announcement in the memento box, too."

"What did your mother say about your marriage?"

"Oh, I suppose she was glad to know I wouldn't be a spinster. I wrote my parents, of course, but I think it was Nate's letter praising Wheat that assured the folks I had a good man."

Ivy let Ellen put a hand under her elbow as they returned to the car. "You can tell me to mind my own business," she began, "but this talk of weddings has me wondering if you have a young man. And I don't mean one of those fellows your mother's picked out for you."

Ellen realized she should have expected Ivy to be curious. Miss Jewell had already skirted the subject. Audrey had asked straight out. Ellen opened the car door for Ivy. "Well, there was this one, but we had a falling out over me working." Ellen walked around the car and slid into the driver's seat. "He says he wants me to have a writing career, but I don't know how I can do that and be married with a house to look after—not to mention the kids that are bound to come along."

Ellen glanced at Ivy, who angled her head to one side as if studying the problem. "I don't give advice on matters of the heart. You're bound to get blamed if things don't work out. So, all I'll say is that it's up to you what happens, and nobody else."

Having said her piece, Ivy settled back. Ellen let the words sink in as she turned the car around and headed back the way they'd come on the river road. Before they reached the road's intersection with the highway, Ivy asked Ellen to stop. She pulled to the shoulder and into the shade.

"That grove of trees there is where the Fourth of July picnics were held." Ivy pointed. "But people stopped coming here after the town park was built."

Ellen picked up the notebook. "I've driven by the park but never stopped to walk around."

"Not every town had a park, but Sylvester Vine wanted one for Opal's Grove. And it had to be the best. Some folks disagreed with him, but he usually got his way. When it was finished, people came from all around this part of the state to see the walking paths lined with flowers and the occasional bench. A rose garden was arranged around a white marble fountain. There's a band shell and a picnic ground. After a few years, the city put in a children's playground. You should go see it, even though the drought and dust storms have wreaked havoc on the flowers. Constance is on a committee to restore the plants, but so far the only plan they've come up with is women taking their dirty dishwater out to the park and dousing the flowers. "She chuckled. "Most of the time, they forget, so the plantings languish."

Ellen started to close the notebook, but Ivy had more to say. "When we first moved to the claim, Clara and I would walk down to the trees along the river. It was about a mile from the soddie, but sometimes we just couldn't take the open land and skies another minute. People said there were women who went crazy from the openness. I believe it. Clara and I would wrap our arms around the trees, rubbing our hands across the bark. It lifted our spirits to stand in the shade with the sound of leaves rustling in the breeze. That's how we met John Featherstone."

Ellen stopped writing and looked at Ivy in surprise. "I saw his collection in the library."

Ivy was pleased. "He had a little place at the edge of town, a kind of leather shop with living quarters in back. He sold harnesses and saddles—that sort of thing—and repaired them if somebody brought something to him. He took in Ezra Coombs to learn the trade. With Ezra around, Mr. Featherstone had more time to follow his interest in hunting fossils and looking for Indian goods like arrowheads and such. If I came upon him along the river, he'd show me what he'd found and explain what the things were. Sometimes, I'd walk with him in his searches. Some people thought he was an eccentric, but he didn't seem that way to me. I liked his company, and I think he enjoyed mine."

"The county history said he was a mountain man."

"Oh, he did lots of things. He was a fur trapper. That's how he came to meet people from different tribes and got interested in Indian goods. When the trapping trade began to slow, he turned what he'd learned about the country into working as a scout for soldiers and scientists on surveys and scientific expeditions. His interest in fossils began on those trips. I don't think he had much schooling, but he taught himself. By the time I knew him, John Featherstone was even writing to college professors about some of his discoveries."

"The label with the collection said he believed that an old Indian village was located somewhere close. Too bad he never found it." Ellen saw a closed look pass across Ivy's face.

"He found it, didn't he?" Ellen barely breathed out the words.

Ivy fidgeted in the seat. "Iris Hewitt came asking me that once, and I'll tell you what I told her: he never showed me such a thing. And you can write that down." She jabbed a finger at the notebook.

Ellen jotted down the words before turning toward the woman. "But that's not the same as knowing there was one."

Ivy looked away, chuckling in spite of herself. "You're a bright one. Iris Hewitt never figured out how I talked around her question. Now, don't write this down, and don't ever tell anyone I told you so. He found something." She paused. "It was about a year after Wheat and I married. We'd come to town for supplies, and Wheat wanted to see Mr. Featherstone about a horse collar. When their business was finished, he invited us to follow him into this shed he'd built behind his store to hold all the things he'd found. I remember a table covered with bits of pottery, but on one end there were a few small bowls and a couple of little figurines. He couldn't have found those just picking along the river. When I looked at Mr. Featherstone, I knew from the gleam in his eye that he'd made the discovery he'd always hoped for.

"Finding it was enough for him. He kept a few pieces but left everything else in place. He covered it over and walked away. He didn't tell us where. Said he'd take us to see it sometime, but that never happened. He died in his bed two months later. Poor Ezra found him one morning when he went to work. In his will, Mr. Featherstone left the business to Ezra and most of his collection to a college. The remainder was given to the town. That's how it came to be displayed in the library." Ivy fanned her face. "In a way, I'm glad he never told me or anyone else. I like the mystery of it."

Ivy motioned for Ellen to start the car. "Let's go home and get something cold to drink."

"Thank you for telling me about Mr. Featherstone." Ellen put the car in gear.

"He wouldn't mind my telling you. In fact, I expect someday his discovery will be unearthed."

CHAPTER 15
ELLEN AND THELMA

Saturday night supper was mashed potatoes and gravy, leftover meatloaf, and a salad made from new lettuce and radishes from Miss Jewell's garden. Audrey was in a fine mood after her talk with Iris Hewitt. The woman had been sympathetic and most agreeable to giving Audrey what help she could to find a library job.

"We're on a roll," Audrey declared over supper. "I've got Mrs. Hewitt and you've got Mr. Calley."

Audrey suggested they go to the movies as a little celebration. Ellen half-heartedly agreed. She was tired and had already seen the picture, but the night before she'd begged off to work on the article promised to Mr. Calley. She didn't want to refuse a second night and dampen the general good mood.

They were just finishing their meal when the hall phone rang. Its shrill tone brought Miss Jewell bustling out of the kitchen, wiping her hands on a stained apron. Another house rule was that no one but Miss Jewell answered the telephone.

"It's for you, Ellen," the landlady said as she returned to the kitchen. "It's Mrs. Hamilton," she said over her shoulder.

Ellen gave Audrey a puzzled look before taking the call.

"Agatha and I have a bit of a problem," Ivy began, her voice sounding strained. "Thelma's car has broken down. I mean to say her family's car, and we have no other means."

"Miss Ivy," Ellen broke in, "what would you like me to do?" She listened as the woman at the other end of the line took a deep breath and explained why she'd called.

After Ellen hung up, she searched for Audrey and found her outside under the arbor with a cigarette. She apologized for upsetting their plans. "Mrs. Hamilton asked me to come over. She thought of a few other things she wants to add to the interview." Ellen briefly thought about her capacity to make up little white lies on the spot, but Audrey didn't seem bothered by the news. "I don't mind going to the movies alone. Maybe I'll see people from work there."

Unh-uh, thought Ellen. Maybe you'll see Ralph, or maybe that was the plan all along.

Ivy Hamilton was waiting outside her kitchen door when Ellen pulled into the woman's driveway. Ellen shook her head and smiled. Ivy and Agatha were full of surprises. She never would have guessed what they were up to.

Ivy hurried forward as Ellen exited the car. "We can't thank you enough. Thelma couldn't ask Bill for his car. He has to use it when the sheriff puts him on night duty, and we just couldn't think of anyone else."

"I'd love to help." Ellen didn't add she felt warmed by their trust. She followed the woman into the kitchen, where seven paper bags, with names printed on the side, sat lined up on the table.

"It's just that we have things delivered most every Saturday, and there are some folks that count on us."

"Even if they don't know who's behind the food and clothes." Ellen finished the thought with a smile. "I'm proud to help," Ellen reassured her, glancing at the sacks. "Did you sew all this?"

"Oh, no," Ivy said, chuckling. "Some is my work, but mixed in are things from the church basement. And this bag here is just diaper cloth for the Allens, who just had their first baby—a boy."

Ellen hefted a sack under each arm. Ivy followed with another. When the bags were loaded onto the back seat, Ellen slid behind the wheel. "Thelma's waiting for me at Mrs. Bright's?"

"Yes, and thank you again." Ivy gave a small wave.

In less than ten minutes, Ellen pulled into the driveway at the Bright house. As soon as Thelma heard the car, she was out the back door, carrying a sack of groceries. She was wearing a dark, sleeveless blouse, trousers, and her brother's hand-me-down black, lace-up basketball shoes.

She nodded to Ellen, the dimple flashing when she smiled.

"You have a tire iron," she said as a statement of fact, not a question. "Get it, and put it on the front seat." She opened the car's back door and pushed the sack to the middle of the floorboard.

Puzzled, Ellen retrieved the iron from the car's trunk, tossing it on the front seat before joining Thelma, who was back in the kitchen, where Martha was folding down the tops of bulging grocery bags. Agatha was giving directions from her seat at the head of the kitchen table.

"You're a godsend," Agatha said when she saw Ellen, drawing her forward with a wave. Gently catching Ellen's wrist, Agatha stuffed a few dollars into her hand.

Ellen protested, but Agatha insisted she take the money for gas. Then she turned to Martha. "Give that list to Thelma. They should get started before it gets too dark for them to get around on those country roads."

When they finished loading the backseat of Ellen's car, Thelma and Martha squeezed into the front with Ellen. Thelma held the tire iron on her lap. Martha had to be taken home before they started the deliveries.

"Why the iron?" Ellen asked as she backed out onto the street.

"Protection. Just in case."

"Protection?" Ellen's head jerked for a quick look at Thelma. "You're teasing. Aren't you?"

Martha, who had yet to say a word, glanced at her sister and smiled.

"I had some trouble on the road one night," Thelma answered casually. "The McAllister brothers. They're a couple of toughs, always getting drunk on bootleg whiskey and acting stupid. I was going slow, coming back into town, and the two idiots tried to jump on the running boards."

"What happened?"

"Oh, one of 'em was so tipsy, he couldn't get his balance and fell off into the ditch. The other one went flying when I reached out through the window and hit him in the gut with the tire iron. I keep it right beside me on the seat."

The sisters giggled.

Martha was still smiling when they let her off in front of the Weaver home. Thelma's brother, Hugh, was in the driveway, working on the family car. He waved an oily rag in their direction. Her mother was seated on the front porch.

"Ma, I won't be late, and, Martha, say hello to Chester," Thelma called out as Ellen pulled away.

Thelma directed Ellen to take the highway north. Sometimes the deliveries were south of town, made more difficult with the bridge work, and some Saturdays, the route was east. Tonight, the women's list was for places to the north and west.

"Chester is Chester Welch, a barber here in town," Thelma said without Ellen asking. "He and Sis have been keeping company for five years. He comes over, and they sit in the parlor and listen to the radio, or they see a picture show. Sometimes they go for a drive on Sunday afternoons."

"For five years?" They reached the outskirts of town. In the west, the sunset lit the sky with startling shades of pink and turquoise.

"It suits them," answered Thelma. "Sis wants to live at home, help Mom, and work for Miss Agatha. Chester likes his bachelorhood, living alone above his barber shop."

Ellen mulled this over. "So there's no talk of marriage?"

Thelma hooted. "If there was, they'd both run in opposite directions. Maybe that'll change, but for now, they like things as they are."

They left Opal's Grove behind. Thelma leaned forward, getting her bearings. "It's about five miles before we take a county road on the left. Mrs. McNulty lives farthest out, so we'll start with her and move back toward town. She's one of the regular stops when I come this direction," Thelma offered. "Her husband died some time ago. Her son's in jail for trying to rob Miss Agatha's bank. He never had a bit of sense. Tried to make his getaway on a bicycle. Miss Agatha bears no hard feelings, and she worries about Mrs. McNulty living out here like a hermit, ashamed to show her face in town."

Thelma raised a finger to her cheek as if something else had just come to mind. "Gee, I hope she's got her dogs tied up."

"I hope you're joking," said Ellen. "I don't mind sneaking along back roads and leaving things on people's porches, but being chased by dogs that are probably rabid makes me nervous."

Thelma giggled. "Sometimes she forgets, but the dogs are old. We can outrun them if we have to."

"Wonderful," Ellen muttered.

To think of something else besides what awaited at the McNulty house, Ellen asked about Bill. "Sometimes your fiancé drives for you?"

"He did a couple of times, but then we got worried. If Sheriff Logan found out, he might not like Bill being involved." Thelma paused. "Not that this is illegal."

"Of course not," Ellen answered, wondering if it was against the law to steal up on people's porches uninvited. Nancy would know. Probably, thought Ellen, it was against the law. Trespassing. That was it. Ellen wished she hadn't remembered.

"But we were afraid Bill might lose his job," Thelma continued. "Besides, lots of weekends, the sheriff has Bill working. Most every Saturday night, there's trouble at this rough joint east of town. It's called the Hurley-Burley. Miss Agatha says there's been a Hurley-Burley there since the early days. The first one burned. This is the second or third."

"They sell liquor? That's illegal in this state."

"Malt beer is legal. You know, what they call three-two beer." Thelma corrected her. "It's the hard stuff that's illegal, and Bill says there's a pretty good trade for it out the back door. Once in a while, there's a raid just to slow down the bootleggers and moonshiners."

Thelma pointed to a side road, and Ellen made the turn onto a surface that was more washboard than gravel. She kept the car to a crawl. When they reached Mrs. NcNulty's, she drove slowly past the dilapidated clapboard house with a sagging front porch. It was best, cautioned Thelma, to go on to another driveway and turn around so they were facing back the way they'd come.

Ellen agreed with the strategy. The last of the evening's sunset was fading. Better to be headed out than down some unfamiliar country road in the dark.

Ellen let the car glide slowly back past the house and stopped. Thelma scrambled out, quietly opened the back door, and grabbed two grocery sacks.

Ellen watched her dash across the dusty yard to the porch. Just as Thelma set down the sacks, there was a sharp yelp and then a snarl.

Ellen jumped at the sound. She put the car in gear and was

already moving forward when Thelma jumped into the front seat.

"That dog Lucifer was under the porch. Almost got a piece of my ankle." She tried to catch her breath.

"Did he bite you?" Ellen shouted as she pushed down the gas pedal, spraying dirt and bits of gravel in the car's wake.

"No." Thelma sat back. "But he scared the crap out of me."

Her hands flew over her mouth. She peeked over at Ellen, not sure how this college-educated girl would react. Nice girls weren't supposed to say such words.

"Scared the crap out of me, too!" Ellen shouted over the noise of the motor. They looked at each other and burst out laughing.

Driving down one farm road after another, leaving a sack of groceries here, a bag of clothing there, Ellen and Thelma settled into a friendly companionship. Thelma talked about Bill and the wedding. Miss Agatha was giving them money to pay three months' rent on a little house. Miss Ivy was making Thelma a floor-length dress of white satin with a lace bodice. Bill had a new blue suit. Thelma wouldn't have minded if he wore his duty uniform, but everyone else connected to the nuptials, including the groom, had voted her down.

"I don't understand it," Thelma told Ellen. "Who doesn't like a man in uniform? I once got on a Greyhound bus and rode all the way to the Colorado line just because the driver looked so snappy in his uniform, and for a while I had a terrible crush on the usher at the movie house here in town. He wore this red jacket with gold buttons."

"So, you're marrying Bill because he wears a uniform?"

"No, silly. He's the guy for me. The uniform is a bonus."

Ellen smiled to herself. Who could argue with that?

When Thelma asked if Ellen had a boyfriend, her first thought was to brush off the question, but in the face of Thelma's openness, she heard herself talking about Jason and their breakup.

Thelma sat back, folding her arms across her chest. "So, you don't have a boyfriend."

The words hit Ellen like a bucket of cold water. Until that moment, she realized, some part of her believed the breakup was temporary. But she'd told him to go, and he had. She suddenly wondered if she had done the right thing.

They made the last country delivery and headed back to town.

"How long have you been doing this?"

"About a year. When Miss Agatha's son took away her car, she asked me to take over."

Ellen cut her eyes to Thelma and then back to the road. "Are you telling me Miss Agatha used to be out making her own deliveries?"

"Just about every Saturday night, her and Miss Ivy would pack up that Oldsmobile and head out."

Ellen shook her head. "That's crazy. They could have had an accident. Been hurt. Chased by Lucifer or run into one of those drunks you were talking about."

Thelma shrugged. "Maybe so, but if Miss Agatha still had her car, those two ladies would be out here instead of us. You should know by now you can't tell them a thing. After Bill and I get married, he won't want me doing this, so we've already arranged for Martha and Chester to take over."

Ellen couldn't picture Martha rambling around on country roads but didn't say so as they drove into town. Thelma directed her as they detoured down side streets and alleys to make their deliveries. Finally, there were two sacks left, one of groceries and one filled with boys' shirts and overalls.

"These go to the Picketts," said Thelma, directing Ellen to stop midway down an alley. Ellen kept the motor running while she slipped out of the car, opened the back door, and grabbed the bag of clothes. Thelma snatched the other sack, and they pushed through a back gate and across the yard to a concrete stoop in front of the kitchen door. Through the open windows, they heard a radio playing and little-boy voices.

Their last delivery finished, they scrambled back to the car. Ellen put the Packard in gear and eased down the alley.

"Thanks for helping," Thelma said when Ellen stopped in front of the Weaver house. "It's sure easier with someone else along."

"I loved it. Can I come with you on the next run?"

Thelma sat back and laughed. "I don't know why not. For a college girl, you're okay. I thought you might be a snob and look down on people like me. I should have known that if Miss Ivy and Miss Agatha liked you, things would be fine."

Ellen didn't know what to say but decided to take it as a compliment. "Just remember to call me about next time. I'll be disappointed if you don't."

CHAPTER 16
ELLEN

It was another Friday and another week closer to the end of the work in Dobbs County. Ellen thought she should have a sense of growing panic, but she couldn't muster more than a mild concern as she went through days of listening to stories that mixed grief with happiness, loneliness with just getting by. The article she promised Grover Calley appeared in Wednesday's edition of the local paper, along with the first two settler interviews. And the newspaper man made good on his promise to Ellen. He liked her writing style well enough to give her the name of two friends, one at a St. Louis newspaper and one in Chicago. He told her to mention his name in her letters but cautioned her not to get her hopes too high. "Stringers are a dime a dozen, and you've got to be good—I mean *really* good—to get noticed."

Ellen knew what he left unsaid: it was even harder for a woman. He was trying to prepare her for disappointment, but she would have none of it.

When she wasn't at an interview or typing up the results, she worked on two articles to include with her letters. The first, she decided, would tell readers about the interview project from the WPA workers' point of view, including comments from Audrey, who was more than happy to oblige, and from the professor, who huffed and puffed before agreeing. She wished she could write about the nighttime deliveries for the second story, but that was out of the question. She settled on the clothing bank, emphasizing the helping hand offered to friends and neighbors when times were hard.

For that piece, Ellen wanted to talk to Ivy. She drove to the house late on Friday afternoon but was disappointed to find her gone. She was returning to her Packard when a next-door neighbor, watering potted geraniums on her front porch, called out to Ellen.

"Mrs. Hamilton's gone to visit Mrs. Bright. Her daughter-in-law picked her up not more than fifteen minutes ago."

Ellen thanked the woman and started the car. She'd planned on visiting Agatha anyway. Her interview had appeared in that day's paper, and Ellen was anxious to know what the woman thought of seeing her words in print.

Ellen drove back to the old residential part of town. She found Ivy just where she hoped, rocking beside Agatha on the woman's front porch. As Ellen exited the car, the women called for her to join them.

"We were just talking about you," said Ivy when Ellen took a seat beside her. "You did such a nice write-up about the project, and Agatha's just as pleased as can be with her interview."

"I can speak for myself." Agatha tapped her cane for attention. "And I agree with everything Ivy just said. I've had phone calls all afternoon from people saying how much they liked it."

"My daughter-in-law Constance is fit to be tied because Agatha got her name in the paper before I did." Ivy laughed with delight.

"I can talk to Mr. Calley about running your interview sooner than he planned," Ellen offered, but Ivy wouldn't hear of it.

Ellen would willingly have put in a word with the man, especially since she had a favor to ask. She explained about the possibility of writing for the newspapers Mr. Calley suggested and outlined her idea for the articles. "But I need more information on the clothing bank."

"Well, that's easy enough," Ivy answered. "We'd be only too happy to help you whatever way we can."

Ellen pulled a pencil and her dog-eared notebook from the satchel that she was beginning to think of as an extension of herself. She never seemed to be without it.

"We started the bank back in '32," began Ivy. "The crash on Wall Street in '29 didn't hit us all of the sudden. It was more like when you throw a rock in a pond; it takes a while for the splash to move out in bigger ripples."

"Some people thought we'd be safe," broke in Agatha, "but my son knew better, and he took all the precautions he could think of to keep the bank solvent. It wasn't too long before people around here began to feel the financial pinch, and then the weather turned against us." She nodded to Ivy to continue.

"There was the long drought, and the dust blowing in all the way from Oklahoma and western Kansas. Some people quit coming to church because they were ashamed to be seen in threadbare clothes, and we heard of a girl, bright as a penny, who quit high school for the same reason."

Agatha picked up the story. "Several of us ladies at the church got together and went to the minister. It's not an original idea, the clothing bank. One of us, I'm not sure who, heard about one in Calvert City. We decided to try the same thing here. At first, not many people came. Folks just don't want to feel like they have to take charity, but, as this Depression keeps on and people get more desperate, more come."

Agatha stopped for a breath. "Of course, it helped draw people in when it got around that we had more than hand-me-downs. We had clothes sewn from scratch by Ivy Hamilton." She gave her friend a big smile.

Ivy turned her head, embarrassed by the compliment. "Other ladies make clothes. I'm not the only one."

"No. But you've got a reputation for being the best."

"I'm sure that's true." Ellen put away the notebook and thanked them. She started to leave, but Ivy and Agatha protested. She had to have a lemonade.

Ellen volunteered to fetch the drink, rather than Agatha calling Martha with the bell that sat on the table between her and Ivy. After returning with a large glass and a tray of gingersnap cookies, Ellen resettled herself.

"Now, tell us about Mae Swenson," said Agatha.

Ellen laughed and shook her head. "It's a mystery to me how you two can sit on a front porch and know everything that's going on in town. I just heard about her this morning at our meeting with Mrs. Hewitt."

"Oh, I'm sure we don't know everything," answered Agatha, "but we like to keep informed."

She didn't have to add that the information helped them decide who needed a sack of canned goods or a new shirt.

Ellen took a long drink. The cool lemonade felt wonderful sliding down her throat. "I don't know what you've heard, but Mrs. Hewitt, with the blessing of the WPA woman in Topeka, let Mae go. This morning, Mrs. Hewitt divvied up her remaining assignments among the rest of us."

"But why was she fired? It's true she sometimes acts like she's in another world, but she means well," said Agatha.

"Sometimes her mother has to remind her to eat," Ivy piped in. "And when Mae's husband went out for a paper one day and just kept on walking, she didn't miss him for two days."

Ellen gave Ivy a sidelong glance to see if she was exaggerating and saw by the look on her face she wasn't.

"Surely, she's capable of writing down what people say to her," Agatha chimed in.

Ellen shook her head. "That's the problem. She did two interviews the first week, and only two this week. It's just not that she's slow. She wrote down what people told her and then she turned it all into rhyme. I've been assigned the job of trying to salvage the interviews she turned in." Ellen raised a hand before either woman could interrupt. "When Mrs. Hewitt tried to explain Mae's poetry wouldn't do, Mae accused her of stifling artistic expression." A look of mischief stole over Ellen's face. "Since we're good at secrets, I know you won't repeat this, so let me give you some examples of what she turned in. I read through them after lunch." Closing her eyes, she leaned back in the chair. She began to recite a few of the lines, although she hadn't intended to memorize them.

"First," she said, "this is from Mrs. Wentz's interview: 'The settlers did quake, as the snow fell in big flakes.' And there's this: 'Grasshoppers hopped, they hopped along the floor, they chewed up my green curtains, and then they asked for more.' "

Ellen kept her eyes closed, but there was no mistaking Ivy's chuckle or Agatha's low laugh. "Wait, one more." She held a finger in the air and concentrated to get the right cadence. "This line is from the Harry Oliver interview: 'In wagons they came, the prairie for to see, when they reached Opal's Grove, Harry said, "Ma, I got to pee." ' "

Gales of laughter filled the porch. Ellen opened her eyes. She loved to watch people when they laughed, looking at each other to share the moment.

"I shouldn't laugh," choked Ivy, wiping tears from her eyes. "Mae really is a dear person."

"I know," agreed Agatha, getting herself under control. She exchanged looks with Ivy and burst into laughter again.

As they quieted, Ellen stood. She had to be on her way. Miss Jewell served supper early, and she wanted to get to work on the article.

She stopped on the top step and turned. "You probably already know this, but just in case you haven't heard the good news, Jess Smith got a job with a Kansas City newspaper. It's temporary, but it may turn into something permanent."

The women were slightly disgruntled that this piece of information had escaped them, but they recovered. They were happy for the young man. His father was a plumber by trade, but jobs were few these days, and the family struggled to get by. As Ellen made her way down the sidewalk, she heard them conspiring over how best to get him a new suit of clothes and a little spending money before he left for the big city.

At the boardinghouse, Ellen found two letters waiting for her on the hall table. Fanning them, she went through the kitchen, saying hello to Miss Jewell, who was cleaning vegetables, and on to the backyard. Audrey was already there, reclining in her usual chair, a wet washcloth covering her face.

She pulled the cloth away when she heard Ellen. "Doesn't this heat beat everything? I'd strip down to my unmentionables, if it wouldn't scandalize Miss Jewell."

Ellen sat, pulling her skirt up to mid-thigh. Stripping down didn't seem like a bad idea. She waved the letters in Audrey's direction. "One from my mother and one from my friend Nancy in Topeka." She opened the one from home.

Halfway through the letter, Ellen looked up, chuckling. "Sam Danner's off the marriage market."

"Who?" Audrey swung her legs around to sit upright.

"The mortician Mom thought I should snap up for a husband. Seems he's engaged to Holly Spears. She teaches piano and sings in the church choir. She's perfect for Sam. Now they won't have to pay someone to provide the music for viewings and funerals."

"You know who another perfect wife would be?" Audrey didn't wait for Ellen to answer. "A beautician."

Ellen stared.

"Not that a funeral director isn't trained for arranging the dearly departed's hair or dabbing on rouge to give that healthy glow, but I'd want somebody like Angie at the Beauty Hut to fix me up when I go." Audrey patted her hair, which no longer looked chopped and lopsided.

Ellen smiled and went back to the letter. "Oh, my goodness!"

"What? Bad news?" Audrey leaned forward.

Ellen shook her head. "No, but very unexpected. Remember I told you about my cousin Louise?"

Audrey nodded eagerly.

"Well, Louise is back in Tulsa, but not for long. She's on her way to Hollywood where the saxophone player's band is going to be in a movie. And"—Ellen drew out the word—"she's got a two-year-old son she plans to leave with his grandparents. Until Louise walked through the door, they didn't know this little guy even existed."

Audrey lit a cigarette. "I hate to say this, Louise being your relation, but she doesn't sound like a very nice person, leaving her child."

Ellen had to agree. "Maybe it's best, though. If you're going to get left on somebody's doorstep, you couldn't do better than Uncle Frank and Aunt Viv."

"On the other hand," Audrey continued, "Louise being in Hollywood would be a break for you. I mean, if you decided to go in that direction and work as a screenwriter."

"I don't think it's the place for me." Ellen put the letter aside and opened Nancy's, certain it would be an amusing ramble. She smiled as she read. Nancy was going to her father's office three mornings a week. When she wasn't fetching her father iced coffee, which he had recently discovered, she read law books in the firm's library. She had spent several afternoons playing tennis at the country club. She and Franklin played bridge with his parents, and Nancy had managed to drag him to a charity event to raise money for the soup kitchen.

Ellen came to the end of the letter, frowning at the postscript. Nancy had seen Jason when he was in town with his father for a meeting of some sort. Nancy said they'd run into each other by accident. Ellen doubted that, especially since Nancy made a point of giving him her address at Miss Jewell's.

Ellen let out a sigh. She wished Nancy had left things alone, but, still, she couldn't help but feel a little pleased that Jason knew she'd found a job.

Audrey waited, but when Ellen didn't offer to share what was in this letter, she casually asked if Ellen had plans for the evening.

Ellen eyed her warily.

Audrey ignored the look. "The town band is giving a concert tonight at the city park."

Ellen groaned and made a face.

Audrey didn't miss a beat. "I wouldn't mention it, except Miss Jewell seemed awfully disappointed because the friend she goes with is tied up with relatives from out of town. I thought, since she's been so nice to us . . ."

Ellen thought of Miss Jewell letting Audrey commandeer the writing desk in the living room for her typewriter and the old card table she'd brought up from the basement for Ellen's use. After it was washed and hauled up to the bedroom, it made for a good typewriter stand. Then, of course, there was the woman's general good nature.

Ellen gave in.

Later, as the landlady chirped excitedly through supper and then dressed for the outing, Ellen felt a twinge of guilt that she'd almost refused. It was little enough to pack three folding chairs from the backyard into the trunk of her car and drive the threesome to the city park.

Ellen supposed she and Audrey should have realized there would be a large turnout. People unable to find seats on the wooden benches facing the bandshell fanned out on chairs and blankets brought from home. Miss Jewell had a favorite spot. By the time the band was assembled, she was in her lawn chair, Audrey and Ellen on either side.

Ellen looked around, recognizing several faces in the crowd, including Ivy and Agatha seated near the front with their sons and daughters-in-law. She caught a glimpse of Iris Hewitt but had no clear view of the woman's husband, who, according to Miss Jewell, sold insurance and liked to dabble in local politics. Ellen realized that after only a short time in Opal's Grove, she wasn't entirely an outsider.

The city band was an assorted mix of old and young, male and female, and musical skills. The evening's entertainment began with a labored rendition of the "Star Spangled Banner," but the band charged through "Stars and Stripes Forever." A polka, a waltz, and then a popular romantic tune followed. Despite the occasional squeak or offbeat of a drum, Ellen had to admit she was enjoying herself. Miss Jewell happily tapped a foot to the beat of each song.

One musical number followed another. As the evening wound to a close, the conductor, who Miss Jewell explained was the high school music teacher, turned to the audience.

"We've got a special treat for you tonight," said the middle-aged man, his forehead shining with perspiration. "A few of our musicians have been working with one of the WPA workers who just came to town. When he's not talking to the older folks, he's playing a guitar and singing. So, here, with some of our band members, is Cowboy Joe."

The conductor stepped back as musicians moved to the front and Joe bounded onto the stage all smiles.

Ellen felt her jaw drop. She leaned around Miss Jewell to see Audrey was just as surprised.

"You didn't know?"

"No idea," answered Audrey.

Joe stepped close to the microphone, swinging his guitar into place. "We're gonna play a couple of tunes you folks have been hearing on the radio," he announced. With a nod to the musicians gathered around him, the group swung into a song about somebody being stranded on the highway of love. Ellen didn't know the song, but she'd heard the next one, "Tumbling Tumbleweeds," several times on that radio program Miss Jewell liked so much. When the song finished, Ellen and Audrey cheered and applauded with the rest of the crowd. Joe really should be on the radio, Ellen thought.

When Joe thanked the crowd and tried to leave the stage, people shouted for just one more song. Smiling sheepishly, he looked at the other musicians and nodded. At the first notes of a well-known hymn with a rousing melody, the crowd got to its feet. Some people sang along. Others simply clapped to the rhythm. When the song came to an end, several people approached the stage to shake Joe's hand.

"Well, I never expected that." Ellen turned to Audrey, but she was gone, one of the many heading toward the bandshell.

Miss Jewell stood, fanning herself with a hankie. "My goodness, that was exciting. I can't thank you girls enough for bringing me along."

"I'm glad we didn't miss it," said Ellen, folding up the chairs. She stood on tiptoes searching for Audrey and had almost given up on finding her when she saw Audrey pushing back through the crowd with Joe in tow. Following in their wake was the professor, looking unhappy and overheated. While most men in the crowd were in their shirtsleeves, Ralph wore his shabby tweed jacket like a badge of the professor he used to be. Ellen wanted to throw up her hands. The man was hopeless.

"Ellen!" Audrey gushed, breathless, pulling Joe by an arm. "Joe and his group are going on to the Hurley-Burley to perform. He wants us to come along." Ralph hung back.

Ellen looked past her roommate to a smiling Joe. "You were wonderful," she said. "Miss Jewell thought so, too." Ellen moved slightly to one side to include the woman in their group. "But I don't know about the Hurley-Burley." She gave Audrey a look, hoping she'd get the hint. It didn't work.

"Well, I'm going. Joe will give me a ride, or maybe Ralph." She turned to the man as if just remembering he was there. "See ya later," she said, turning to walk away with the two men.

CHAPTER 17
ELLEN AND JASON

Miss Jewell didn't utter a word until they were almost back at the boardinghouse. "I wish Audrey hadn't gone off to that place," she said at last, her good humor gone. "Something's bound to happen that'll end her up in trouble."

Ellen couldn't have agreed more. She had no explanation for Audrey's behavior. One minute, she was earnestly writing publishers about her book or sending letters to librarians. Then, she'd turn around and do something that might get her fired from this job and maybe ruin her chances for another.

"I don't know what goes through her head, Miss Jewell. I'm just going to keep my fingers crossed she gets home safely."

Jerusalem Jewell was silent. Ellen shared the woman's displeasure. She wanted to get her hands on Audrey and give her a good shake. She turned down Miss Jewell's street and slowed to park in front of the boardinghouse. Ellen drew in a breath when she realized she knew the car sitting just ahead at the curb. She'd recognize it anywhere, even with its Iowa license plate.

"Who's that sitting on my porch?" Miss Jewell asked as she climbed out of Ellen's Packard. In the deepening twilight, only a silhouette of a man could be seen, sitting on the porch swing.

"Jason Davis. He's a friend from college," Ellen explained as she joined her landlady on the sidewalk.

Jason pushed himself out of the swing. Even in the dim light, Ellen could see the shock of dark hair that stubbornly fell across

152

his forehead. She watched as he crossed the porch, his movements unhurried.

She'd told herself that if she ever saw Jason again, she would be casually friendly. Bygones were just that, but that's not how it felt, seeing him step off the porch.

Miss Jewell huffed and raised an eyebrow. "Was he expected?"

"No. I'm as surprised as you are." Ellen tried to reassure her, but the woman was in no mood to be mollified.

"First, it's the Hurley-Burley, of all places," she huffed. "Now, a gentleman caller. I've a good mind to speak to Iris Hewitt. I run a respectable boarding establishment."

The woman marched toward her house, arms swinging. Ellen followed behind her. Jason met them on the sidewalk halfway to the porch.

Before Miss Jewell could say a word, Ellen was beside her. She stumbled through the introductions. "Miss Jewell, this is Jason Davis. Jason, Miss Jewell, owner of the boardinghouse."

Jason briefly took one of the woman's hands, although she had not offered it.

"Miss Jewell, it's a pleasure. I hope you don't mind that I took the liberty of enjoying your porch swing, but I'm passing through town on business for my father and thought I'd stop to see Ellen. Your neighbor across the way said you went to the park for a concert, so I decided to wait. I hope you don't mind."

The woman melted under his smile. Jason moved to her side, gently leading her up the porch steps and to her door.

"Would you mind if Ellen and I sat out here for a little while? I don't have much time to visit. I'm staying at the hotel downtown. I would have waited till morning to stop by, but I have to get an early start."

"Not at all." The woman beamed at Jason. "You visit. I'll just turn on the porch light and leave you two alone."

A moment after she was gone, the porch light flickered on in a yellow glow. Seconds later, lamps in the front room were switched on, spilling light across one end of the porch. Jason smiled at Ellen and whispered, "I guess that means no hanky-panky."

Ellen shook her head. The man was irrepressible. She wanted to be angry at his sudden appearance, at least a little cross. He had some nerve just dropping back into her life. She turned toward the street. "I have to get the chairs out of the car."

He caught her hand, leading her into the shadows and the swing. "That can wait. C'mon, aren't you a little glad to see me?"

"Surprised." She pulled her hand away and sat.

Jason settled beside her, all nonchalance gone. "Look, I have to say this quick, or it won't come out at all. Mile after mile in the car, I've gone over what I was going to say when I got here. Maybe I'm being a sap for showing up like this, but I'd like to try to set things right."

Ellen felt glued to the swing. Even if she wanted to follow Miss Jewell into the house, she couldn't. It was like being at a movie that, no matter how awful, you had to stay for the ending.

When Ellen didn't move, Jason plunged ahead. "I'm on my way to Oklahoma. Dad's thinking of buying a radio station there. We've got one in Iowa, and it's doing well. As I've been learning, it's not just about giving farmers useful information but also providing good all-round programming." He stopped. "Sorry, I'm rambling. The thing is, Dad wants me to look at this station in Ponca City, and I had your address."

"From Nancy," Ellen interrupted. "She wrote me."

He took a deep breath. "I thought since I had to drive through Kansas anyway, I'd swing by here."

Ellen smiled and cocked her head. "This is a long way from the Oklahoma line, but I appreciate you taking the time. It's good to see an old friend."

He groaned. "Look, I'm sorry about the way things ended up with us. It's just that . . ." He stopped, unconsciously pushing that unruly lock of hair back from his face. "Ah, hell, Ellen, I miss you. I can't talk to anyone else the way I can with you. I never said you shouldn't have a career. You're the one that said it had to be either that or me."

Ellen started to snap that he hadn't listened or tried to understand, but she stopped before the words were out.

"Ellen, I owe you an apology. I took your talk about working too lightly. I didn't begin to understand how you feel until I met two of the women who write for Dad's publications. If there was a place for you on one of the papers, you'd have it." He paused for a breath. "The point is, I've watched these women at work. I've gotten to know them a little. I see it's not just a job to them. It's important and satisfying. That's what you want."

She felt a catch in her throat. It had taken a lot for Jason to say that. She wasn't going to push for more. "Yes, it is something I want." She shifted uncomfortably. "Tell me about your job."

Jason followed her lead in changing the subject. "I like the work fine, but some of the fellows who've been at the paper for a long time think I'm just there because my old man gave me a job. I've got to prove myself to them. It hasn't been easy." It was something he'd admit to Ellen but no one else.

"I'm sure it will work out for you," she answered. "Sooner or later, the skeptics will realize you've got a talent for the job."

Jason lightly touched her arm. "Thanks for the vote of confidence, but enough about me. Tell me about this." He flung out a hand, meant to take in the whole of Opal's Grove.

Ellen hesitated. She was tempted to talk about Mr. Calley and his newspaper contacts. She had such great hopes, but she would keep those close to her heart. There had been too many times she was sure something would come her way, only to be disappointed.

"Tell me about this interview job." He began to gently push the swing with one foot. The old ease of being together settled on them.

"There isn't enough time to tell you everything about the people I work with or the woman in charge." Ellen smiled. "But you might get a kick out of knowing some folks have the idea President Roosevelt will see their interviews. And one or two, being lifelong Republicans, have complained about that."

Jason laughed with her as she told him about the man Ralph had interviewed.

"There are two ladies in particular I've gotten to know," Ellen continued. "To see them rocking on a front porch or handing out clothes in a church basement, you'd never guess what they've lived through. But they just get on with life. They're smart and funny and always trying to help somebody. I hope I can be like that when I'm eighty."

"They sound great." Jason leaned closer.

"They're special, and most of the people I've interviewed have been the sort you'd like to know. But not all."

She told him about Nettie and the train.

"You were bound to run into somebody like that," he reasoned. "As some people get older, they live more in the past. I remember this man down the street when I was a kid. He couldn't remember what he ate for breakfast, but he could tell you every detail of his days in the Union army. All us kids would sit on the man's porch and listen to him, just fascinated."

"I suppose Miss Vine is fascinating, but not in the way you'd want to spend much time with her." Ellen stood. She didn't want to waste her time with Jason discussing the woman.

In the far distance, there was a flash of lightning.

"Rain would sure be welcome," said Jason.

"I better get the lawn chairs." Ellen got up and went down the front steps to the car. Jason followed.

"Here, let me help," he said as she opened the car trunk and grabbed for a chair. Jason reached around her. She felt his breath on her cheek.

She scooted to the left, letting him remove the chairs. As he closed the trunk, she lifted one chair under an arm and indicated he could bring the others. She led him along the side of the house to the backyard. "Just put those under the arbor next to this one," she said.

Night had fallen. The moon was obscured by clouds scuttling in from the west. The vines covering the arbor filtered out the light shining from the kitchen.

Jason stepped into the space. "Very cozy."

"At the end of the day, my roommate and I sit out here with Miss Jewell in the shade." Ellen righted a chair, putting distance between herself and Jason. The arbor had suddenly become too cozy.

"Where's the roommate?" Jason set down the chairs he carried.

Ellen shook her head. "At a beer joint out on the highway, and Miss Jewell is fit to be tied. I'm not too happy about it either. She could get fired. I could get fired just for knowing about it."

She took a step. "We better go back. I don't want Miss Jewell to find us here. With the mood she's in, she might send me and Audrey packing."

"Sure, whatever you say." He reached for Ellen. She tried to step back, but he pulled her a step closer. "Just tell me this trip wasn't wasted."

"I don't know. You complicate things."

Jason ran a finger along Ellen's cheek, stopping at the tip of her chin.

Ellen knew he wanted to kiss her. When he hesitated, she acted for him. The peck on his cheek lingered before she stood back at arm's length.

"Well, that's a start." He gave her one of his devilish grins. "I guess that means you do want to see me again."

"Not at all," she answered, skirting past him with a smile. She paused, her eyes twinkling with mischief. "It was the only way I could think of to get you out of the backyard."

"I guess that's what I get for thinking I could sweep you off your feet." He took her arm as they walked to the front. "Can I stop and see you when I head home in a week or so?"

Ellen shook her head. "I honestly can't decide if that's a good idea. Just when I think things are going in the direction I want, you show up and I get confused."

He reached out and put his hands on her shoulders. "I'm coming back. You're not quite rid of me."

With a brush of his lips against hers, he was gone. Ellen watched him drive away before walking back to the house. She found Miss Jewell in the front room, putting away some mending.

"Seems like a nice young man," she offered. "What line of work is he in?"

"His father owns the Farm Land Newspaper Company. Jason works on one of the papers, but it sounds like he might be getting more involved in the company's radio business."

Ellen could see her landlady was impressed. "It looks like it might rain. Want me to help close windows?"

Miss Jewell said they'd worry about the windows when, and if, the rain came.

"Okay, then. I'm going to sit out on the porch for a little while."

"You go right ahead. I'm heading to bed." Miss Jewell stopped for a moment. "Tell Audrey I'm upset with her. She's too impulsive. I had a teacher boarder like that once. She fell head over heels for a book salesman, and the next thing you know, she lost her job and was living in a home for unwed mothers."

Ellen worked to keep from laughing. "Yes, ma'am, I'll tell her."

She flipped off the porch light as she returned to the porch. As she settled back on the swing, she wondered how she was ever going to get any sleep after Jason's sudden appearance. She tried to sort out her feelings, but every rational reason she could think of for keeping Jason out of her life was countered by arguments for why he should stay.

An older car pulled to the curb, interrupting her thoughts. Audrey reached through the open window to pull the door handle from the outside. She said something to the driver before stepping out of the vehicle.

Ellen went to stand at the top of the porch steps. She said a prayer of thanks that Audrey didn't look tipsy, but when she came close, Ellen smelled beer and cigarettes.

"Waiting up for me?"

"No, just sitting here thinking." She walked back to the swing.

A clap of thunder and a flash of lightning made both of them jump. "Maybe we'll get some rain," Audrey said hopefully.

"Maybe." Ellen began to rock the swing. "How was your evening?"

Audrey plopped down on the top step. "Joe was great. The crowd loved him. We were having a wonderful time. I even got Ralph to dance with me a couple of times. Then, these two women got into a fight, pulling hair and throwing beer at each other. Of course, that got the men they were with started, and then somebody else threw a punch. I grabbed Ralph by that scruffy jacket he wears. I swear I'd like to burn that thing! Then, we hightailed it out of there."

"What happened to Joe?"

"Oh, he's fine. He and the band ran out through the kitchen when the fight started. He jumped in the car with us before the police got there."

Ellen bit back the impulse to lecture Audrey on what could have happened if she'd landed in jail. At the very least, she'd be fired. And there was the bigger picture. Iris Hewitt was unlikely to help Audrey find other work.

"Are you angry with me? What about Miss Jewell?" Audrey's expression was that of a child hoping to talk her way out of a scolding.

"I'm not really angry. But I am upset with you. So is Miss Jewell. She likes you, and she doesn't want you to end up like one of her boarders." Ellen told her the story.

"What!" The shout reverberated down the quiet street. Audrey clamped her hands over her mouth and started to giggle. "That's the last place I'll end up."

"I think she meant it as a cautionary tale," Ellen offered.

Audrey rolled her eyes. "I'll consider myself warned."

Ellen was quiet for a moment before she asked if something was going on between Audrey and Ralph.

Audrey looked startled, and Ellen worried she'd stepped into something that was none of her business.

"What!" Audrey managed not to shout this time. "Like boyfriend and girlfriend? Oh, no, no, no." She shook her head vehemently. "I told you: I like being on my own. I just gave myself the job of being Ralph's friend. He needs one. I tease him when he's being self-important and encourage him when he's in the dumps about finding another teaching job. He still hasn't heard from that college he has high hopes for, so it's a chore being positive."

Ellen was sorry she'd asked and said so.

"That's okay." Audrey waved a hand in the air. "I'm not trying to change him into someone different. He is who he is, but maybe now that he's loosened up and danced at the Hurley-Burley and almost got punched in the face, he'll start acting more like a regular person."

Ellen smiled back at Audrey. She was finding it impossible to stay mad at her.

"Just talk to Miss Jewell tomorrow and set things right. Now, let me tell you about my evening," she said.

Another roar of thunder and streak of lightning sent them rushing inside.

CHAPTER 18
NEAR OPAL'S GROVE, 1936

Audrey easily worked her way back into Miss Jewell's good graces, and things seemed to return to an even keel. Ellen busied herself redoing Mae Swenson's interviews and keeping up with her own. She sent off the articles to Mr. Calley's contacts. Almost a week after Jason's visit, she decided he wasn't coming back and tried to keep thoughts of him pushed to the back of her mind.

Thursday morning was spent in the courthouse basement, typing one interview and then another. At half past eleven she emerged to a calliope of horns and the sight of cars and trucks of every description maneuvering for space as they circled the courthouse. Getting to her car parked across the street was going to take some quick footwork. She started to cross the street but was forced back by one car and then another. She had never seen this much traffic in Opal's Grove, even on Saturdays when the farm families came to town to trade. Was this Thursday some sort of special market day? Maybe there was an exciting court case she hadn't heard about. She shook her head. Surely, she would have seen an announcement in the paper or heard people talking on the street if something special was happening.

Just when she decided to take a chance and dart through the traffic, there was a screech of brakes.

"Get in," Thelma shouted from behind the wheel of her family's newly repaired automobile. Sitting beside her was Agatha. In the backseat was Ivy, frantically waving for Ellen to join them.

Without hesitation, Ellen hugged her satchel to her body, wrenched open the passenger door, and hopped into the back beside Ivy. Ignoring the blare of horns behind her, Thelma pulled into the parade of traffic, taking the highway south out of town.

"Where are we going?" Ellen turned to look out the back window. "Where is *everybody* going?"

"The bridge!" Thelma had to shout to be heard over another horn blast and a rattle that sounded as if it was coming from the engine. "They were breaking up rock down by the river and found bones."

Ivy turned to Ellen. "There's a skeleton. Or a part of one."

Thelma watched the road while she continued. "Cecil Phelps was using a pickax to break the rock, and when he pulled it up to take another swing, there was a skull stuck on the end of the axe. It just came up out of the ground like a Halloween ghost. Cecil clutched his chest and fainted dead away."

"How do you know this?" Ellen leaned over the front seat.

"My brother Hugh was right there. Everyone thought Cecil had a heart attack, so Hugh drove him to the hospital. While Hugh was there, he called Mother. She called me and Martha at Miss Agatha's. It's all over town now, and people want to know what's happening. Including us."

Both Agatha and Ivy nodded. Some things, you didn't wait on the front porch to hear secondhand.

They passed the train depot on the left, slowly bounced over the railroad tracks, and continued past the city limits. Cars and trucks began to slow and bunch together, bumper to bumper.

"Automobiles are coming back this way." Ellen pointed. "It looks like the police are making people turn around."

Ahead, they could see two deputies waving cars to stop and

turn back toward town. For some drivers, it took more than one try to pull forward, back up, and then swing into the northbound lane.

Thelma leaned so far forward, her chin almost bumped against the steering wheel. "Oh, look! One of the deputies is Bill. Don't worry, ladies. Now, we'll find out what's going on."

At the barricade, Bill motioned for them to stop.

"Oh, for God's sakes, Thelma, what are you doing out here?" he moaned as he approached the driver's side window.

"Bill Snyder, I would thank you not to swear in front of these ladies." Thelma puffed.

"Sorry." He leaned down to look through the window and tip his hat.

Thelma's fiancé was square-jawed and broad-shouldered. Ellen was reminded of a recruiting poster for the Boy Scouts. Or the army. The thought sent a shiver down her spine. Already, some politicians and newspaper columnists were warning of another war.

"Don't worry about it, Bill." Agatha leaned across the seat to see him. "This must be very trying, and I apologize for adding to your troubles."

He shook his head. "It's been like a circus out here. And it's not just the sightseers. The coroner got here right behind Sheriff Logan. Grover Calley showed up but left after a few words with the sheriff. Right behind him was that beady-eyed funeral director. He went off steaming when the sheriff ordered him to turn his hearse around and go back to town. Then Iris Hewitt threw a hissy fit."

"Iris Hewitt?" Ivy called from the backseat. "What was she doing here?"

Bill ignored the traffic jam building up behind Thelma's car. "She heard about this and came roaring out in that big Buick she's so proud of. She parked in the middle of the highway, buttonholed the sheriff and started talking a mile a minute about the skull coming from an Indian burial. She kept going on about an Indian village. When the sheriff told her to leave, she gave him a piece of her mind. She left about twenty minutes ago, yelling about calling an archaeologist at the state college."

"What's the sheriff going to do?" Ellen asked. She wondered if he gave any credence to Mrs. Hewitt's theory.

"Well, he sure isn't going to wait for Iris Hewitt, if that's what you mean." Bill grimaced at the very idea.

"He's got the coroner, that Dr. Page, here to look things over; although I'd say from the looks of things, this isn't anybody that got killed and buried recently. Whoever it was has been dead for a long, long time."

Bill wiped beads of sweat from his forehead with the back of his sleeve. "Now, please, Thelma, get this car out of here."

"Of course, Bill," she said, smiling prettily. "You've been so sweet."

The others thanked him as Thelma put the car in gear and began to maneuver the turnaround.

"Look." Ellen pointed to a Ford approaching in the opposite lane. She knew that car. "There's Mrs. Castle with Miss Vine."

All heads turned in that direction. If Nettie noticed them, she gave no sign, but Stella Castle nodded before inching her auto forward.

Ellen felt the atmosphere change around her. Neither Agatha nor Ivy were chirping away with comments about Iris Hewitt or speculating about the unidentified skeleton. Thelma must have felt it, too, driving with her eyes straight ahead and her mouth tightly shut.

Thelma let Ellen out near her parked car. She thanked the women for taking her along, but it was plain their earlier enthusiasm for the outing had soured. "Don't forget Saturday. Come for supper," Agatha called as Thelma pulled away.

"Hartley!" The bellow made Ellen jump. Behind her, Grover Calley stood with an oversized notebook in one hand. "You keep some interesting company," he said, watching Thelma's car disappear around the corner. "You been out gawking with the rest of the town?"

"Yes, sir. I heard you were there."

"One of the first ones, but the sheriff says there's nothing to report until the doctor looks things over. There's more than just a skull. Looks like there might be a whole body out there. I came back to talk to the man they took to the hospital."

"Was it a heart attack?"

"No. He just had a bad scare, pulling that skull up the way he did would do that to a man." He eyed Ellen for a moment. "You want to be a reporter. Tell me what you saw."

She listed the men that surrounded the sheriff behind the barricade. She then repeated what Bill had said. Calley jotted down a few notes.

"I was there when Iris Hewitt was carrying on. She's got a bee in her bonnet about locating that Indian village. Then I remembered that interview you did with Mrs. Hamilton. We're printing it in tomorrow's paper."

Ellen could guess what was coming next.

"I didn't know until I read her interview that Ivy Hamilton knew Featherstone fairly well. I've been over to the library to look at that collection. Haven't paid attention to it in years, but now I'm wondering if he didn't find something." He gave Ellen a long stare. "Did you ask her?"

Ellen stared back, slightly insulted by his implication she had done a poor interview job. "Yes, I asked. He sometimes showed her the things he collected, but as she said in the interview, he never took her to see any Indian village or told her where one might be found." Ellen calmed. She eyed the traffic and wondered about making it to her car. "Now I'm going to the boardinghouse for lunch."

"I'm going to get a sandwich myself, but afterwards I'm going back out to the bridge." He paused. "Want to go out with me? Might be something there you could pick up for one of those stringer stories."

"What time do I meet you at your office?" she asked, fighting down a wave of excitement.

"Make it forty-five minutes," he answered. "I hate to eat and run. Whatever's out there isn't going anywhere soon."

CHAPTER 19
NEAR THE RIVER,
OPAL'S GROVE, 1936

Ellen arrived at the newspaper office wearing an old blue dress and walking shoes. Her satchel was slung over one shoulder. In one hand she carried a thermos of ice water; in the other was a wide-brimmed garden hat borrowed from Miss Jewell. Calley nodded brusquely and introduced her to the man waiting beside him on the sidewalk. "You remember Maynard. He's our photographer." The man was younger than Calley, with a strong, craggy face that didn't seem to change expression. He carried a big, boxy camera. Hanging from a strap around his neck Ellen recognized a Leica camera.

Ellen did remember the man working over the composition table in the newspaper's back room, but she didn't know if Maynard was a first name or a last. They climbed into Calley's Studebaker. The short trip to the construction site was made in silence.

Bill and another deputy were still turning away onlookers but waved Calley through. "Now, Maynard, you know what to do," Calley said after he parked and got out of the car. "I want pictures. If the sheriff says 'no,' put that box away like you agree with him and shoot with the Leica. Just don't let him see what you're up to." Calley turned to Ellen. "And you, be a reporter."

He hooked a thumb toward two cars just arriving. "Looks like we got here just in time."

Iris Hewitt climbed out of her Buick. Out of the other automobile emerged four men. All wore safari-style khaki shirts and pith helmets. Maynard quickly snapped a picture. Iris stopped to introduce Calley to the professor of archaeology, a Dr. Wales, and his three graduate students. Iris gave Ellen a questioning look before leading the way to where the coroner and Sheriff Logan stood, mopping sweat from their faces.

The sheriff welcomed the archaeologists, not because he thought there was anything to this Indian business, but because he was a practical man. Only a few vertebrae and a collarbone were exposed when Cecil pulled out the skull. If the professor and his crew had any ideas on how to uncover and extract the bones without damage, the sheriff wanted to hear them.

Dr. Wales, middle-aged with the sinewy look of a man who spent more time working outdoors than in the classroom, asked the group to stay back while he and his students surveyed the area. Ellen followed Calley's lead and began to make notes, although there didn't seem to be anything of import to record. Wales and his students walked around the site. In hushed voices they conferred. Wales dropped to one knee and began to feather loose dirt away from a clavicle. After another brief conference with his team, Wales returned to the group gathered around the sheriff. He and his crew would lend their assistance, but the tools they'd brought were limited. One of his men would have to return to the college for more equipment. They needed drinking water, and perhaps the sheriff could locate a tent to shade the work site.

There was a sudden flurry of activity as people scurried off. The coroner left to placate the town's funeral director and, in return, get the use of the man's canvas tent used to cover newly dug graves. Iris Hewitt was right behind the coroner, sent to bring back an ice chest of sodas and canisters of ice water. Calley motioned for Maynard and Ellen to join him near his car, but not before the sheriff spotted the box camera and shook his head at Maynard.

"Not to worry," said Calley as they gathered in a tight knot. "I'm going back to town for more water and to tell the boys they may be working the press late tonight to get out tomorrow's morning edition." He dropped into the driver's seat. "I'm leaving you two at the CCC camp. See if any of those men have something to say about this. Probably nothing there, but you never know."

By late afternoon, Ellen and Maynard were finished with the CCC workers. They'd returned to find men working under a cover propped up with metal poles. On sheriff's orders, everyone else had to stay some distance away. With little to see or do, Ellen and Maynard retreated to the tree line for shade. Ellen perched on a small boulder. Maynard sat propped against another, bits of gravel digging into his backside.

"That doesn't look very comfortable," Ellen offered. In answer, Maynard pulled his hat down over his face.

"Do you think Mr. Calley will use those pictures you took of the CCC workers?" Ellen persisted.

Maynard pulled off his hat, giving Ellen a dour look. "I don't like chitchat. But you've got a way about you, I'll give you that. You didn't pepper those CCC boys with questions, which was smart. All it took was one little comment from you about how hard the work must be, and it was like turning on a spigot. Not only did those men tell you what they did—or did not—see this morning, but some tongue-tied guy far from home recited his life story. And another spent ten minutes showing you pictures of his family back in Indiana."

"I'll take that as a compliment." Ellen was rather proud of herself. She'd gotten information for Mr. Calley, and the men at the camp had given her another idea for an article.

"You could at least tell me your full name," Ellen prodded. She was curious because now he'd become a challenge.

Maynard sat up, pulling off his hat in irritation. "My name is Maynard Knudson. I'm thirty-eight years old. I live with an aunt and uncle who raised me after my parents died. I've got a little photo studio. I develop my pictures for the paper, and, once in a great while, people pay me for their wedding portrait or a picture of their darling baby." He glared.

Ellen studied him for a moment. "You forgot to mention that award-winning photograph of a dust storm." Before he could interrupt, she rushed ahead. "Your last name gave you away. I suddenly realized it was you who took the picture. We talked about it in one of my classes. Your photograph made the blowing dust look like a living thing, ready to reach out and snatch those poor children running in terror across the playground."

Maynard sat dumbfounded. Ellen decided it was her turn to ignore him. She pushed herself off the boulder with a little jump and walked away.

"We should probably see what kind of progress they're making," she called over her shoulder. She headed for Calley, who was standing with the man in charge of the bridge construction. Beyond them, Iris Hewitt had settled herself on a camp stool beside the ice chest, a parasol brought from home protecting her from the sun. The sheriff and coroner stood apart from the rest, occasionally mumbling to each other.

Ellen walked as close as she dared to the tent. With its canvas sides rolled up, there was a clear view of the workers and a portion of a skeletal frame. She could see exposed vertebrae and the rib cage. Portions of both arms had been exposed. As two workers continued uncovering the rest of the arms and the hands, another brushed loose soil away from the pelvis. Dr. Wales sat back on his heels, wiping dirt-stained hands on his trousers. He pushed himself to a standing position, told the others to keep working, and motioned everyone to join him. Like schoolchildren obeying a teacher, they gathered around him in

171

a semicircle.

"From what we've seen thus far, I conclude that this is a male," he said, addressing his comments to the sheriff. "Is it a native Indian? Most people think all skeletons look alike, but we can tell a person's race by the shape of the skull, its size, the shape of the eye sockets, and so forth."

Sheriff Logan scowled as he wiped the back of his neck with an oversized handkerchief. "If you were to hazard a guess?"

"Don't need to guess." Wales gave a dry laugh. "Let me explain one or two points. This skull has sloping eye orbits, and its shape indicates a long, narrow face. These are characteristics of someone with European ancestry. With a native inhabitant, you are more likely to find round eye orbits and a wider face surface. There are other factors, but without getting too technical, that's it in a nutshell."

"So, this is not an American Indian," the sheriff finished for the archaeologist.

Iris opened her mouth to speak but was silenced by a stern look from the sheriff.

The man nodded. "There's also the matter of what we are *not* finding. A native burial should have grave goods. Those might be small pots, arrowheads, or other fighting weapons. Certainly, we could expect beads or fragments of shells that ornamented necklaces or clothing." He looked around the group to see if they were following. Satisfied that they understood, he continued, "Now, if you look there, at the material just visible near the rib cage, you'll see a few bits of cloth, possibly wool."

They all leaned forward, following the man's pointing finger. "I would need to analyze these pieces in my laboratory, but my guess is they come from cloth manufactured on an industrial loom. Of course, native groups had these sorts of goods after contact with whites, but I stand by my first assessment. This is not an Indian burial. Nor is there any immediate indication of a native habitation."

Iris Hewitt could no longer remain silent. She sputtered with indignation, steadily finding traction for her rage. Maynard positioned himself to one side of Ellen and a little behind her. "Don't move," he muttered out of the corner of his mouth. A brief nod of her head told him she understood. He was using her as a shield as he lifted the Leica from beneath his shirt. There was a small click and then another. Iris Hewitt was captured on film, standing toe to toe with the archaeologist, her mouth open in angry argument.

Wales took Iris's onslaught in stride, apologizing for dashing her hopes. Then, holding up a finger to silence any more protests, he turned to the sheriff. "Based on what I see, I'd say this is a Caucasian male. He's been in the ground for at least half a century. Very possibly longer.

"I find it quite curious there is no indication of such things as coat buttons, a belt buckle, or leather such as you would find with a belt or shoes. Perhaps this is a victim of robbery. We hear of people being killed today for a pair of shoes or a coat. I don't imagine it was much different back then. But it beats me why someone would strip a man completely naked before burial."

Ellen glanced at Calley, who, for once, seemed surprised by something he'd come across in life. The sheriff had the look of a very unhappy man, made even more so when Wales pulled him over to observe a gouge along the edge of one rib, which the archaeologist suspected had been caused by a bullet or long-bladed knife. The sheriff nodded, stood, and walked away, shaking his head.

"I'd like to get a shot of the bones," Maynard mumbled. Ellen nodded, moving away from the knot of people caught up in the drama of the archaeologist's revelations. Maynard ambled beside her as she walked to the far side of the work area. Stopping near one of the student assistants, she dropped down beside him.

He turned, earnest blue eyes staring out from a sun-browned face dripping with sweat. Ellen ignored his protests that she leave, talking over him as she explained she was with the newspaper, writing a story about archaeology as a sidebar to this discovery.

Ellen was elated to find that the student, who introduced himself as Owen Bushnell, needed little prodding to expound on burial and habitation sites unearthed in Kansas and how they compared to those discovered in other parts of the country. He'd visited several and worked on others. He'd even spent part of the previous year in Central America, which, he assured Ellen, was the place to be for some dramatic discoveries, even when your life was in danger from disease-carrying insects and poisonous snakes.

It was only after Ellen heard the last of the Leica's soft clicks that she gently interrupted Owen's enthusiastic descriptions of the jungle and the Mayan ruin it concealed.

"I heard the professor tell the sheriff about a nick on the rib. What do you think caused it?" She gave Owen her full attention, pencil poised above her notebook.

He beamed, clearly pleased to be asked his opinion. Pointing toward the rib in question, he began to explain. "It's chipped a little. A knife or other sharp object, like a screwdriver, might cause that. But my best guess is a bullet."

"Have you found one?"

The young man shook his head. "Not yet. We'll probably have to sift the dirt to find it, if it's here. The man could have been shot somewhere else. If the bullet passed through, it won't be found. I don't know that much about firearms and their capabilities, but I've seen what a lance or arrow can do to a bone. This doesn't look quite the same."

Ellen thought it all sounded reasonable. From the corner of

her eye, she caught a glimpse of Maynard casually walking back the way they'd come.

She stayed for a few minutes longer, asking Owen what he might conclude about John Featherstone's collection and the possibility of an Indian village. "I'm not surprised that things like that would be found around here," he answered. "There may be a village site near the river. But this isn't it."

She thanked him and stood, brushing dust off the hem of her dress.

Calley and Maynard, she saw, were walking back to the car, with Calley impatiently gesturing for her to catch up.

"Got to get back to the paper," he urged, opening the passenger door for her. Ellen slid into the front. Maynard took the back. She fanned her face with the notebook. The car was like an oven. There was a general sigh of relief when air began to circulate through the open windows as Calley maneuvered the car around the barricade and picked up speed on the paved road.

"Maynard!" he shouted over his shoulder. "Tell me about the shots!"

The man leaned toward the front seat and Calley's ear. "I've got general shots of the site. Took some pictures of two CCC boys who were there when the skull was discovered. I also got Iris Hewitt spitting mad." Maynard couldn't stop himself from smiling at what he knew were great pictures.

Calley barked a laugh. "She's going to be even madder when she sees herself in the paper."

"The last shots I got were close-ups of the skeleton," Maynard said. "Ellen, thanks for keeping that kid occupied."

She turned sideways in the seat, surprised and a little pleased he appreciated her help. "You're welcome. As for the kid," she turned to Calley, "he gave me a lot of information you could use in a sidebar about archaeology. Maybe it would soothe Mrs.

Hewitt's feathers a little to include the places in Kansas where burials and villages have been found. The 'kid,' who hopes to have his doctorate next year, gave me county locations where he said indigenous artifacts have been found."

Ellen flipped the pages of her notebook, ready to read off the names, but Calley broke in. "He used the word 'indigenous?' " He laughed again. "That'll get our readers going to their dictionaries. And don't change it when you write that up!"

Ellen nodded, as if she'd expected all along to write the piece when, in fact, she'd only told Owen about a sidebar to get his cooperation.

"There's something else," Ellen added. "The student thinks that the nick on the rib was caused by a bullet, not a sharp object. He seemed pretty confident about it, but they haven't found any bullet."

Calley seemed to be digesting this news as he sped into town. The car rumbled across the railroad tracks. He didn't slow down until they reached the town square. As he pulled into a parking space, he gave Maynard instructions and asked Ellen to follow him into the newspaper office. He wanted her to start working immediately on her piece.

Once inside the building, Ellen walked past Calley, straight to the restroom hidden under the stairs. She was hot, sweaty, and knew she must look a fright. The mirror proved it. She let out a little yelp when she saw her reflection. She washed away the dirt and grime as best she could before brushing out her hair. When she emerged a few minutes later, Calley was still standing in the newspaper's reception area. Ellen was aware of him watching her as she tossed her hat on a desk and claimed a typewriter.

"Was there something else, Mr. Calley?" She turned in his direction.

The man nodded as he pulled a ten dollar bill from his money clip. "You did a good job out there." The man's voice was gruff. "You didn't complain about the heat. You used your initiative to start a story, and you're not whining about missing supper. On top of that, you somehow got Maynard, who's always a loner, to treat you like a partner."

He tossed the bill next to the typewriter. "If it wasn't for this damned Depression, I'd hire you. But I can't, so here's a little something for a day's work."

He walked away so fast, Ellen wasn't sure he heard her call out her thanks.

CHAPTER 20
ELLEN

As the WPA workers filed into the basement on Friday morning, Iris Hewitt's greetings were subdued. Ellen attributed it to the events of the previous day, but Audrey saw it differently. She leaned over and whispered, "Bet you a milkshake we're getting the axe. Iris is afraid to tell us."

In a few moments, Audrey's prediction proved true. Iris faced the group and clapped her hands for attention. The word had come from Topeka. The project would not be extended to other counties.

"You are all to be commended for what you have accomplished here. However, the state historical society says it has more than enough pioneer stories for its archives, and the editors for the WPA's state guide report they have enough material to include in their publication. For its part, the WPA wants to use its limited funds elsewhere. If any of you wish to apply for new work, you must contact Mrs. Fletcher in Topeka."

Iris stopped, expecting a volley of questions and perhaps an angry outcry. None came. "Well, I must say you are all taking this much better than I anticipated."

"We didn't expect this work to last too long. I think we've all been trying to plan ahead." The science-fiction writer didn't go on to share what he intended, only hinting that it might involve going to Hollywood.

Jess raised his hand to get their attention. "I had a piece of luck." Sounding both proud and still a little dazed, he recounted his trip to Kansas City. He had a temporary newspaper job, covering sports. Applause broke out. Audrey stuck two fingers between her teeth and whistled.

"I've got plans, too." Cowboy Joe stood.

"And what are those?" Ralph's tone was condescending.

Audrey blew out a breath, irritated that her reclamation project on Ralph had just taken a backward step.

"Gonna sing on WIBW in Topeka. They got this program called 'Jamboree.' " Joe's smile was wide as a country mile. "A man from the radio station offered me the job after he heard me sing."

More applause filled the room. Ellen noticed Joe deftly avoided mentioning the man had no doubt heard Joe during one of his weekend performances at the Hurley-Burley.

After receiving her paycheck, Ellen headed out of the courthouse. She had an interview with a man she'd inherited from Mae Swenson's list. Ewell Morgan lived with his widowed daughter and two grown grandchildren in a narrow two-story house in the area the locals called "south of the tracks." In this part of town, residential blocks were occasionally interrupted by the appearance of small businesses. The Morgan house, weathered gray, sat between similar houses. Across the street was a mechanic's shop that did double duty as a place for tire repair.

Ellen's knock brought a sprightly middle-aged woman to the door. "Come on in. Dad's been waiting for you," she said, smoothing the front of her apron with a hand. "He's just here in the front room. Thought it might be quieter to talk in here than in the kitchen where the girls and I are making strawberry jam." She led Ellen to a room on the left, called out to her father that his company had arrived, and excused herself.

People said Ewell Morgan had once been a muscled, barrel-chested man, like his father before him. He was still a big man, taking up a large part of a cushioned chair, but the years had chiseled away the hard muscle and whittled away at his strength. He motioned Ellen to take a seat on a sofa that was old but comfortable. It matched the homey feeling of the tidy room.

"Glad you came," he said, nodding. "Thought I was gonna get stuck with Mae Swenson. She's a nice enough lady, I guess, but doesn't know which way is up, if you ask me."

Ellen let that go and introduced herself.

"You're the one in the paper!" Ewell grabbed the morning paper from its place on a side table and stabbed a finger at Ellen's article about archaeology in Kansas. "You were out there when they were digging up that skeleton! Now, isn't that something?" He leaned forward. "You know, if my dad was alive today, he'd be real interested in those bones."

Ellen hastily pulled out her notebook and pencil. "Why is that?"

"Well, he might have some ideas about who those bones belong to."

Ellen struggled to hide her excitement. What a coup it would be to present Mr. Calley with an article identifying the buried remains. She took a deep breath and told herself to go slowly and get the man's story from the beginning. Lay the groundwork, she told herself, before grabbing for the prize.

"I truly want to know what you think your father might have believed, but let's take one step at a time. Why don't you begin with who your father was and how your family came to be in Opal's Grove?"

The man nodded. "Dad was Henry Ewell Morgan. My mother was Mary. We came to Opal's Grove from Indiana in the spring of 1868. I was eight years old. So you see, I was old enough to have some memory of the Civil War, mainly of the soldiers, like Dad, coming home. Dad was a blacksmith by trade. He could have picked up where he left off in our little town, but he couldn't seem to get settled after the war. He started to look at moving west. The question was where."

Ellen nodded encouragement, taking it all down.

"There were so many town companies advertising in newspapers or mailing out handbills, it seemed like a fella had his pick of places. As I recall, Dad saw a handbill for this town and wrote to Sylvester Vine. He wrote back, and, before you knew it, we were on a train with all our belongings, including Dad's tools, boxed up in a baggage car. The town seemed better than some of places we saw from the train, and Dad said we'd stay. Mr. Vine and Mr. Bright at the bank helped Dad get set up, and we had a little cottage back of the blacksmith shop. For a little while, we were strapped for money, but things picked up. My older sister, Dorie, got a job helping in one of those big houses north of the courthouse. My younger sisters helped Ma at home, and Mr. Hill, who opened up the Railroad Hotel, took me on to do odd jobs and run errands like going over to the depot to collect or send telegrams for the guests." Ewell stopped to take a breath and shout in a bellowing voice for his daughter to bring him a glass of water.

In a few moments, the woman who had greeted Ellen at the door arrived with a glass of water for her father and one for Ellen. As she handed her father his glass, she gave his shoulder an affectionate squeeze.

Ewell drank deeply, giving Ellen time to ask about school.

He wiped the back of a hand across his mouth, shaking his head. "When they started a school, Dorie refused to go. Said she was too old, but Ma laid down the law with me and my younger sisters. Most of the time I liked school, but I didn't go very long. Quit at age eleven. I knew how to read, write, and do sums. What else was there to know? Seemed to me I should be working with Dad and learning the trade, and he agreed. To earn a little extra, I sometimes still helped out at the hotel.

"By the time I was twenty-five, Dad had turned most of the work over to me. Over the years he did less and less, but he was at the shop every day until he came down with pneumonia and died at the age of seventy."

"And you had a family." Ellen wanted to include this before they returned to the subject of the skeleton.

"Married Kristina Anderson, one of the Swedish immigrant girls. She only knew a few words of English, and what I knew in Swedish had to do with things I made, like horseshoes and barrel hoops. But we got along fine. When we got married, I rented this house. After a good long while, I managed to buy it. Brought up five children here. I'd say I've had a good life. Never rich, but never too poor. And the wife and I raised a good family." He sat back with a smile of satisfaction. "Now, let's talk about those bones."

Ellen laughed and gave in. "Okay. Why would they be of such interest to your father?"

"Dad may have been a blacksmith by trade, but there were times when the sheriff called on him to be a deputy. Dad was a big man, but it wasn't just his size that got people's attention. He was respected around these parts. So, if there was trouble, Dad was a good man to have on your side."

Ellen waited while Ewell downed the remainder of his water. He leaned forward. "You see, hearing about that skeleton reminded me of a time when one particular fella in town just seemed to take off without saying a word to anybody. Now, I'm not saying this was all that unusual. Why, I can name five or six families that up and left the county without even a goodbye wave to their neighbors. But I recall Dad didn't agree with folks, including the sheriff, who thought this fella had just skedaddled."

"Did your father have a reason?" Ellen was sitting on the

edge of her seat.

"Sure did. This fella made furniture. Nothing fancy, you understand, but it was sturdy. He promised my mother a whatnot shelf to sit in the corner of the living room, but when the man's boss went looking for him in the little workshop he had, there was Mom's shelf half-finished and another lady's linen chest without a finished lid. Dad couldn't believe this fella would just up and leave things the way they were. I remember Dad saying the man was a bit of a rascal with the ladies, but that didn't mean he wasn't a hard worker. He told the sheriff what he thought, but Showcross, that was the sheriff, didn't want to hear it."

"What was the name of the man who disappeared?" Ellen took a deep breath.

"That's what's driving me crazy. I can't exactly recall. Seems like it was McMahon or maybe it was Monahan. Something like that. Maybe you could find out."

"I'll try. I might find a newspaper story, and if there are city directories, those would have the names of people and their occupations."

Ewell shook his head. "The first city directory was 1885. I know that for a fact, because I asked my wife if I should buy an advertisement in it. The smallest one cost two whole dollars, and I thought that was too much, but she told me to go ahead. It was good for business and showed our civic pride." Ewell laughed. "At least I think that's what she said. Her English got better over the years, but sometimes I misunderstood her."

"Do you recall the year this happened?"

"Well, it was only a year or two after we got here. I know that because we didn't have that much furniture, and Mom was counting on that shelf to dress up the living room."

Ellen closed her notebook and promised she would do some research. Despite the lack of a specific name, she thought Mr.

Morgan had given her a good start.

Ewell called out to his daughter that their guest was leaving, and the woman appeared, her hands stained strawberry red. At the door she thanked Ellen for coming and added, "Sorry Dad couldn't stand to greet you the way a gentleman should, but he's chair-bound. Usually, he's in a wheelchair, but he insisted you see him in a regular chair."

Ellen shook her head slightly. These old pioneers never ceased to amaze her. "Tell your father that if I come up with a name, he'll be the first to know."

Before going to the courthouse to type up Ewell Morgan's interview, Ellen went to see Grover Calley. She expected him to be impressed with the information she'd uncovered and was disappointed when he only raised an eyebrow.

"Pull up a chair," he growled, pointing to a straight-back chair in a corner. "I've known Ewell Morgan all my life. He's a steady sort of man. Not given to flights of fancy. In fact, I doubt Ewell has an ounce of imagination in him. So I believe what he says, but he doesn't remember an exact name.

"Meanwhile, Iris Hewitt is downstairs going through old newspapers. She's been at it most of the morning. She's popped in here twice to give me an update." He made a face as he readjusted his spectacles and waved a sheet of paper at Ellen. "So far, she's come up with a man who took off when the wife he abandoned in New York showed up at his door here in Opal's Grove. Iris is of the opinion that when the man tried to leave town, the jilted wife followed him and took her revenge with a gun. Then she found a newspaper story about a man named Meeker, who stole money from his employer and hightailed it out of town. The sheriff and his deputies chased after Meeker but never found him." Calley put the paper down. "Those are just the ones she's found this morning. Lord knows what she'll come up with next."

Ellen started to speak, but Calley cut her off. "Wait, there's more. When I talked to the sheriff this morning, his office had already heard from three people. A woman down in Williamsville says it's her great-grandpa. A family the next county over believes it's great uncle Herbert, who was known to take a drink or two and wander off when inebriated. My favorite is the high-school teacher who claims the skeleton was stolen from his classroom by some prankster students, and he wants it back."

Ellen had to smile at that but said she was determined Mr. Morgan's story not be ignored. Calley agreed. "I'll pass it on to the sheriff. He'll probably go see Ewell, and, when the interview you did gets to my desk, we'll put it in the paper, just like all the other pioneer stories. Satisfied?"

She wasn't, but carefully reading through decades of old newspapers would take more than a few days. Besides, Iris was already going through the earliest issues. If the man Mr. Morgan remembered was there, she was sure to find him.

Deflated, Ellen saw her big scoop slipping away. She thanked the newsman and got up to leave.

"Heard the WPA is shutting the project down," said Calley, sitting back.

"It wasn't such a big surprise. We knew when we were hired the project might not last longer than a month or two. I'm hopeful I'll find something before too long."

"That's the spirit." He pulled his phone across the desk. "I'll call the sheriff right now." Ellen took that as a dismissal and left the room.

CHAPTER 21
AUDREY

Ellen returned to the boardinghouse, still brooding over the chances of identifying Ewell Morgan's mystery man. Normally, she might discount Iris Hewitt's research abilities, but she knew the woman well enough by now to concede that Iris had the drive to scour the newspapers for possibilities.

As she stepped onto the porch, Audrey came bounding out the front door.

"You'll never guess!" She pulled Ellen into the house, down the hall, and into the dining room, where Miss Jewell was setting out lunch. The landlady's smile was almost as bright as Audrey's.

"Remember this morning when Mrs. Hewitt called me aside after the meeting?" Audrey didn't wait for an answer as she paced around the room. "Well, she gave me a solid lead on a job. She's been talking to a woman at the state historical society about sending the interviews to Topeka. And Iris, bless her heart, asks the woman if she knows of any librarian jobs." Audrey stopped to take a deep breath. "And the woman says, what a coincidence, a position just opened at the historical society. Can you believe it?"

"That's wonderful!" Ellen dropped into a chair. "So, you're going to call or write this woman?"

"Already done!" Audrey finally took a seat. "Mrs. Hewitt was in a terrible hurry to get to the newspaper office, but she took me over to the library and let me use her personal telephone to call this woman, who passed me on to a man named Grayson. And Tuesday morning I have an interview." Audrey threw up her arms like a runner who just crossed the finish line.

Ellen clapped and cheered. Miss Jewell applauded, too.

Even if this job didn't pan out, it was a tremendous boost for Audrey, and Ellen realized there was one way she could help. Promising Miss Jewell to pay for the call, Ellen went to the hall telephone and asked for long distance. As she waited to be connected, she hoped that either Nancy or her mother was home.

When the call went through, Ellen was relieved to hear Nancy's voice. Her friend's shout of surprise reverberated down the line.

Ellen assured her there was nothing wrong—something people tended to assume when they received a long-distance call—and told Nancy what she had in mind.

Nancy agreed, and, after they discussed the details, Nancy turned the subject to Jason, asking if he had stopped in Opal's Grove.

"Yes," Ellen answered. "I'm not going to run up a bill giving you the details, but you'll be pleased to know we didn't fight. In fact, it was nice to see him, but don't get any wild ideas like planning my wedding." She laughed, thanked Nancy again for doing the favor she asked, and called the operator to know what the charges were. She dug the coins out of her satchel, which she realized was still slung over one shoulder.

Returning to the dining room, where Audrey had already started her lunch, Ellen took her seat. "It's all set. I called my friend Nancy in Topeka. She's going to meet you at the train station on Monday. You'll stay with her, and she'll get you to your interview and then back to the station."

"You did that for me? I don't know what to say. Are you sure your friend doesn't mind?"

Ellen shook her head. "She's thrilled to do it and says she

can't wait to meet you. I have a feeling you two will get along just fine." Ellen reached for her ham and cheese sandwich. "You should wear that dress you got at the church basement. It's very becoming, and you'll need a hat. I don't know why women are expected to wear hats, but they are, especially when they want to look fashionable or, in your case, professional. I've got a little straw one that will go great with that dress."

Ellen realized she was almost as excited as Audrey.

CHAPTER 22
NETTIE

It was time for another run of Saturday deliveries. Ellen was looking forward to it. At Agatha's insistence, she'd brought Ivy and her parcels to the Bright house. They would have supper together before Ellen and Thelma set out in Ellen's Packard. She thought it was safer than taking a chance on Thelma's heap of a car. Although it was running, Hugh wouldn't guarantee it would last much longer, and Ellen hadn't liked the sound of the motor when Thelma drove them out to what people were now calling the Indian burial.

Iris Hewitt was responsible for that, and not even Grover Calley's front-page story in Friday morning's edition could change a name that had already stuck in people's heads. He reported every word uttered by the archaeologist. In Saturday's edition there was a follow-up story, sketching out the plans to transport the skeleton, once it could be moved, to the funeral parlor. The sheriff's department, Calley reported, was making every attempt to identify the remains, but Sheriff Logan could already say that, going back some thirty years, there were no unsolved missing person cases in the county.

Finding earlier cases was going to be difficult. Older records were gone, if they ever existed, and the sheriff was hearing the same from officials contacted in surrounding counties. Ellen noticed Calley had chosen not to enumerate the possible identities being offered up by private citizens or those put forth by Iris Hewitt.

Around the supper table in Agatha's dining room, Ellen was praised for her story about Kansas archaeology, and there was some talk of the sheriff's angry reaction to Maynard's photos of the skeleton in the paper, not to mention Iris Hewitt's threats to cancel her subscription when she saw the front-page picture of her facing down the archaeologist, her face contorted in fury.

"Mrs. Hewitt hasn't entirely given up," Ellen told the ladies. She went on to recount the woman's newspaper search, as well as her own discovery from the Ewell Morgan interview.

"We'll probably never know," Agatha said as she glanced at Ivy seated to her right, who'd grown quiet and seemed to have lost some of her healthy color.

"Aren't you feeling well?" Ellen asked, concern creeping into her voice.

"Just a little tired. It's the heat, I expect."

"And the phone calls," inserted Agatha.

Ivy gave her friend a small smile but seemed to perk up. "Since my interview appeared in yesterday's paper, I've heard from people I haven't seen in years. And, of course, Constance is preening like it was her interview, not mine."

She looked at Agatha. "What a relief she and Dell already had plans to visit those friends in Wichita this weekend. I don't think I could take another day of her calling me 'pioneer mother.' "

Ellen relaxed. This was the Ivy she knew.

With supper finished, Ellen and Thelma, who'd just said goodbye to Bill at the back door, carried the last of several sacks to the car. Through an open kitchen window, they could hear Ivy and Agatha talking with Martha. Words were punctuated with laughter.

"They're having a grand time with this," said Ellen, a bag of groceries in each arm.

Thelma nodded. "Miss Agatha says it keeps her young. Let's put these on the floor of the back seat," she suggested.

Ellen carried her bundles to the passenger side, while Thelma took the other. Together, they loaded the bags, pushing them toward the middle and packing them together as tightly as possible.

Ellen stood up and peeked over the top of the car. She felt rather than saw a whisper of movement. "What was that?"

Thelma struggled to right a sack that threatened to spill its contents across the car floor. "Did you say something?"

Ellen shook her head. "I felt something go past."

Just as the words left her mouth, she caught a flash of white outside the kitchen door. Then, there was the sound of the door banging shut and cries of surprise from inside.

Thelma rose off her knees while Ellen scurried around the car. They raced toward the sound. Just as Thelma reached to open the door, Ellen pulled her back. She gestured toward the figure standing just inside the kitchen. The bird-like woman's hands were extended in front of her. She held a small gun. Agatha sat at the far end of the kitchen table, Ivy next to her. Martha stood backed up to the sink.

Ellen focused on the weapon and the shaky hands that struggled to keep it pointed at Ivy and Agatha. Ellen didn't know anything about firearms, but this looked like a derringer she'd once seen in a movie about a riverboat gambler.

"They found Malcolm. Did you know that, Ivy?" The woman's voice was eerily calm, although her hands trembled. "That fool Iris Hewitt thinks it's some dead Indian, but we know better. Don't we?"

When no one answered, Nettie's voice rose in anger. "Don't we?"

Ellen felt her stomach knot in fear. She put her mouth next to Thelma's ear. "Go next door. Call the police. Tell them Nettie

Vine has a gun."

Thelma nodded, turned, and ran along the grassy edge of the driveway toward the street.

Nettie shouted again. Ellen jerked at the sound. Through the screen door, she saw Nettie pointing the gun at Martha and then panning it back to Agatha and Ivy. Ellen looked around frantically for some sort of weapon. She couldn't wait for the police.

The tire iron! Hadn't Thelma already gotten it out of the trunk and put it on the front seat? Ellen sprinted to the car and leaned through the open window. The tire iron was there. She almost cried with relief. Gripping the piece of metal with one hand, she dashed back to house and threw open the kitchen door.

As Nettie turned in surprise, Ellen brought the iron down on the woman's hands with a smashing blow. The gun went off before hitting the floor and skidding across the room. Splinters of linoleum erupted. Someone screamed; Ellen thought it was Martha.

Nettie came at Ellen with clawed hands, trying to scratch and tear at her. Ellen dropped the tire iron and threw her arms around Nettie, pinning her arms to her sides. The woman struggled with rage, and Ellen found herself hanging on for dear life. As Nettie bucked to get away, she slipped. They fell to the floor, Ellen on top of the writhing Nettie.

"She won't stop fighting!" Ellen shouted breathlessly.

"This'll quiet her." Martha brought a can of cling peaches down on Nettie's head. There was a groan, a trickle of blood at the scalp, and Nettie lay still.

"You've killed her!" Ivy hurried over, hands to her face in horror.

"No, listen to her groan. At least that got her still." Martha patted the can and placed it on the counter.

Ellen rolled off the woman, breathing hard. She gripped the edge of the kitchen table to pull herself to her feet.

Ellen heard Ivy's voice, and then Agatha's, calling out to ask if she was hurt. Ellen shook her head. She was shaky, but the only visible signs of her tussle with the woman were a few scratches along one arm.

Ellen stared down at Nettie. "We can't leave her there. Martha, help me get her into a chair."

Ellen pulled a chair away from the table. Nettie groaned again as Martha lifted her onto the chair like a sack of flour. The delicate fabric of Nettie's summer dress was torn at the sleeves. Her braided crown of hair hung loose from its pins, falling limply over one ear. With great efficiency, Martha took off her apron and wrapped it across Nettie's torso, tightly tying the apron strings around the back of the chair.

"There," said Martha, brushing her hands together. "She can't fall out of the chair and break her fool neck, and she can't do more fighting when she comes to. Do you think we ought to tie her feet, too?"

The other women stared at the otherwise shy cook with surprise and some admiration. Ellen began to giggle. She realized she sounded slightly hysterical. She clamped a hand over her mouth and looked around. Ivy wet a dish towel and handed it to Ellen with instructions to clean the scratches on her arm. Martha was sent to Agatha's medicine cabinet for a bottle of iodine. Meanwhile, Ivy used another towel to wipe away the blood along Nettie's scalp.

From outside came the wail of a police siren. "Now this is what we have to do." Agatha pounded the table with her cane, taking charge. "Sounds like the sheriff is almost to our door."

Ellen pushed back a strand of hair. "Thelma ran next door to call the police."

"Well, I guess that can't be helped," sighed Ivy. She moved

away from Nettie and picked up the gun, where it lay against a baseboard. Holding it gingerly with two fingers she carried it to the counter and placed it in the sink.

Agatha again rapped the cane. "Martha, please call Dr. Fox. Tell him this is an emergency, and, if he's not here within five minutes, he won't see one cent of my money for that new hospital wing. Then call my son and tell him what happened."

Just as Martha hastened to the phone in the hall, Thelma pushed through the kitchen door. "Sheriff Logan just pulled up." She stopped short and gasped at the sight of Nettie Vine hog-tied to the chair.

"Tell the sheriff we're fine and to come on back," Agatha commanded. She glanced at Ivy. "Things will be fine. Don't worry."

Thelma went outside, and the women heard her calling to the sheriff. Then he was there, stepping into the kitchen. Standing over six feet and strongly built, he blocked the door. Ellen had only a glimpse of Bill Snyder hovering outside. There was no sign of Thelma.

From the look on Sheriff Ben Logan's face, it was clear that during his many years in law enforcement, he had never expected to find one of the community's grande dames trussed up like a Thanksgiving turkey in the kitchen of another of the town's well-to-do women.

As the sheriff shook off his surprise, the doctor came striding into the kitchen from the front of the house, followed closely by Thomas Bright Junior. Tall and lean, with just a touch of gray at the temples, Agatha's son went directly to his mother and knelt down on one knee. "Are you hurt?"

Agatha patted his shoulder. "Just fine, thanks to Ellen and Martha."

"What Martha told me on the phone didn't make any sense." He turned to survey the room.

The doctor frowned as he bent over Nettie, pulling up one eyelid, then the other. She moaned. As she slowly regained consciousness, she began to mumble that there were murderers in the house. Ellen slipped beside Martha and whispered, "We should have gagged her, too."

The sheriff wearily swiped a hand across his chin. He'd rather deal with hobos camping down by the tracks or kids joyriding in their daddy's car. But it seemed the town had gone wacky. First, there was that damn skeleton. Now this.

"Will somebody tell me what happened here?" The sheriff fought to keep his voice steady and patient.

Agatha leaned around her son. "We'll be happy to talk to you, but first the doctor must attend to Miss Vine. Now, Doctor, I'm sure it would help in your examination to know that Miss Vine is groggy because she was hit with a can of peaches. It was peaches, wasn't it, Martha?"

Martha nodded.

"And her wrists may be broken," added Ellen. "I hit her with a tire iron." She pointed to where it lay under the table.

Questions exploded. The doctor's face registered shock. The sheriff glowered and raised a hand, demanding silence. But, again, it was Agatha who took control. "Tom Junior, why don't you help the doctor move her into the back parlor? While you're doing that, we'll talk to the sheriff."

Logan stepped farther into the kitchen, allowing his deputy and Thelma inside. Thelma came over to stand between her sister and Ellen. "I closed the car doors," she whispered. Ellen nodded. She'd completely forgotten the open car and the sacks filling the back seat. At least Thelma was thinking straight. It just wouldn't do for the prying eyes of neighbors, who were surely gathering in the street, to get a glimpse of their cargo.

"Mrs. Bright, if you please." The sheriff stood waiting.

"Well, I don't want to tell you how to do your job. But it occurs to me that Nettie somehow slipped past Mrs. Castle. Shouldn't someone check on her?"

The sheriff immediately gestured to Bill, sending the young man out the door.

"Thank you, Mrs. Bright. Now, if you'd please explain what happened here."

Agatha nodded. "Ellen and Thelma were putting some things in the car for me. Martha, Ivy, and I were here in the kitchen talking while Martha finished washing the supper dishes. Suddenly, and I must say quite unexpectedly, Miss Vine burst through the door with a pistol in her hand. She threatened to kill us . . . well, maybe not all of us—I think she was mostly interested in Mrs. Hamilton. But, instead of firing at us, she shot a hole in my linoleum. Ellen surprised her, she dropped the gun, and Martha valiantly stepped in to help subdue her."

"Why would she want to hurt any of you?"

The women looked at one another.

"I suppose you'll have to ask her," Agatha answered for them.

The sheriff didn't look happy. "The gun?"

"In the sink." Ivy pointed.

A low growl of frustration rumbled in the man's throat as he walked to the sink. The growl grew louder when the sheriff saw that Ivy had dropped the gun into a dishpan of dirty water and soaking pots. He deftly retrieved the weapon, water dripping, and stared at the double-barrel Remington derringer, which looked to be about as old as the woman who'd been carrying it. Logan deftly checked for another bullet and found it. He shook his head, before glancing at Tom Junior, who had returned to his mother's side. The look passing between the two men made Ellen shiver.

The gun was ridiculously small in the sheriff's hand. It looked like a toy, but Nettie had intended it to be deadly. Ellen gripped Thelma's arm to steady herself.

The sheriff pocketed the bullet. He wiped the gun with a dish towel before placing it on the counter. "Now, ladies, do any of you know why someone like Miss Vine would suddenly decide to do something like this?"

Agatha stood her ground. "I can only repeat what I said before. You will have to ask her."

"Didn't she say anything when she burst in here? Give any reason at all?"

"Well, yes, but it was garbled. And we were so frightened! It was impossible to concentrate on what she was trying to say."

With that, Agatha pushed back her chair and stood with the help of her cane. "We're going to my husband's old study to recover from this ordeal. Ladies, come along."

One by one, they silently trooped out of the kitchen and down the hall to the study, with its dark leather furniture and walls lined with shelves of leather-bound books. The smell of Thomas Bright's vanilla-scented pipe tobacco had penetrated the room's very fiber and still lingered. Once Martha closed the door behind them, Agatha directed her to a leather sofa and told her to rest. Then she turned to Thelma.

"Come help me with the refreshments. In times like this, brandy is a great restorative; I'm sure the doctor would recommend it." Agatha opened the glass doors to a high-backed secretary. With Thelma's help, she retrieved a cut-glass decanter and short balloon-shaped glasses. Agatha poured the amber liquid while Thelma passed the glasses around.

Ivy took one of the leather chairs beside the fireplace. Agatha settled into another, while Ellen took a seat next to Martha, leaving room for Thelma on the sofa. In unison, they raised their glasses to their lips. Ellen grimaced at the taste, but the liquid's warmth was a pleasant surprise. The women tasted their brandies or simply held their glasses, breathing in the liquor's rich aroma.

"Who's Malcolm?" The night's events had shaken Martha out of her usual shy self.

Agatha glanced at Ivy and sighed. "Many, many years ago, he was one of the young men that courted Nettie."

"So he jilted her," Thelma threw in.

"Nettie never took me into her confidence, so I cannot say." Agatha's tone made it clear she would say no more, and Ivy changed the subject by suggesting they cancel that night's deliveries.

Ellen and Thelma disagreed. Sunset wouldn't come along until close to eight. There was plenty of time to make their run. Both Agatha and Ivy looked relieved. "Wait a little, until we find out what's happening," Agatha advised.

Agatha's son knocked before stepping into the room. "Brandy. What an excellent idea." He walked over to his mother and kissed her forehead.

He turned to face the group. "First of all, Stella Castle is safe. Deputy Snyder found her locked in the pantry. She is understandably upset. I've arranged for her to stay with a friend from her church for the time being. Sheriff Logan has left. He is not happy, but he saw how impossible it would be to question Miss Vine. And I convinced him it would serve no good to charge Martha and Miss Hartley with assault."

"What!" Ellen and Martha cried. Ellen sank back into the sofa, covering her face with one hand. This couldn't be happening. She had worried Audrey would get both of them fired, but now she'd done it to herself. Iris Hewitt wouldn't overlook the fact that one of her WPA workers had wrestled Marie Antoinette Vine to the floor and then stood by while she was bound to a chair.

"Arrest them? The nerve!" Agatha struggled to rise from her seat.

The banker put a hand on his mother's shoulder, gently pushing her back into the chair. "I promise he won't do anything. They were clearly acting in defense of you and themselves. He knows that, although he hemmed and hawed, because it seems he should arrest somebody when a gun's involved. But he'll have to content himself with the bullet he dug out of the kitchen floor and with the confiscated weapon. Right now, he and the deputy are dispersing the crowd that's blocking the street."

"Oh dear," Agatha worried.

"There will be rumors, of course," continued Tom Junior, "but no one but you ladies truly know what happened here. I suggest the less said, the better."

There were nods around the room.

"Lastly, we come to Miss Vine." He reached for Agatha's glass and took a sip of brandy. "The doctor has examined her injuries. The cut was slight. One wrist is broken, the other badly bruised. The biggest concern, of course, is her state of mind. She is obviously a danger to others, and perhaps to herself. The town has come to accept her eccentricities, but this is beyond the pale. Dr. Fox has called a private hospital in Topeka where she can receive the sort of care she needs. The doctor will take her to his surgery to attend to the broken wrist. She will rest there tonight. Tomorrow, the doctor, accompanied by his nurse, will drive Miss Vine to Topeka, highly sedated, I might add."

"She's not coming back, is she?" Ivy knew the answer before she asked.

"No," said Tom Junior. "I've asked Mrs. Castle to pack things Miss Vine might need or want. I'll have the house closed up until her lawyer and her only close relative, a cousin in Philadelphia, decide how to handle the property and its contents for her continued financial support."

"Poor Tom," Agatha shook her head. "Saddled with that woman's affairs even after she's gone."

He didn't comment but turned to Ivy. "Should I call Dell to

take you home?"

"He and Constance are in Wichita. Ellen brought me, and she'll take me home."

Tom Junior shook his head. "I want Mother to stay with us tonight, and I would feel better if you joined us."

"Nonsense!" Agatha protested. "I am perfectly fine. We will proceed as if nothing happened."

Ivy agreed, and Tom Junior threw up his hands in surrender.

His mention of a phone call reminded Ellen of Miss Jewell and Audrey. They knew she was having supper with Agatha. If rumors were spreading around town, and Ellen was sure they were, she needed to call. She asked to use the phone and excused herself, followed by Tom Junior, who intended to stay with the doctor until the sheriff cleared the street of gawkers.

"Miss Hartley," he said, taking her hand, "I cannot begin to thank you enough for your quick action. When I think of what might have happened . . ."

"I don't want to think of it either." She inclined her head toward the study. "Those women are very dear to me."

"I suspect they feel the same about you," he said. "And I suspect you and Thelma have errands to run tonight. Please, be careful." He gave her a wink.

"You know?"

"Don't tell Mother. It would spoil things for her. And, I have to admit I'm a little embarrassed it took me some time to realize what she's been up to."

"What gave her away?" Ellen lowered her voice.

"Grocery bills. She spends far too much on canned goods and dried beans. When I added that to the stories I've heard around town of people finding sacks of things at their door, it suddenly struck me that Mother was the culprit. It wasn't too difficult to figure out who her partners were." Tom Junior jerked his head toward the study and smiled. Without another word, he turned on his heel and retraced his steps down the hall to where the doctor worried over Nettie Vine.

CHAPTER 23
IVY AND AGATHA

The doctor left with Nettie. The crowd in front of the house was gone. From her phone call to Miss Jewell, Ellen learned that rumors were indeed spreading. One story had Nettie Vine shooting out street lamps before breaking into Agatha's kitchen to take potshots at her electric icebox. Ellen assured her landlady that nothing of the kind had happened, saying only that Nettie had appeared with a gun but was disarmed before she hurt anyone. She told Miss Jewell not to expect her back at the boardinghouse for some time.

Ellen went back to the study. "You won't believe what people are already saying." Ellen repeated Miss Jewell's story.

"The sillier, the better," said Agatha. "By this time tomorrow, there will be so many stories, no one will know what to believe, even if they hear the unvarnished truth."

"We just don't add fuel to the fire," volunteered Thelma.

Over the last of their brandies, the women agreed.

Martha announced she was going to straighten the kitchen, and, when that was finished, she would call Chester for a ride home. Thelma and Ellen were anxious to make their deliveries, but, before Ellen left the room, Ivy motioned her over. "Don't forget that you're taking me home. I'll wait here with Agatha until you return."

They made the deliveries as efficiently as possible. The evening's events had cast a pall over the adventure of stealing around in the night, and neither wanted to hash out what had happened. When they did speak, it was to comment on the weather or the expression on someone's face when they found a sack of groceries or newly made shirts on their porch. The only lapse came when Ellen dropped off Thelma at home. As Thelma said goodnight, she touched Ellen's shoulder. "You did real good. And Martha! I wish I'd been there to see her thump Miss Vine upside the head."

Ellen could feel the tension floating out of her body. She was laughing when she left Thelma, and she was still smiling when she returned to Agatha's, where she found Martha sitting with Chester in the kitchen.

"I didn't want to leave the ladies alone, and Chester came to keep me company." Martha tipped her head toward a man with an open smile, ruddy cheeks, and carefully clipped brown hair.

"I offered to stay the night," Martha continued, "but Miss Agatha won't hear of it. She and Miss Ivy are still in the study." With that, she and Chester said goodnight and were out the door.

Ellen found the women seated as she had left them. Ivy said she wasn't quite ready to leave, motioning Ellen to take a chair.

Ivy and Agatha glanced at each other. "We've been talking," Ivy began, "and decided that you deserve an explanation."

"But we must have your solemn promise that what we say here goes no further," Agatha interjected.

"We trust you already, but I'm afraid we must ask for your promise," Ivy added.

Ellen nodded and promised, even raising her hand as a sign of taking an oath.

"Martha asked about Malcolm," Ivy said, clearing her throat. "There's more to him than being one of Nettie's admirers. Everything begins and ends with him." She glanced at Agatha, who gave her a nod of encouragement.

Ivy's voice grew stronger. "Ewell Morgan is more right than we would like people to know."

Ellen felt a chill as she remembered the words of Nettie Vine. Maybe they weren't out-of-control ravings. Was it possible Ivy knew the identity of the skeleton? If so, that could only mean Agatha did, too. Ellen faced the women, not sure she wanted to hear what they had to say.

"Ewell almost got the name right," Ivy began. "The last name was Mahan—Malcolm Mahan. He showed up in Opal's Grove sometime during the autumn of '69 and got a job at the lumberyard. As a little side business, he built simple pieces of furniture—just like Ewell remembers. Malcolm seemed a pleasant sort, always ready to trade jokes with the men and pay compliments to ladies. He was quite good-looking."

"Knew it, too," interrupted Agatha.

Ivy smiled at her friend before continuing. "Mrs. Archer practically swooned the first time he came into the store. He had dark hair that curled over his collar and the kind of long eyelashes that any girl would envy. He was beyond handsome."

"I think Ellen gets the idea," Agatha prompted. "Go on with what you need to say."

"Despite his good looks, I stayed clear of him. Early on, he tried to cozy up to me. Even if I'd never met Wheat, I wouldn't have been interested in Malcolm Mahan. He was too friendly, if you know what I mean, and I didn't like the way he eased his conversations around to money. He hinted about how well I must be doing as a seamstress and how prosperous my Uncle Nate looked when he came to town."

"I didn't like him, not that he would have paid any attention to a married woman like me," interjected Agatha. "But from what Ivy told me, and the few times I saw him at community events, I thought there was something hard and calculating under that jovial manner of his. I've seen some con men in my day, and he fit the bill."

Ivy picked up the story. "I can't be certain of when he met Nettie, but I would guess it was when Sylvester Vine invited the whole town to the homecoming reception he threw for his wife and daughter when they returned from Philadelphia."

Agatha dismissed that with a sniff, catching Ellen's eye. She knew without being told that this was on the heels of Nettie's rumor mongering.

"Wherever Malcolm and Nettie met doesn't really matter." Ivy shifted in her chair. "He began to visit the Vine home, which seemed perfectly natural when Nettie held one of her social evenings or Saturday afternoon parties. These weren't as well attended as in the past. I never went, but I knew our crowd was breaking up, going their separate ways to get married or earn a living. Two or three of the boys went off to college. But Nettie persisted with her picnics and evenings of parlor games.

"In pretty short order, Malcolm began to call on Nettie as a suitor. Mr. and Mrs. Vine were not happy. It was fine to include Malcolm in a group of friends, but he wasn't acceptable as a son-in-law. For one thing, Mrs. Vine would have been horrified to introduce her upper-crust Philadelphia relatives to a young man with rough, calloused hands and unsure manners. Malcolm wouldn't have known a soup spoon from a ladle. His dress-up clothes were cheap and garish, although I suppose he thought he looked quite the man-about-town.

"Both Agatha and I heard snippets of gossip. A word was dropped here and there among Agatha's friends at afternoon teas. I heard things when my clients had a fitting or when a word was dropped by shoppers at Archers. It was said that Mr. Vine put his foot down—Nettie was not to see Malcolm; he was no longer welcome in the Vine house."

Ivy's voice tensed. "I tried to piece together in my mind how things happened the way they did. Maybe they argued because

Malcolm decided to leave town without Nettie. And I suppose it's possible they planned to run off together, but something went terribly wrong." Ivy took a deep breath. "I just happened to be there when it did."

Agatha leaned forward and patted Ivy's knee in encouragement.

"It was late in March 1870. I had been out at the claim helping Clara with spring cleaning and going over plans for my wedding. Riding back to town, I came upon Malcolm and Nettie. They were standing down amid the trees along the riverbank near the place where the country road meets what is now the highway. Nettie's ridiculous pony cart was just off the road, with Malcolm's horse tethered nearby. My first thought was a lovers' tryst, and I felt embarrassed to come upon them. I could have avoided them if I had taken off over a planted field, but I worried about my horse trampling a crop the farmer had worked so hard to get in. I could have turned back to the soddie, but I did neither.

"I had so much to do in town. I told myself if I rode at a steady pace, and kept my eyes forward, I could pretend not to notice them." Ivy made a noise to express her own foolishness. "As I came closer, I heard their voices. Nettie's was angry and accusing. Malcolm's voice was lower, as if he was trying to calm her. From the few words I heard, I guessed Nettie was accusing Malcolm of breaking a promise to her.

"I should have spurred my horse and ridden away. That I didn't is the reason for what happened today." Ivy stopped to catch her breath.

"At first, I wasn't noticed. But then, Malcolm looked up and saw me. He laughed, called my name, and threw his arm out in a big wave. Nettie turned. When she saw me, the anger seemed to roll right off her. Her voice rose, ever more agitated. I saw Malcolm turn back to her. He reached out a hand to soothe her. Maybe he intended to pull her into his arms. But, in that moment, Nettie reached toward the holster hanging about Malcolm's waist and grabbed for the revolver. For a split second, my only thought was how odd it was for Malcolm to be wearing a gun, but then, lots of men who normally wouldn't show a pistol or shotgun in town carried them when out in the country.

"As he tried to wrench the gun out of Nettie's hands, it went off. I can still see the look of surprise on his face. He stumbled back a few steps, grabbing at his side, and that's when Nettie pulled the revolver straight up toward his chest and fired twice more."

Ellen's hand flew to her mouth to smother a gasp.

"I screamed and jumped from my horse, and that's when Nettie turned and raised the gun in my direction. I threw myself to the ground just as John Featherstone came running up behind Nettie. He knocked her flat and relieved her of the weapon." Ivy smiled for the first time. "Your technique tonight was very similar to Mr. Featherstone's."

"She killed him?" Ellen's voice was a whisper.

"Oh, yes. Malcolm Mahan was quite dead. I believe he might have survived the first shot, but not the others." Ivy sighed, her story almost finished.

"Nettie was on her hands and knees, trying to claw her way along the ground to her pony cart. Mr. Featherstone grabbed her around the waist and lifted her upright. She kicked at him. I'll never forget the scream that came out of her. It was a long, horrible wail. Mr. Featherstone shouted for her to quiet down, but she was out of her head. She kept fighting him, and there didn't seem to be anything to do but bind her hands and feet. With one arm around her waist, he managed to yank a leather strap out of a coat pocket. His pushed her to the ground and tied her hands, and then her ankles. Finally, he tied an old bandana over her mouth, but not before she began to scream that I had killed Malcolm. Maybe the holstered gun I always wore when I rode alone gave her the idea that I fired the shots. She was hysterical. In her mind, I killed Malcolm out of jealousy because he preferred Nettie over me."

"To think Ivy would give that man the time of day, let alone encourage him, was preposterous," said Agatha, giving Ivy a thunderous look. "You should not blame yourself for what happened."

"Over the years, I've made a point of avoiding her, which was easy enough seeing how there were few opportunities for our paths to cross. But, more than anything, I've felt sorry for her." Ivy looked at Ellen. "There's nothing left of the high-spirited girl who enjoyed the fun of parties and made people laugh. It's sad what became of her, and I hold Malcolm responsible for teasing her with the idea that I was a rival and perhaps making promises he had no intention of keeping."

Agatha was not in the mood to forgive Nettie or make excuses for her. "None of that erases the fact she wanted to make you the killer."

Ellen turned to Ivy. "But the sheriff back then couldn't have believed that."

"He never knew. Mr. Featherstone was afraid to go the sheriff. His name was Showcross, an ex-Union officer appointed by Sylvester Vine to the job of law enforcement when the town was first established. After the local government got organized, Mr. Vine made sure Showcross kept his office, although some people thought he was too heavy-handed in the way he carried out his duties.

"Mr. Featherstone was sure the sheriff would side with whatever Nettie said, and Sylvester Vine would protect his girl. If it came to my word against Nettie's about Malcolm, I'd lose."

Ivy sighed. "So, I did what Mr. Featherstone told me to. I

went back to town, trailing Malcolm's horse behind. It had to look as if he had returned the animal to the livery stable. When I left my mount at the stable, I tied Malcolm's to a post outside. Sooner or later, the livery owner or the boy working for him would spot the animal and think the worst of Malcolm for not bringing it inside."

"As for the rest, Mr. Featherstone never told me the details of what he did or how Nettie ended up back in her home. As for me, I told three people. I had to tell Wheat, of course. I told Agatha, because I couldn't be her friend and hold back that sort of thing. I knew she would insist on Thomas being told, because she refused to keep anything from him."

"The skeleton . . ." Ellen began.

Ivy and Agatha nodded in unison. "We believe it's Malcolm," said Ivy. "Nettie must think so, too. Somehow, its discovery and all the talk about it has brought everything back to her, or at least the part she wants to believe that I killed the man."

Ellen felt the reporter in her begin to tug.

"Surely, people wondered where this man was. His employer and friends must have asked questions."

"At first they did, but people came and went all the time, sometimes without a backward glance. Malcolm's things disappeared from the boardinghouse. I never knew how that came to be, but I suspected John Featherstone somehow managed to remove them, with no one the wiser. Ewell Morgan's father may have had doubts, but it was easy for people to assume Malcolm just packed up and left town, especially when the stationmaster remembered him buying a rail ticket. The man didn't recall seeing Malcolm board a train, but he could have missed him in the crowd of people that left and arrived on any given day."

"Let me tell the rest," Agatha broke in. "Sylvester Vine hustled his wife and Nettie out of town. His explanation was that Nettie was feeling poorly and would benefit from the sea air at a relative's place on Nantucket. They stayed over a year. I can't say I missed them."

Ivy leaned back in her chair. "I'm sorry that I brought this down on you."

"I'll always be grateful you told me this story." Ellen rose, still reeling from Ivy's revelation. She resisted the urge to go to the woman's side and offer a hug of support and sympathy. The display would have embarrassed Ivy.

CHAPTER 24
NEAR OPAL'S GROVE, 1870

The seamstress trembled as she got back onto her horse. Tears welled in her eyes as she promised to do as he said. Featherstone didn't watch her ride away. He wanted to hurry and finish the dirty business before him.

The Vine girl was tied at her hands and feet. Otherwise, he had no doubt she'd try to get away. The bandana muffled her cries. He picked her up like a sack of potatoes and carried her to the pony cart, where he dropped her behind the driver's seat. Nettie immediately began to pound her feet against one side. She struggled to a sitting position.

Featherstone slapped her across the face, not hard enough to really hurt but enough to get her attention. Her eyes opened wide in surprise. Never in her life had anyone laid a hand on her.

"Be still." The man's voice was rough. "I've never hit a woman in my life, but I'm making an exception for you. If you don't stay absolutely still, the next lick will be with a fist. Do you understand?"

Nettie's eyes showed fear. She nodded.

He scanned the road along the river and then the main one from town. He had to get the girl and the dead man away from this spot. He picked up Malcolm and laid him in the cart beside the girl. She suddenly sat still as stone, her head turned away. Featherstone took the pony's reins and walked through the woods to where his own mount was tethered.

He'd come to this spot several times, always finding fossils. Today, he'd happened on what looked like a giant turtle. He'd been carefully digging for it when he heard the shots.

Featherstone looked around. Satisfied that they were hidden from the view of any traveler, he picked up the shovel he'd been using to unearth the turtle and walked farther along the river. He began to dig.

When the grave was ready, Featherstone lifted the man from the pony cart and laid the body out on the ground. He bent down and began to strip away the dead man's clothes. As he did, he went through each pocket. From inside the jacket, he removed a leather pouch. A look inside revealed that some of the folded papers were letters written by the Vine girl. He put those aside and reached into another pocket. Out came a fat wad of greenbacks. In one of the trouser pockets was a small bag filled with silver coins. Featherstone sat back on his heels and frowned, wondering where somebody like Mahan got that kind of the money.

He stuffed everything, including the dead man's clothes and revolver, into one of the gunny sacks he always carried for his collecting. With some regret, he loosened the saddle on his horse, pulled off the blanket underneath, and wrapped it around the man. With a heave, he dumped the body into the grave and began to fill it.

Thunder rolled in the distance as Featherstone covered the grave with brush and river stones. When the job was done, he tied his own horse to the back of the cart and gave its nose a pat. Rain began to fall in a steady downpour.

Featherstone hauled himself onto the cart's seat and looked back at the girl. Her clothes were soaked. She watched Featherstone, blinking back water running into her eyes. Her stony-eyed stare had given way to a look of defiance.

He flicked the pony's reins and sadly shook his head. She

knew what she'd done. Now, the girl was counting on her daddy fixing things. She was already planning how to make life miserable for that seamstress. Featherstone was going to make sure that didn't happen.

The downpour lessened. By the time he reached town, the rain had turned into a light mist. Keeping to the side streets, he made his way to the alley that ran behind the Vine mansion. At the carriage house near the back of the property, Featherstone hopped out of the cart and tied the pony's reins to a post.

He walked toward the house, stopping when he came to the side door that led directly into the room Sylvester Vine used as his library and office. Featherstone banged on the door with a fist and stepped back.

Vine opened the door with a look of irritation. "I was just going into supper. What do you want? Don't you know that decent people don't call at this hour?"

Featherstone stood silently, waiting for Sylvester to stop blustering.

"You'll want to close the door and come with me," Featherstone said quietly. "It's your daughter."

Vine angrily pulled on a coat and grabbed a hat off a peg near the door.

On the walk to the carriage house, Featherstone matter-of-factly told the man every detail of what had happened.

When Sylvester Vine saw his daughter, trussed up and gagged, he rounded on Featherstone, shaking a fist and threatening to call the sheriff.

"You don't want to do that." Featherstone's tone was flat. He slowly walked behind the cart and untied his horse. As he mounted, he gave the man a long, hard look. "I don't want any of this coming back on me or on that seamstress girl. And there are lots of reasons you don't want people, including the sheriff, to know about what's happened. You may think you own the man, but you don't own the town. There are people hereabouts that won't put up with your daughter getting away with this." He let the threat hang in the air.

When the man dropped his head, refusing to meet his gaze, John Featherstone reined his horse to one side, ready to leave this sorry mess behind. Suddenly, he paused. "One more thing. In the gunny sack you'll find the effects of the man your daughter killed, including the money. I could be wrong, but I figure you paid off Mahan. Told him to leave town and never see your daughter again. Now, thanks to her, you won't have to worry about that money-grubber again."

The men glared at each other, neither seeing Nettie Vine trying to scream through the old bandana.

CHAPTER 25
NETTIE, 1936

Nettie lay in the guest bedroom. Dr. Jonathán Fox had wanted to take her to the town hospital, not his surgery, which consisted of an office and examination room attached to his private residence, but Tom Bright overruled him. He wanted Miss Vine to have total privacy, out of sight and away from everyone but the doctor. Fox hadn't liked the idea, but the prospect of Bright money for a new hospital wing was a powerful argument. Nettie was treated in the surgery before being moved to the upstairs bedroom prepared by the doctor's wife. Fox called in Nurse Ames, and together they alternated turns at Nettie's bedside.

Sedated and then given something for the pain, Nettie willingly submitted to the doctor's care and then her move to bed, wearing a cotton nightgown belonging to Mrs. Fox. In the early hours of the morning, Nettie began to stir. She groaned and opened her eyes. A woman's face seemed to float over her.

"Doctor, she's coming around." There were footsteps, and then a man's face appeared. Nettie couldn't make out his words. She closed her eyes, drowsy and comfortably drifting in a fog cocoon.

The man's voice jolted her back. He said his name. Did she remember what had happened? Did she know where she was?

She nodded dreamily. Of course, she knew where she was. She was reclining in a chair at that quiet place on the Hudson River. At first, she was angry with Mother for deceiving her. She'd said they were going to Nantucket, not this place where a doctor talked to her most every day and where she was forced to sit in mineral baths and drink water that smelled of rotten eggs.

She was overjoyed when Mother came to fetch her, saying she was well enough to travel. She didn't remember being ill, but she didn't dare ask and risk being left in this place that, for all its picturesque beauty, felt like a prison.

"Miss Vine. Do you know who I am?"

Nettie wanted to swat at the man who kept breaking into her dreams with questions.

When he asked again if she recognized him, the place on the Hudson faded away. Nettie focused on the face hovering above her. "You're Dr. Fox. Was I in an accident? My wrist hurts. And my head aches."

"You had a fall."

"Rubbish. I never fall." Her words slurred. "I'm graceful. Like a ballerina. That's what Mother says."

The man cleared his throat. "Be that as it may, you have a small cut on your head to which I have applied a dressing, and your right wrist is broken. It is bandaged with a light cast. Nurse Ames and I are looking after you."

She let the doctor's words wash over her. She closed her eyes and dreamed. She was in Nantucket. She was alone, walking along the shore. The tide was out. When she looked back the way she'd come, she could see her footprints in the sand. That made her smile. So did the white and pink shells she'd gathered in a basket. She enjoyed walking on the beach almost as much as driving her cart across the prairie.

She turned toward the dunes and her aunt's summer house just beyond. She had to change for dinner. Tonight would be just the family, for which Nettie was grateful. When they first arrived on the island, she'd welcomed the excitement of summer parties and picnics, but now she was weary of them and the men her mother insisted she meet.

Nettie stopped at the wooden steps that led up from the beach. There were voices just above. Her mother and Aunt Ruth. She ducked into a stand of seagrass, straining to hear their conversation. As she suspected, she and her prospects for marriage were again being discussed. Mother had become obsessed with having Nettie engaged by the end of summer. Nettie wished Mother would find something else to occupy her time.

"Not one serious suitor!" Her mother's voice carried down to her. "It's incomprehensible that Marie Antoinette should remain on the shelf."

Mother's words rose above the sound of wind and surf. "I took this up with Sylvester in my last letter, and I am shattered by his reply."

Nettie edged closer to the steps. What could Papa have said that would so upset Mother?

"I could hardly believe it! Our Marie Antoinette is not to be married—ever! He demands there be no more talk of marriage. He believes our daughter is too fragile in disposition to manage married life."

Her aunt's reply was lost in the wind. It hardly mattered. Nettie slowly dropped to her knees, oblivious to the sharp edges of the seagrass that surrounded her. She sighed with happiness. Papa refused to let her marry. She no longer had to contend with talking to men who did not interest her. She no longer had to pretend gaiety when she felt none. Best of all, there was no reason for her mother to play matchmaker, eyeing every eligible man as a prospective bridegroom for her daughter.

The anger Nettie felt toward her father receded. He had her best interests at heart, after all. When Malcolm returned, he wouldn't find her burdened with a husband. She would be waiting for him, and they would go away together just as he promised.

Hovering on the edge of consciousness, Nettie heard the doctor say something and a woman's voice answer. She wished they would go away. Tuning out the voices, she gave herself over to a luxurious sense of well-being. Somewhere, Malcolm was waiting for her.

Chapter 26
Ellen

At precisely nine o'clock on Sunday morning, Grover Calley rapped on the boardinghouse door. He wanted a word with Ellen, if Miss Jewell would be so kind as to fetch her.

Ellen wasn't altogether surprised that Calley sought her out and said so when she joined him.

"I like walking around town on nice Sunday mornings like this one," he said, stepping off the porch and indicating with a swing of his arm that he expected Ellen to join him. "Walking gives me time to reflect, and to indulge in a good cigar." He pulled a plump Havana from his jacket's inside pocket. After inspecting the cigar with some care and biting off one end, he brought a silver lighter to the tip, puffing his cheeks in and out like a squeezebox.

Ellen waited for him to finish, stuffing her hands into the side pockets of the beige dress with elbow-length sleeves that covered the scratches from the night before. Satisfied that the cigar was burning, Calley set a leisurely pace down the quiet street. "I'm still writing my story for Monday's paper about what happened over at Mrs. Bright's yesterday. Nobody answers the door at the Vine house. When I stopped by Ivy Hamilton's this morning, she said she was too flustered to talk, which is a pile of horse manure. I don't think you could ruffle her feathers if you tried. Why, she once shot a coyote trying to carry off a calf. Didn't bat an eye. Her son Dell told me that story and was real sorry it wasn't in her interview." He puffed. "Mrs. Bright politely told me, through her cook, who glared at me through the screen door, to go away.

"Then, I talked to Sheriff Logan again. Last night he said, and I'm paraphrasing here, 'Miss Nettie Vine, for reasons known only to herself, entered the kitchen of Mrs. Agatha Bright without invitation. She brandished an old firearm, which accidentally discharged. No one was injured.' He said the same thing this morning."

Ellen willed her expression to show nothing.

Calley glanced at Ellen as he took a long pull on the cigar. "The sheriff wouldn't tell me who was in the house at the time, but I talked to some of the neighbors. They saw Tom Junior leave about half past seven. You left with Thelma Weaver a little later. I know for a fact that it was the Weaver girl who called the sheriff. I was wondering how you happened to be there."

"Did you speak with Thelma?"

Calley nodded. "She told me to go fly a kite."

Ellen didn't try to hide a smile. "I was invited to supper."

"Like I said the other day, you've made some interesting friends in this town. Mrs. Bright and Mrs. Hamilton are well-liked around here."

She gave the man a big smile. "Yes, I enjoyed interviewing them very much."

"You interviewed Miss Vine, too. Want to tell me what happened yesterday? Any idea of why she went busting in like that with a gun? Surely, you formed some impression of the woman."

Ellen refused to be pulled in so easily. She'd give Calley something else to stew over. "Did you know Miss Vine has been going to the depot?"

Calley nodded. "I play poker with the stationmaster and a few other gentlemen most every Thursday night at the Elks Lodge. He mentioned it. Then, reading her interview, I recalled my father talking about her going down to greet newcomers. He thought it was a fool thing to do. I was also reminded of the fact that she's done that off and on for years but stopped; that is, until recently." Calley puffed. "Any ideas?"

Ellen wasn't going to share what she really thought, not after what she'd heard last evening. Nettie wasn't reliving the days when she waved to passengers. She was expecting to meet someone who would never show up. Ellen shrugged at Calley's question. "I'm thinking that sometimes she doesn't know if she's in the past or present. She gets confused, and these interviews with all their talk of the old days reignited memories."

Calley eyed her. "What sort of memories? Did you leave out things she said in the interview?"

"I wrote it down exactly as she told it," Ellen retorted.

He believed her and took another tack. "Neighbors also said Doc Fox and Tom Junior arrived about the same time as the sheriff. When I called Tom, he asked me to leave it be, and the doctor isn't home. His wife said he was called out of town, and she doesn't know when he will return. Any ideas about where he might have gone?"

They were now three blocks from the boardinghouse. Ellen stopped. "You'll have to talk to the doctor or Tom Junior."

Calley eyed her for a moment. "Listen, kid. "He tapped the cigar, sending ash spiraling into the gutter. He was clearly annoyed with her. "You could write up this story with an insider's view. I bet the bigger papers would pick it up. This could be your ticket to a real job as a reporter."

Ellen turned to walk back. The man was right. In her mind's eye, she saw the byline, her name in bold print. Above it was the headline "Secrets and Confessions in a Kansas Town." The story was sensational enough to be picked up by other newspapers, maybe all over the country. Who could resist a mystery skeleton and a gun-toting woman? Her mind swirled over the possibilities. Maybe she could change the names in the same way she did when writing those stories for pulp magazines. But, no, that wouldn't work. As a reporter, she had to tell the facts. Ivy and Agatha would understand.

"Well, what do you say?" Calley stumped alongside her, frowning.

His voice snapped her back to the present. Overwhelmed with shame that she had considered for even a moment betraying the women she cared about, Ellen straightened her shoulders. She was disgusted with herself and upset with the newspaperman for dangling a carrot in front of her face.

She took a deep breath. "Mr. Calley, there's no big story here, unless you want to read about an elderly woman who, I would guess, is unstable and has been for a very long time. You could write about how she's always had people looking after her. She's been protected from the world outside her door. I wonder if she even knows there's a Depression." Ellen paused. "I can't add anything to your story, except to say that the hardware store can expect a visit from Agatha Bright in the next few days. She needs a new linoleum covering for the kitchen."

Ellen reached out to shake the man's hand. "Mr. Calley, I've enjoyed this Sunday morning walk, and I truly want to thank you for giving me the names of those editors. Maybe something will work out."

He shook the offered hand, then paused. "Indulge me one more minute, if you please."

Ellen crossed her arms, as if to ward off what he had to say.

"When I was a young man, my dad sent me off to work on a big-city newspaper. He said the experience would be good for me. It was. I met all sorts of reporters, and I found there's one type that'll do anything for a big scoop. They'll sabotage their colleagues, lie to their families, and misuse their friends to get the story." He stared at the cigar, which had gone out. "You're never going to be that kind of reporter."

Ellen kept her arms crossed. "You're telling me I should look into another line of work." She couldn't hide her disappointment.

"You're trying my patience," Calley almost growled, before calming himself. "What I'm saying is that you just discovered you can't be a hard-hitting, damn-everyone-else journalist. Now that you've eliminated that, concentrate on what you can be."

"Okaaayy," Ellen drew the word out slowly.

"Now, before I continue my little trek around town, I've got a piece of news for you. I got a call from my friend in Chicago. Wanted to know about you—if you were reliable, that sort of thing."

Ellen nodded numbly.

"He's going to call you this afternoon at three. I gave him the boardinghouse number. I should let him tell you himself, but I thought I'd give you time to think this over before he calls. He doesn't want you in Chicago. He wants you to stay out here and write the kind of things you sent him. Stories about real people, ordinary people. He's going to call it 'Correspondence from the Plains,' or some such rot."

She asked him to repeat every word. "I can't thank you enough," she stammered.

He waved his hand, refusing to accept any gratitude. "I should head back home. The wife will be wanting to get to church."

Ellen almost ran to the boardinghouse. Ten minutes ago, she wouldn't have bet a nickel on her chances of finding this kind of job, and then suddenly there was this opportunity. She slowed her steps and told herself to take deep breaths. She had to be prepared for the call with some ideas for future articles.

The man in Chicago called exactly at three. Ellen was anxious but felt prepared. She'd spent part of the afternoon practicing with Audrey what she would say to the man. And Audrey helped soothe her nerves by playing her part to the hilt. She asked rapid-fire questions as she expected a newsman might do, and when she decided the best thing for Ellen was to relax, Audrey affected a Donald Duck voice that had them both laughing.

Ellen hung up the phone, took a deep breath, and walked slowly through the dining room and kitchen. The conversation had been surprisingly easy. The man was certainly businesslike as he laid out what he expected for publication, and she felt she held up her end by asking the right questions and offering her ideas for articles.

She was still thinking of what had been said when she stepped onto the narrow back porch. She took another deep breath and reached for the banister post to steady herself.

Audrey gave a cry and ran to her side, slipping an arm around her waist. "Don't tell me that man called all the way from Chicago just to give you the cold shoulder!"

Ellen let herself be led to a lawn chair, where she collapsed with a nervous laugh. "No. It's all set. A contract for ten articles. Another one if those catch on. On top of the paycheck, there's a little travel money to cover going to Oklahoma or Nebraska or wherever I want to look for a story."

Ellen stopped, staring wide-eyed at Audrey and Miss Jewell, who was hovering in the background. "I can hardly believe it!"

"Whew!" Audrey dropped back into her chair. "The look on your face had me scared out of my wits."

"You need iced tea." Miss Jewell hurried to the house.

"With a beer chaser!" Audrey called after her.

Ellen fell back in the chair, laughing.

"Everything okay now?" Audrey still looked worried.

"Fine. I was just overwhelmed for a minute. This has been quite a weekend. A job comes along when I least expect it, and then there was last night. That was the last thing anyone would have expected. One minute, we're having a lovely time at Mrs.

Bright's, and, in the next instant, there's Nettie Vine."

Miss Jewell returned with the tea. "Sorry, no beer." She glanced at Audrey and giggled. "I heard what you were just saying. I hope the ladies have recovered today."

Ellen took a long drink before answering. "Tom Junior called while you were at church. His mother and Miss Ivy were at his house. They were going to have Sunday dinner and then go for a ride in the country." Ellen didn't add that he had again expressed his gratitude.

"It's all anybody talked about after church. Most of what they were saying was pure nonsense, of course, but folks are wondering where Miss Vine got to." Miss Jewell settled back into her chair and looked at Ellen expectantly.

"Dr. Fox took her to his surgery. I guess he's still looking after her." She knew that, sooner or later, people would realize Nettie was no longer home and would not return, but they would not hear a whisper about it from her.

Ellen drank the remainder of her tea. She still felt a little shaky when she thought of wresting the pistol from Nettie, but she certainly didn't regret her actions. Ivy and Agatha were safe, and, in her own way, so was Marie Antoinette Vine.

CHAPTER 27
ELLEN AND JASON

On the Thursday evening before their last official day of employment with the WPA, Ellen and Audrey arrived at the Smith house for a farewell party being thrown by Jess's parents. Neighbors, Jess's friends from high school, and the WPA workers crowded into the family's backyard to congratulate Jess, offer advice on life in the big city, and, in some cases, slip a little spending money into his shirt pocket.

People stood in small groups, talking over one another. Laughter mixed with exclamations at the variety of sandwiches, cold salads, and desserts—many brought by friends—arranged on a table constructed of a long board resting on sawhorses. Ellen and Audrey's offering to this potluck supper was a raisin and custard pie, prepared by Miss Jewell, who refused to relinquish her kitchen to her boarders despite their reassurances they knew their way around a stove.

Ellen thought of this as a going-away party for all of them. Cowboy Joe was on his way to Topeka. So was Audrey. She had the job at the historical society and, with Nancy's help, had found an inexpensive furnished apartment. In the serendipitous way things sometimes happened, Ellen mused, she was going to stay in Opal's Grove at Miss Jewell's. Although Nancy begged her to return to Topeka, Ellen had given it considerable thought and decided she could work from a small town just as easily as from a city. Certainly, she would be more productive than if she went home to the distractions of family and the soon-to-arrive baby.

Ellen nibbled on a pimento cheese sandwich. She nodded to Mae Swenson, who'd been invited because Jess didn't have the heart to leave her out. The woman seemed to flit from one party guest to another, like a butterfly that couldn't seem to find a place to land. Mae stopped for a moment beside Ralph, said something, and moved on.

Ellen was pleased to see the professor had finally exchanged his shabby jacket for one more suited to the summer heat. That was Audrey's doing, dragging Ralph to the church clothing bank. Audrey's influence seemed to have paid off in other ways, too. The man was still without a teaching job, but he was less prickly. In fact, he looked almost relaxed as he chatted with the science-fiction writer about staying on with the WPA to collect material in western Kansas for the state guide.

Iris Hewitt sidled up to Ellen. With her WPA duties reduced to packing up the interviews for transport to Topeka, Iris informed Ellen she had temporarily dropped her quest to locate the Indian village.

"I know it's there, but identifying the remains takes priority." Iris was sure the sheriff had overlooked some vital bit of information, and she was determined to put a name to the bones, which were recently reburied in the town cemetery.

Ellen listened with only half an ear until the woman began to name the six possibilities she'd found in her newspaper search. She waited tensely for the name of Malcolm Mahan to come. When it didn't, Ellen breathed out a sigh of relief.

She mumbled that it was all very interesting and tried to politely step away from the woman, but Iris was not finished.

"Have you heard anything about Miss Vine? There's a rumor she's left town for good." Iris didn't wait for Ellen to respond. "If she's gone to a hospital, like some folks are saying, I wonder what will become of her home. The Vine mansion would make a wonderful museum. You've been inside the house; what do you think?"

Grover Calley came to Ellen's rescue. "Excuse me, Iris, I wonder if I could steal Miss Hartley away for a moment." He lightly took Ellen's arm and maneuvered her to a spot away from the crowd.

"Thank you." Ellen nodded toward Iris, who had latched onto a woman bringing another tray of sandwiches to the table. "She's always planning something, isn't she? Since I'm going to live here for a while longer, I better learn how to avoid her. Otherwise, I'll find myself on a committee trying to talk Tom Bright into turning the Vine house into a museum."

Calley laughed and shook his head. "Is that what she's up to? I wouldn't think she'd have the time, but Iris always has to be doing something. Between her and Constance Hamilton, this town never lacks for projects and committees." He raised his glass and took a taste of the ginger-ale punch being served by Jess's aunt. Calley made a face, turned away from the crowd, and tossed the remainder of his punch into a nearby peony bush. "Blah! Almost the same as that stuff the Ladies' Literary Club serves at its annual spring tea, except theirs has scoops of sherbet ice cream swimming on top."

"I've had that. It's called 'Floating Island Punch.' "

"Well, I call it 'Carrie Nation Punch'; not a drop of alcohol in it. Mind you, I'm not much for drink, but it seems to me a little vodka would go a long way toward improving the taste." Calley huffed. "Now that I'm thinking of it, I best give Jess a lecture on the evils of drink before he leaves. Some reporters can really toss it back."

"It's a nice thing you did for him. I know I said it before, but I'll say it again. The same goes for all the help you gave me. I am so grateful."

"Stop being grateful. I'm sick of hearing it. I'd hire you if there was money for it. Maynard gave me an earful about bringing you on. Surprised me no end, but he thinks you've got what it takes."

He raised a hand to stop Ellen from interrupting. "Then, there are those friends of yours. Before they heard about that Chicago arrangement, I was invited over to Mrs. Bright's. I had hopes she was going to tell me about that ruckus with Miss Vine; I should have known better. Mrs. Bright set out a very nice afternoon tea, complete with cucumber sandwiches, and had Ivy Hamilton there, too.

Ellen waited, wondering what those two ladies were up to now.

"After a few pleasantries, they asked me to hire you. No, that's not right . . . they demanded. It was all very polite, of course, but there was no misunderstanding they expected me to do what they asked. They even offered to pool their resources and pay half your salary."

"You didn't agree!" Ellen was appalled at the thought of taking the women's money.

"Of course, I refused. But it's downright difficult to say no to those two, so we compromised." He patted his jacket pocket for a cigar, then thought better of it. "We agreed that since Jess is going, there will be times when Arnie Stanhope will have to cover sports, not his usual beat of city council meetings and general news around the county. When someone is needed, you get the assignment with the understanding you get paid by the story, not a fixed salary, and that the Chicago job comes first."

Ellen stuck out her hand. "It's a deal. And I'm not going to say I'm grateful, although I am."

They were interrupted by the strum of a guitar that caught everyone's attention. Cowboy Joe stood and made a brief speech, wishing Jess well. To punctuate his remarks, Joe began to play "So Long, It's Been Good to Know You." The tune began softly, slowly building to an upbeat rendition. As he sang, Joe made his way to the gate leading into the side yard. Ending the song with a flourish, he bowed to the applause, and then he was gone.

As she watched Joe's retreating back, Ellen caught a glimpse of a figure stepping back to let Joe pass. Excusing herself from Calley, she wove her way through the partygoers until she was past the open gate.

"Jason," she let out the name with a deep breath. "What are you doing here?"

"Your landlady told me where you were. She even drew me a map so I wouldn't get lost." His irresistible smile dimmed when her frown didn't turn into a look of delighted surprise. "You look great, by the way."

"I mean, what are you doing in Opal's Grove?" She didn't add she'd given up seeing him again.

He reached out and took her hand. "I told you I'd be back. Everything just took longer than I expected. Lawyers in Tulsa. Lawyers in Oklahoma City. A disgruntled and, as it turned out, petty criminal of a station manager trying to sabotage the whole deal. Thought I'd never get things finished."

Ellen pulled back her hand, speechless.

Jason glanced at the gathering in the backyard. "Miss Jewell told me about the party. Aren't you going to introduce me to the honoree? I'd like to meet your friends."

"No." She could think of any number of reasons not to take him around. At the top of her list was someone—probably Mr. Calley or Audrey—mentioning Ellen's plans to stay in Opal's Grove. She wanted to tell him herself, and in her own way.

Ellen lightened her tone. "Let's go somewhere quiet where we can talk. Just let me thank the Smiths for the party and say goodbye to Jess."

Ellen quickly found Jess. Just as she finished wishing him good luck, Audrey was at her side, tugging at an arm.

"Is that him?" She nodded in Jason's direction. "Not what I expected. Too good-looking, and I bet he's got loads of personality. I figured you went for those scrawny, intellectual types with spectacles."

Ellen couldn't help but laugh. "I think you just described the bookkeeper Mother had lined up for me, although I'm not sure about the intellectual part."

"Aren't you going to introduce me?" Audrey waggled her eyebrows.

"No. Absolutely not." Ellen dug into the small shoulder bag that had replaced her satchel for the evening. Pulling out her car key, she handed it to Audrey. "Here, take my car when you leave. Jason will bring me home."

"You aren't going to do something foolish, are you?"

Ellen shook her head. Audrey was trying to nudge her again. "What did you have in mind?" she asked.

"It would be foolish to tell that man to get lost. He looks like somebody you might like to keep around. But don't go to extremes and run off and marry him."

Laughing, Ellen turned on her heel and walked to where Jason stood smiling and nodding to anyone who happened to look in his direction.

Ellen took Jason by the arm and steered him toward the street. Another spectacular sunset filled the western sky, but Ellen had other things on her mind.

"Where are we going?" Jason allowed himself to be led. "Back to the boardinghouse?"

Ellen shook her head. "I thought you'd drive us over to the city park. There will be a few people there, out for an evening stroll, but we won't have Miss Jewell or Audrey hovering around the windows pretending not to be interested in us."

Jason heartily approved, and within a few minutes, following Ellen's directions, they turned onto the street bordering the south end of the park. Ellen pointed toward a parking area near the bandstand. "I was at a concert there the first time you came to Opal's Grove," she said matter-of-factly.

"Seems like ages."

She gave Jason a sideways glance. "Yes, it does."

He parked and helped Ellen out the car. With the exception of two women strolling in the rose garden and a man walking his dog along a path on the opposite end of the park, they were alone.

Jason glanced around. "Pretty place. I'm surprised that those flowers—are they daisies?—look so good. You'd think the heat and drought would have killed them."

"Dishwater. Buckets of dishwater." Seeing his confusion, she repeated what Ivy had told her about Constance's committee to water the plants with dirty dishwater. "At least some of the ladies are following up on the plan." She took the arm Jason offered, and they walked to a path bordering the concert grounds.

"You got the inside scoop, huh? Know all the secrets of the beautification committee?" Jason teased. "You sound like a girl who's gotten to know this little town pretty well. All settled in, just like home."

"Not like home." Ellen didn't add "thank goodness." "But I am settled in, as you say, and I'm going to be here for longer than planned." She pointed to a bench sheltered beneath a bur oak tree.

When they were both seated, Jason's body angled toward her with an arm draped across the back of the bench, Ellen told him about the Chicago newspaper, the articles she was already planning, and the occasional assignments from Grover Calley for the local paper.

Jason dropped a hand to her shoulder, leaned closer, and

hugged her to him. "Good for you! I mean it. I know this didn't just fall into your lap. You worked for it."

"You bet I did. But if it hadn't been for that skeleton, I might not have made an impression on Calley. Oh, he liked the article I did about the pioneer interviews, but it was the way I handled the skeleton story that caught his attention."

Jason withdrew his arm to hold up both hands. "Whoa! Back up and explain."

Ellen poked him in the chest. "You've been busy. I've been busy." She launched into the story of the skeleton's discovery. Taking a breath, she thought she might as well tell him about Nettie Vine barging into Agatha's kitchen.

"Then, the sheriff came, and there was Mrs. Bright's son, and a doctor for Miss Vine," she finished. "And that's all."

"That's all?" Jason's voice rose. "What more could there be, unless she actually shot somebody?"

"Well, nobody was shot, and Miss Vine is being looked after in a special hospital." Ellen kept the end of the story to herself. It wasn't hers to tell. It never would be.

Jason sat back, shaking his head in disbelief. "You're going to write about this for the Chicago paper, aren't you?"

"No," Ellen said more stridently than she intended and then tempered her tone. "I won't take advantage of a confused old woman. As for the skeleton, there's no conclusion. The remains haven't been identified, and it's unlikely that will happen. And the last thing this town needs is a bunch of outsiders pouring in trying to solve the case, or worse, digging around on private property hunting for an Indian village that could be anywhere along the river. Before you know it, there will be a rumor of a hidden treasure."

"Fortune hunters and a treasure map. Has all the makings of a radio play; don't you think?"

"I believe that's been done more than once." Ellen smiled.

233

"Yes, but you could put a new angle on it." Jason shifted, his arm once again encircling Ellen across the back of the bench. "Driving up here, I thought I had a great job to offer you. The radio station in Oklahoma broadcasts a radio play once a week. They're rotten. The station manager, whom I personally had the pleasure of firing for general laziness, drunkenness, and stealing from petty cash, was using a thirty-year-old book of plays meant for high-school performances. That got me to thinking. Those stories you write for the magazines are similar to radio plays. So, why not hire you to write plays for the station? But you've made other plans."

Ellen was flattered he thought of her and saw any value in her writing, but her focus had to be the newspapers. He'd expected as much.

"While I was in Oklahoma, I thought about you."

Ellen raised an eyebrow, wondering at the shift in conversation. "I imagined you sitting in the backyard at the boardinghouse, and I wondered how things were going with the interviews. Sometimes, I'd ask myself what you would do if you were in some of the situations I got into."

Ellen tensed. "Jason . . ."

He reached for her hand. "I'm trying to tell you how I feel." Ellen was suddenly reminded of Ivy saying how grateful she was that Wheat never said flowery, romantic things to her. Some people had to hear the words, but Ellen realized she wasn't one of them.

"Don't look so anxious. I'm not leading up to a proposal of marriage."

Seconds ticked by as they stared at one another. Suddenly, they both burst out laughing.

"I admit it; I did think that's what you were about to do. It was a little frightening."

"I thought about it driving up here. But these last couple of weeks taught me a few lessons. The first being that I'm not as smart as I thought I was. I have a lot to learn if I'm going to run Dad's business someday. It wouldn't be fair to leave my wife alone while I work long hours and spend a great deal of time at our new station in Oklahoma."

"And I'd like to see what happens with the newspapers." Ellen stopped. "You're going to Oklahoma? I plan to do some stories from Oklahoma."

"Just what I was thinking. Lots of things to write about there."

Jason hugged Ellen to him. "We might figure this thing out yet."

"We might." Ellen pictured herself stepping off a cliff, but she didn't mind the sensation. With a start, she realized she didn't mind that she would never be like Nancy, with plans laid out like stepping-stones into the future.

Jason kissed the top of her head. "I can stay around for a couple of days. Have any plans?"

Ellen situated herself to look at Jason. "As a matter of fact, after tomorrow morning I am no longer being watched by Iris Hewitt and the WPA, so I would like to go to the Hurley-Burley and see what all the fuss is about. And, Saturday night—how would you like to go for a little ride in the country?"

ABOUT THE AUTHOR

M. J. Holt is the author of seven books on historical subjects that include studies of children's Western experiences in the 1800s and the changing lives of farm women at the turn of the 19th century. She has been a research consultant for PBS documentaries, including "The American Experience," and for Kansas PBS stations' programming on local history. She appeared on C-Span's "First Ladies Series" in connection with her biography of Mamie Eisenhower. Her books have been recognized by the Illinois, Kansas, and Oklahoma Centers for the Book, and her book *Indian Orphanages* received the Oklahoma Historical Society's Book of the Year Award. A native of Illinois, she has lived in Kansas for the last thirty-plus years.

The employees of Five Star Publishing hope you have enjoyed this book.

Our Five Star novels explore little-known chapters from America's history, stories told from unique perspectives that will entertain a broad range of readers.

Other Five Star books are available at your local library, bookstore, all major book distributors, and directly from Five Star/Gale.

Connect with Five Star Publishing

Visit us on Facebook:
https://www.facebook.com/FiveStarCengage

Email:
FiveStar@cengage.com

For information about titles and placing orders:
(800) 223-1244
gale.orders@cengage.com

To share your comments, write to us:
Five Star Publishing
Attn: Publisher
10 Water St., Suite 310
Waterville, ME 04901